The Adventures of Captain Star & the Amazing Dr. Zuntor

The Adventures of Captain Star & the Amazing Dr. Zuntor

Gene Anderson

TheGeneAndersonStory.Com

First Printing, 2026
Amorphous Publishing Guild
Buffalo, New York USA

www.Amorphous.Press

CONTENTS

Part I: Killer Drymahords

Deep in outer space, on a faraway planet in another solar system, on the other side of a black hole three uncharted planets away from Pluto, a conversation between two scientists was taking place. They were conversing about a new scientific experiment that was about to happen in an underground laboratory that had been especially designed to keep out the rays of the three red moons. These moons only revolve around their planet once every sixty years in Earth time.

The relevancy of the timing of these experiments with the revolution of their planet and the three red moons was that the moons at that specific time increases the gravitational pull by a 100,000-degree force. This once-in-a-lifetime experiment requires this increased pressure mode to cause a fusion of the ingredients that had secretly been developed.

"Dr. Zuntor, I must extend my compliments to you and your engineers on the speedy completion of this fabulous underground laboratory", said Dr. Mingerzor. It had taken twenty-nine (earth) years to complete the underground laboratory, with its fifty floors, all below the surface of the planet Duderyon.

Dr. Zuntor was one of seventeen pods that had been born to a pair of Duderyons. Unfortunately, all seventeen pods were exposed to the rays of the three red moons. The pods were unearthed during an earthquake, which at the time of his birth had not yet been controlled. During the mating season of the Duderyons, a special section of the planet was made available to its inhabitants for breeding.

During this earthquake, the mound in which the seventeen Duderyon pods broke open, and the gravitational pull created such friction that the heat of the exposed planet surface reached 2,000 degrees or more. When the explosions occurred from the mound full of Duderyon pods, only two were able to survive the blast. It was only because the explosion raised such an enormous cloud of dust that it filtered out enough of the rays for two of the seventeen pods to survive: He and his brother Pelcozor.

As they grew older, Dr. Zuntor and his brother Pelcozor became two of their planet's most successful and influential scientists. Both brothers had to be registered with the Supreme Intelligence Council — a group of interplanetary scholars whose purpose is to accommodate and develop the most intelligent youths in their immediate solar system. The two brothers were under constant supervision, due to the fact that they were two of the most brilliant of all the young students in their solar system.

But in time, it was discovered that there was a major difference between them. Zuntor was very studious and had dreams of being a major influence on the development and preservation of their solar system. On the other hand, his brother Pelcozor was just the opposite of Zuntor. Even though he was mentally qualified to do work on the team of scientists assigned to special projects, he was always trying to find ways to capitalize on his advantages. He was always looking for an opportunity to take over and become "The Supreme Ruler" of all the planets in their entire solar system.

In another section of the underground laboratory, Dr. Pelcozor was having a meeting with two of his colleagues concerning the takeover of the new serum that the Institute was developing.

"If we get hold of the formula and the ZYM23Ø.6 Serum, then we will, at long last, be able to take control of all the planets in our solar system. With this ZYM23Ø.6 Serum, we will be able to control the growth patterns, and all the major physiological systems in the bodies of all the incubations on our planets. With this power, I will be able to cure all diseases that I will invent. I'll be able to make our civilization weak at will, and then rejuvenate it after I take control", said Pelcozor. He then began to giggle like a man on a manic high who was very pleased with himself.

"Dr. Zuntor, we're ready. The neurophysiologist has just made the two new specimens ready for your final test", said one of his assistants.

"Thank you, Miss Uzar", answered Dr. Zuntor, as he headed for the elevator and descended down to a lower level where the two huge Drymahords were waiting. In appearance, they look like a cross between an ape and a hog; their bodies are similar to an ape, yet they have the face of a pig. One was a male, the other a female; they could be used for breeding when the experiments were concluded. Their weight is approximately 200-300 pounds.

Excited about the arrival of the two Drymahords, Dr. Zuntor rushed to their force-fielded cages. Looking in on them, with a sigh of amazement, he asked his assistant, "How were we able to get these two off the planet Getnor, without starting a war with the Getnorites, Miss Uzar?"

"Oh, Dr. Zuntor, everyone in the entire solar system is aware of your work, so for the first time, we were able to get the cooperation of the Getnorites."

"Well, Miss Uzar," said Dr. Zuntor, "it looks like the importance of our new discovery of the ZYM23Ø.6 Serum has a value, even to the Getnorites."

Miss Uzar inquired, "Zuntor, why is it so important that we use only the Drymahords?"

Looking through his memory retainer slides, as he scanned the hologram screen, Dr. Zuntor said, "The Getnorite Drymahords are the only species that have a life cycle and a system with similarities to the inhabitants of all the planets in our solar system. That's why I'm so excited about their arrival."

"Dr. Pelcozor, they're here! They're here!" shouted one of his assistants, referring to the Getnorite Drymahords, as he stepped off the elevator into the laboratory where Dr. Pelcozor was making plans to steal his brother's serum. Then he only has to finish with the experiments.

Dr Pelcozor turns to his chief assistant. "As soon as we take the serum, I want you, Mr. Lanorque, to be ready with one of the Supreme Provider's space ships. I don't want to take any chances on being late for our rendezvous with the Getnorite scientists."

"How long will it take, Dr. Pelcozor, before you think you'll be able to find the right formula for the reversal agent, sir", asked one of his assistants.

"I don't know for sure, that's why it's so important for us to be on that ship, and on our way, as soon as possible", stated Dr. Pelcozor.

"Why do we have to work with those Getnorites, Dr. Pelcozor? You have the ability to find the Reversal Agent without their help", said Mr. Lanorque.

Answering him with a strange look in his eyes, Dr. Pelcozor explained, "In a laboratory, on the planet Getnor, there is a Dr. Cimjone, who has been working on the ZYM23Ø.6 Serum. But their planet doesn't have the gravity force that ours does. And without this force, it is impossible to manufacture the ZYM23Ø.6 Serum. But they do have the ability to develop the Reversal Agent."

"But, why is it necessary to have a Reversal Serum?" asked another of Dr. Pelcozor's assistants.

"The purpose of the ZYM23ø.6 Serum is to retrogress the body's systems to those of an infant — because an infant's immune system is more capable of fighting off alien bacteria. The ZYM Serum specifically affects the growth patterns, along with the neural, respiratory, glandular, and other major systems of the physical body.

The addition of the ZYM Serum to the now youthful (therefore strong) physical organs and life-giving systems, multiplies the capability of fighting off, or killing, any disease which might attack the body. However, the ZYM23Ø.6 Serum is too strong and will eat up the brain cells, and in time, the personality will become homicidal! And that, my dear Mr. Lanorque, is why we need a reverse serum — to act as an antidote, and return the body to its normal functions before these dreadful side effects become permanent!"

On the planet Getnor, a doctor by the name of Cimjone is in his laboratory thinking; "I know by now that fool, Dr. Zuntor, has received those two Drymahords. What makes him think I'm going to let him have all that power to himself? All he thinks I want, is to to share the credit for the serum's development. He must think I'm a fool. With that ZYM23Ø.6 Serum, along with my Reversal Agent, I can take over all the planets in this solar system. No one will be able to stand up to me and my army. I'll have men that will have absolutely no fear of dying. And with the spreading of germs that I'll inflict upon the entire solar system, all the planets will be so weak, their leaders will have to give in to my demands. My army will know that they won't have anything to fear, because I'll have the two serums, and I'll be able to crush them at will!"

As these thoughts were running through Cimjone's mind, there was a light beam in his face from out of his hologram scanner screen. Throwing a switch, he sees an image of Dr. Zuntor. As Dr. Zuntor sends out his image to Dr. Cimjone, he also receives the image of Dr. Cimjone on his hologram scanner screen. Both Doctors are now looking at each other's full-length, four-dimension, image on their hologram scanner screens.

Once interplanetary enemies, the two doctors, (due to the need for each other's serums) have justifiably become research partners. So, Dr. Cimjone greets his colleague with false sincerity, "How good it is to collaborate with you again, Dr. Zuntor. I hope our Drymahords arrived in time for you to be able to complete your experiments."

"Yes, thank you, Dr. Cimjone", said Dr. Zuntor, looking at Dr. Cimjone's image. "I was hoping you would keep me informed about the progress on your Reversal Agent. It 's absolutely imperative for us to be able to reverse the mutation process immediately; if not, those two Drymahords will have to be destroyed before they develop an immunity to the Reversal Agent. We both know that would make them treacherous and completely out of control. Their thirst for blood would be so addictive, our planet's population could be completely decimated", said Dr. Zuntor.

"Have no fear, Dr. Zuntor, we are about to complete our last test. All that's left to do is to perform the recycling process on a 'baby' Drymahord, to see if the Reversal Agent works the same way as it does on an adult Drymahord", answered Dr. Cimjone. "One of the things that concerns us, however, is if an infant Drymahord doesn't receive the Reversal Agent in time, without a very close monitoring of the physical changes, it will be almost impossible for us to know if its body processes, or its physiological systems, are reaching the normal maturity cycle."

After hearing this, Dr. Zuntor leaned back in his Hydrolaxing chair, and still looking at the image of Dr.

Cimjone, inquired, "Let me see if I understand you properly, Dr. Cimjone. You're saying that if a baby Drymahord that's received our ZYM23Ø.6 Serum and doesn't receive the Reversal Agent in time will grow to full adult size and then, after a short period of time, its body's systems (such as respiratory, endocrine, immune, etc.) will revert back to an infantile stage. Without the physical appearance ever changing, this infant-to-adult-to—infant cycling will take over, and the repetition continues over and over, ad infinitum. Is that correct, Dr. Cimjone?"

"Yes, and not only that", said Dr. Cimjone, "While they are in the adult stage, they will become more cunning and traitorous, with double their normal strength. And if they haven't been monitored properly, we would never know it, but if by chance – only by chance, I said – something unexpected happened, and they would have to be destroyed, is that possible? And if so, how?"

Now looking at the concerned look on Dr. Zuntor's face, he could see stress in his eyes, and wondered what they could do if their serum ever got into the wrong hands. Dr. Pelcozor remarked to his assistant, Mr. Lanorque:

"It's been long enough for those two Drymahords to have been tested, so I think we need to pay my brother, Dr. Zuntor, a visit."

"Doctor, when you spoke to Dr. Cimjone, what did he say when you told him your plans about taking over the underground laboratory?"

"Why!? What business is it of yours, you fool!" He then grabbed his assistant by the neck, and began to strangle him. As Lanorque was on his knees, crawling on the floor, screaming, Dr. Pelcozor, (with the look of a murdering, power-hungry, maniac) could feel the adrenaline rushing through his body, as his assistant begged for his life. Then throwing Lanorque to the floor, he stumbled back against his control table, breathing hard and said, "Don't you ever ask me my plans!" With foam running from his mouth, he screamed "Do you think a fool like you could comprehend my plans? Not only that you already know too much! Maybe you're working for my brother, or even worse, those Getnorites!"

With fire in his eyes, he slowly pulled his laser pistol and was just about to fire, when Lanorque said, holding up his hand in defense, "Dr. Pelcozor, don't do this. Listen to me before you shoot! Please!"

Pausing for a second, Dr. Pelcozor said, as he looked at his begging assistant, "Give me just one reason why I shouldn't blast you! Just one!"

"Doctor, give me a chance to prove that I am faithful. Just one chance! I'll do anything! Just give me one more chance!"

Looking at him, pleading for his life, Dr. Pelcozor began to think, "Yes, I can still use this fool." Pausing for a moment, Dr. Pelcozor says, "Hmmm ... If I let you live, there is something I want you to do."

"Yes! Anything!" answered Mr. Lanorque.

"I want you to take some men, and after my brother leaves his laboratory to pick up supplies, you and your men break into the laboratory and bring me back that cylinder with the ZYM23Ø.6 Serum in it. Also, take a tranquilizer-beam gun so you can subdue those two Drymahords, and bring them, along with that serum, to me." Looking down on Lanorque, who had backed into a corner trembling, he shouted, "You have your orders! Now Move! You fool, Move!"

Getting up off the floor, Lanorque began falling over everything, trying to get away before Pelcozor changed his mind. As he stumbled through the door, he could hear Dr. Pelcozor laughing to himself.

"One more experiment with these Drymahords without the Reversal Agent on hand would be unsafe. Wouldn't you think so? Dr. Zuntor?" asked his assistant as she was handing him the last of the Reversal Agent that had been sent to them by Dr. Cimjone, the Getnorite.

"You're absolutely correct, Uzar", said Dr. Zuntor, answering her, as he reached for the antidote serum with a pair of forceps. Both Uzar and the doctor were extremely fatigued after so many days of concentrated work. During the transfer from one person to the other, the antidote slipped and fell from their hands, hitting the floor and splattering everywhere!

"Oh, Doctor! I'm so sorry!" said Uzar, with tears in her eyes.

"No! No! this can't be true!" He looks at her and down at the floor at the last of the ZYM23Ø.6 antidote agent. Dr. Zuntor had an expression of disbelief on his face. He grabbed his head between both hands, then slumped into a chair. After taking a moment to compose himself, Dr. Zuntor looked at Uzar, who was uncontrollably crying, and said "Uzar! Uzar! Come to yourself! We don't have time for personal sympathy. We have to do something quickly!" Then he began to pace the floor, thinking. After a moment he said to her, "Uzar, go down to the transport floor and make things ready for us to be transported to the next spaceship that is traveling toward the vicinity of Getnor. Then ask for permission to be beamed aboard. Hurry Uzar! We don't have a moment to waste!"

Hastily running over to the hologram scanner screen, he punched in the code for the planet Getnor. A few moments later, Dr. Cimjone appeared. "Dr. Zuntor, I'm surprised to see you again so soon. You work much faster than I would have thought possible."

With stress in his voice, Dr. Zuntor said, "Thanks for the complement, Dr. Cimjone, but it's a little premature. So getting straight to the point — there has been an unavoidable accident. I no longer have enough of your Reversal Antidote Agent to complete my experiments with these two Drymahords."

"Dr. Zuntor, what can I do for you?" asked Dr. Cimjone. Dr. Zuntor explains: "First, I must tell you that we have already given the Drymahords an enormous amount of my ZYM23Ø.6 Serum; too much time has passed, and they have not had their last series of your Reversal Agent."

Thinking to himself for a moment, Dr. Cimjone said, "We don't have but just a little left, and it will have to be tested alongside your ZYM23Ø.6 Serum in order to be sure that it will be a perfect match. But," continued Dr. Cimjone, 'We might not have enough time before the reaction, for not having enough antidote might cause the two Drymahords to become unmanageable and deadly!"

Dr. Zuntor exclaims, "However the case may be, I'll have to come in person to your laboratory. If I have your permission, Doctor."

Dr. Cimjone thinks to himself, "I've got him where I want him. Now he's going to have to come to me with his ZYM23Ø-6 Serum. But I'll not give him mine. Not only that, but I'll have his serum and hold it until the uncontrollable Drymahords cause a panic on their planet! Then, with his serum and him in my hands, I can take over and won't need the help of his brother, Dr. Pelcozor." His evil mind continued to scheme and with a smile on his face, he says to Dr. Zuntor, "Whatever you need, Doctor. Me, my staff, and my laboratory are at your disposal."

Moments after discontinuing their conversation, Dr. Cimjone pushed some buttons that switched him to his transport room.

"Transport Controller. What can I do for you Dr. Cimjone?" Dr. Cimjone gives his orders to the Controller: "I 'm expecting a Duderyon Ship soon, When it arrives, release our planet's protection-force-field, and allow them to enter. After it docks, beam Dr. Zuntor and his assistant to my laboratory immediately!"

"Very good Sir!" answered the controller.

Not knowing that Dr. Zuntor had departed to the planet Getnor in hopes of receiving a replacement for the wasted Reversal Antidote Agent, Dr. Pelcozor was anxiously waiting for Lanorque, whom he had sent on a mission to break into his brother's laboratory. Dr. Pelcozor was thinking, "Hurry, you fools! You are holding up progress." He began to pace the floor. "Lanorque, I'm going to kill you if you mess this one up! For the sake of all the gods, Hurry!!"

As the elevator stopped on the floor of Dr. Zuntor's laboratory, Lanorque and his evil crew were secretly getting off. Making their way down a maze of corridors, they soon arrived at the door of Dr. Zuntor's laboratory. Having been given the access code to the door's beamed lock, the three burglars see the two Drymahords in their laser cages.

Looking around, Lanorque and his men were turning over everything, looking for the serum. One of Lanorque's men was standing in the middle of the floor, looking at the two Drymahords, amazed at the size of them. Tipping up behind him and slapping him upside his head, Lanorque says, 'What's wrong with you, fool! We don't have time to waste!"

"But what in the galaxy are they?" asked the man.

"Doesn't make any difference; just keep looking for that serum!" said Lanorque.

Coming down the corridor was Dr. Mingerzor. Using the access code, he walked into the laboratory, only to be mugged and tied up! Slowly opening his eyes, Dr. Mingerzor sees Lanorque holding a laser gun in his face, and heard him say, "I'm glad you came to our little party, Doctor!" Then, focusing on the doctor, he speaks slowly and quietly, as he says, "If you want to live, tell me where the ZYM23Ø.6 Serum is. Believe me, I'm not playing around with you!" He then slapped him across the face a couple of times.

With blood running from his mouth, Dr. Mingerzor knew that these men were serious. He shakes his head 'yes'. Lanorque, knowing that the doctor believes that it's best to cooperate, unties him. Rubbing the back of his neck, the doctor says, "Do you have any idea how important this serum is to the population of our solar system?"

Slapping him again, Lanorque says, "Don't want to hear any lectures. Just tell me where the serum is." He put the ray gun up to the doctor's head. With fear in his eyes, the doctor gets up, and walks over to a secret compartment behind a wall. He carefully removes a small cylinder and hands it over to Lanorque.

"Now doctor," says Lanorque, walking over, accompanied by his two cohorts, to the cage where the two Drymahords were being held. "Just one more thing I need for you to do, then you are free to go. Unlock this cage", he demands as he points toward the two Drymahords.

"Don't ask me to do that! It's too dangerous!" cried Dr. Mingerzor.

Not understanding what Dr. Mingerzor meant by 'dangerous', Lanorque replies, "Don't try to make a fool of me, doctor. We both know that the Drymahords are the most passive species in the solar system."

"No! It's not that! It's that these two have been injected with the ZYM23Ø.6 Serum, and have not had the Antidote Agent. Without the antidote, they are extremely dangerous! Please don't make me do this — Please, No!!"

This time, full of rage, Lanorque ruthlessly beats Dr. Mingerzor down to the floor. He then drags him over to the cage and says, "This is the last time I'm going to tell you! Now! Do as I say!"

Just barely able to see, Dr. Mingerzor says, "All right ... If this is what you want, I'll do it!" He slowly begins to punch in the combination that unlocks the caged Drymahords.

Meanwhile, on the spaceship, Uzar was asking Dr. Zuntor if he was sure that he could trust Dr. Cimjone with the small sample of his ZYM23Ø.6 Serum that he said he needed to test his Reversal Agent, to see if it would match theirs. "I have to take a chance and give him the benefit of the doubt. I don't have time, and things have become too critical."

"But, Doctor, I'm afraid for your safety", said Uzar, with a look of fear in her eyes.

"Well, what will be will be, Uzar. Besides, we are in their planet's orbit already."

"Dr. Zuntor has just entered our transport beaming area, Sir", announced an assistant. "Do you want us to escort him to your laboratory? If so, I'll bring him to you right away!"

"Very Good", replied Dr. Cimjone. He continued looking through the memory retainer slides of his hologram scanner screen. And as usual, his evil mind was thinking, "When I get my hands on that ZYM23Ø.6 Serum of his, nothing can stop me! The whole solar system will be mine!"

As the arrival of Dr. Zuntor was announced, Dr. Cimjone's face portrayed a beautiful and winning smile as he says, "Dr. Zuntor! How wonderful it is to see you. I hope your trip wasn't too inconvenient for you."

Dr. Zuntor replied, "On the. contrary, Dr. Cimjone, I've been hoping to visit your remarkable laboratory for a long time-"

Dr. Cimjone rudely interrupts, "And who is this lovely person?", smiling at Uzar.

With the sight of Uzar causing an unexpected interest, Dr. Cimjone was thinking, "When I get my hands on that serum, and put Dr. Zuntor in my prison, I'll make her my personal breeding slave."

Answering him, Dr. Zuntor introduces Uzar: "Dr. Cimjone, this is my assistant, Uzar. She's been with me throughout this entire experiment."

Taking her by one hand and kissing it, Dr. Cimjone looks into her eyes (which makes Uzar feel a chill run through her body) and says, "I've never had the pleasure of meeting anyone so beautiful as you, my dear."

Very politely, Uzar says, I've heard so much about you, Dr. Cimjone, that I feel as if I know you." She is still trying to shake off her feeling of insecurity. Noticing the demeanor of them both, and knowing time was of an essence, Dr. Zuntor broke into their conversation.

"Dr. Cimjone, maybe on another visit to your planet, we all might have an opportunity to socialize, but for now, we need to take care of the business at hand."

"Yes, Doctor, you are right. I have The Reversal Agent right over here. And, by the way, did you bring some of your serum with you?" inquired Dr. Cimjone, as they walked to another area of the laboratory.

Cimjone continued looking at Uzar, who was in a semi-telepathic state. (It was unknown to Dr. Cimjone that Uzar was able to read minds, and was now receiving his traitorous thoughts.) Out loud, he said, "Right over here, Doctor." As they were walking, Dr. Zuntor handed the small container of his ZYM23Ø.6 Serum to him.

Greedily holding onto the serum, Dr. Cimjone was thinking, "At last! I've got it!" Before Uzar could react, they were entering a very small room. Standing in the doorway, Dr. Cimjone pushed the both of them into the room. They fell against each other and a nearby wall, falling to the floor. He then hit a button that sealed the room.

Walking away laughing, Dr. Cimjone went to his hologram scanner screen. He dialed some numbers, and within seconds, their image was on the screen. He was laughing as he was looking at them because they were totally in shock. He was very amused seeing them trying to pass through the invisible laser force-field door, and watching them being knocked back down onto the floor. Dr. Cimjone says, "Well Doctor, I hope that you and Uzar are enjoying your accommodations." He began to laugh again.

"Dr. Cimjone, How could you be such a fool to think that you could get away with this?! You, more than anyone, should know that without my help, you'll never be able to make the combination of the two serums work."

Dr. Cimjone replies, "I don't need you anymore because I have a sample of your ZYM23Ø.6 Serum, right here in my hands!"

Dr. Zuntor exclaimed, "Even though you have it, it's not enough to do you any good. And you can't make any more without my help!"

Dr. Cimjone asserted, "Once again Doctor, you are wrong. And I have a little surprise for you." He hit more buttons, which made his hologram scanner screen project another image alongside his two prisoners.

After he removed the force-field that locked in the two Drymahords, Lanorque pushed Dr. Mingerzor out of his way, and said, "You men grab hold of those Drymahords! I'll get the serum and take care of Dr. Mingerzor." He then turned to Dr. Mingerzor and shot him with two long blasts, which incinerated the doctor into dust. As he picked up the serum, he heard screams coming from his men.

Not believing his eyes, he saw his two men being ripped into shreds. Screaming and kicking, the two men began to plead with Lanorque to save them. Thinking to himself, as he was running out the door of the laboratory, "I've got to get this serum to Dr. Pelcozor before he finds out about those two Drymahords getting away. Maybe I can make him understand that they've gone wild and no one can stop them! No One!" He ran down the corridors and jumped onto the elevator that descended to the floors below — to Dr. Pelcozor's secret laboratories.

All through the corridors, then out into the population, the two Drymahords were slaughtering everyone in sight. A general alarm sounded throughout the planet! The Drymahords were completely out of control! Blood was running everywhere they roamed!

"It's Dr. Pelcozor!" Uzar said, as she pulled on Dr. Zuntor's arm.

"Pelcozor, what are you doing? Have you lost your mind?" demanded Dr. Zuntor as he looked on in disbelief.

Watching the three of them on his hologram scanner screen, Dr. Cimjone said, "It looks like we have one big happy family here." He began to laugh. Then, with a serious face, he said, with a snap in his voice, "What do you have to report, Dr. Pelcozor?"

Seeing that his plan of taking over the solar system was taking shape, Dr. Pelcozor said, "I'll have the ZYM23Ø.6 Serum and the two Drymahords in my possession shortly." Then, feeling a sense of satisfaction, he said to his brother, "Well, big brother, how does it feel to be under my control? I always knew that some day you would have to bow down to me."

Dr. Zuntor had tears in his voice as he pleaded with his brother, "Pelcozor, don't let this power-hungry fool lead you astray. Can't you see, he's not to be trusted? Stop while you have a chance."

"How sweet it is!" said Dr. Cimjone, "What a touching scene." Then with a calm voice he said, "If you remember, Dr. Zuntor, I said I had a little surprise for you. Well, as you see, your brother and I are going to work together on the two serums. And as you know, he knows as much about your ZYM23Ø.6 Serum as you. So now, with us working together and you out of the way, the entire solar system is ours!"

Dr. Zuntor, thinking fast, said to himself, "I've got a feeling that both of them are waiting on each other to make a mistake. They are both too greedy to be serious about ruling together. As soon as they both get what they want, they will turn on each other. All I have to do is feed their greedy egos a little. He then said out loud, "I must admit, that I was fooled by the both of you, and I'm certainly not able to compete with either of you. But tell me, which one is going to rule over the other?"

No one said anything for a moment, then Dr. Pelcozor excitedly said, "I have to go now, Dr. Cimjone, and as for those two — do what you must! I've just received a message that my men are back with the ZYM23Ø.6 Serum and the Drymahords. As soon as I organize everything, I'll have you come to my laboratory, and together we will complete the experiments." He faded out of the hologram.

Running through the door with the canister of the serum in his hands, Lanorque stumbles and falls to the floor saying, "Dr. Pelcozor! I have it!"

Dr. Pelcozor looks down with amusement at Lanorque, as he holds the canister of serum in his hands, and says to him, "Good work Lanorque. You will be well rewarded for this." Still beaming with joy,

Dr. Pelcozor asks, "Now where did you put those two Getnorite Drymahords?"

Afraid to tell him, because he knew he didn't have a chance, Lanorque answered, "I ... I ... They got away, Doctor."

The expression changed immediately on Dr. Pelcozor's face. He began to look like the ruthless, evil, madman he was. Grabbing Lanorque up off the floor, he beats him about the head and face quite soundly. Blood is running from his mouth and eyes as he tries to explain, "Dr. Pelcozor, don't! I couldn't help it! Listen! Just give me a change to explain!"

Knocking him back onto the floor, Dr. Pelcozor said, "Give me just one reason why I shouldn't kill you."

Looking up at the insane doctor, Lanorque (laying there terrified and bleeding) said, "I had them, Doctor, but I didn't know they were so strong and dangerous."

Kicking him in the face, Dr. Pelcozor said, "What, do you think I am a fool? You know that a Drymahord is the most passive species in our solar system." He began to beat Lanorque again.

Covering his head, Lanorque pleaded, "Don't Doctor, please! Don't! Let me tell you, please!"

Foaming from the mouth with anger, Dr. Pelcozor stopped beating Lanorque and said, "You have one more chance to tell me the truth."

"Pelcozor, I'm telling you the truth! They went crazy when we took them out of their cages. Lanorque finally remembered what Dr. Mingerzor had said about the reaction of the Drymahords when they were in need of the Reversal Antidote Agent. He quickly tried to explain it to Dr. Pelcozor.

The Supreme Educators were holding an emergency meeting regarding the slaughter that was being caused by the Drymahords. "We must do something about those killer Drymahords! They are destroying everything and everybody in their path! If we don't stop them soon, our planet will be destroyed", warned the Supreme Educator.

"How did they get free?" asked one of the council members.

"As I understand," contributed another member, "they were safely locked up in Dr. Zuntor's laboratory."

Someone else asked, "Where is Dr. Zuntor? I thought he was experimenting on them, and had them under control."

"Has anyone seen him since they got loose?" asked the head of the Space Zoologist Department.

"He has taken a ship to the planet Getnor, to pick up some Reversal Antidote Agent from Dr. Cimjone", reported the Supreme Educator. He continues, "Gave him a ship and permission to go to Getnor, because there was an urgent need to replace the last of the Antidote Agent."

The Chief Scientist of Advanced Neurology spoke up: "There's one thing I don't understand. Why is it taking so long for him to return? Did anyone try to get in touch with Dr. Cimjone to find out what's happening?"

The Chief of Interplanetary Security interjected, "I've been trying to contact him, but his hologram scanner system will not receive our frequency. I've taken the liberty of sending out a patrol to investigate some strange activity that has been observed on and around the planet Getnor."

The Supreme Educator – with a feeling that the Getnorites were about to break the truce between the two planets – said, "I'm in agreement with the Chief of Interplanetary Security. We need to put up all of our defenses, and alert our military to expect some kind of attack from the Getnorites. Especially since those Drymahords are slaughtering our population. By our past experience with them, we can be sure they are going to take advantage of our problems! Therefore, we must get prepared!!"

With the order received to patrol their solar system, the Duderyon Air Force based on the planet took off from their space platforms.

Not knowing that his planet was being monitored, Cimjone was having dreams of grandeur about double—crossing Dr. Pelcozor. As soon as he got what he needed, he would also kill Pelcozor's brother, Dr. Zuntor. And as a bonus, he would make Uzar his queen.

Locked up in that small room, Dr. Zuntor said to Uzar, "Should have listened to you, Uzar You are never wrong when it comes to judging a situation. But I must admit, that deep in my heart, I knew that Dr. Cimjone would always have something up his sleeve."

Uzar, searching his eyes and seeing the sadness, put her arms around him and said, "Don't feel so bad, Doctor; and anyway, I can still be helpful to you."

"What can we do? He's got us locked up and there is no way we can break through this laser, force-field lock", said Dr. Zuntor.

"But Doctor, there's one thing we've got in our favor", said Uzar.

"And what is that?"

"You must have forgotten that I have the power of extrasensory perception."

Looking at her with amazement, Dr. Zuntor said, "That right, Uzar. Now I remember how we use to play around with it back in our laboratory when there wasn't very much to do. Let's give it a try!"

Feeling a little better about their chances of turning the tables on Dr. Cimjone and his brother, Pelcozor, he suddenly appeared to be changing personalities in front of Uzar's eyes! For the first time in her years of assisting Dr. Zuntor, she saw a look in his eyes she had never seen before.

"What's wrong, Doctor?" she asked.

"What's wrong?!" The most naive and vulnerable individual she had ever known, had, in a blink of an eye, changed! Justifiably so, but changed!

Her mouth dropped open in astonishment as she saw what was happening to him. Realizing how people he loved and trusted had double-crossed him so that not only him, but the entire solar system was now in danger, he could feel the bile of hatred rising up within! And now, due to his change of attitude, he could feel a new sensation overtaking his entire body and mind! Remembering, as he stood in the middle of his tiny, prison-room, a seminar, when he and his brother were under the Interplanetary Scholars Development Program ... He had the ability to transform his personality, to whatever degree was necessary, in order to adapt to any circumstance. Now he had become a shrewd, fearless, and powerful, warrior!

Knowing that the timing was right, Dr. Pelcozor boards his spacecraft with Lanorque at the controls. He had allowed Lanorque to live after he understood the circumstances wherein the two Drymahords had escaped. However, he still felt it was best to join Dr. Cimjone as soon as possible.

At last, Dr. Pelcozor's ship was speeding towards Getnor. All of a sudden, he saw some Duderyon warships approaching his craft! After observing them for a moment, he realized they were not after him. It became obvious they were headed for the Getnorite planet!

"Lanorque, we will have to increase our speed to warp 5. 674. In order for us to be admitted entry into the Getnorite's gravitational zone, we must arrive there before their Planetary Defense Air Force gets a fix on those Duderyon War Ships that are rapidly approaching their planet's orbit! Once they notice them, they will engage their Planetary Defense Lock, and no one, including us, will be able to enter their gravity zone."

Back on the planet Duderyon, the killer Drymahords were destroying more and more of the planet's population. Duderyons were being killed by the thousands. They were unstoppable! And due to the ZYM23Ø.6 Serum not being fully understood yet, no one knew anything about the full effects of the serum on the adult Drymahords, especially since the full dosage of the Reversal Agent had not been administered. And there were so many unanswered questions. Each day (earth time), new changes were taking place on the Drymahord's life force.

First, their personality changed from friendly to traitorous. And now they had grown to over 1,000 pounds.

And most amazing of all, through some trick of evolution due to the mutations taking place within their hormonal system, the Getnorite Drymahords had sprouted wings, so that now they could fly!

"Doctor Zuntor, I see your brother, Dr. Pelcozor, is on his way to our planet. As soon as he arrives, there will be no further need for you!" announced Dr. Cimjone. As Dr. Zuntor looked at the hologram scanner screen, he had already devised a plan to lure Dr. Cimjone into their prison room. He gave Uzar the signal.

Relaxing her body and clearing her mind, Uzar began to concentrate on the power of mental telepathy. She directed her power to Dr. Cimjone. Knowing he had a desire to control her for his personal pleasure, she sent a suggestion to him, that now was the time for him to take advantage of her. Deeper and deeper she began to concentrate on projecting this suggestion to him.

At last Dr. Cimjone began to receive the message. He couldn't understand why he was becoming so obsessed with pursuing her. Immediately, Cimjone tried to divert his mind, and the tug-of-war was on. His better judgment was telling him, "No! Not now!" But her power of suggestion was telling him, "Yes! Now!"

When he received the report that Dr. Pelcozor had just docked his ship and was about to be beamed into his transport room, her hold on his mind was broken. "Now let the games begin!" he said to himself. Throwing a switch on his hologram scanner screen, he saw Dr. Pelcozor and Lanorque walking through the corridors of his complex, on their way to his laboratory. Not long after he saw him on the screen, Dr. Pelcozor was walking through the door of the laboratory.

It's so good to see you again, Dr. Peleozor. But I'm surprised you are here after telling me to come to your place, when you received the serum and the two Drymahords, said Dr. Cimjone. (Knowing all the time what was happening on the planet Duderyon.)

Dr. Pelcozor replied, "I know what we agreed to, at that time, but our plans had to change."

Dr. Cimjone demanded, "Why, may I ask, was it necessary for our original plans to change?" Then, softening his tone of voice, he said, "I was looking forward to seeing your laboratory." Dr. Cimjone wanted to hear Dr. Pelcozor himself say that he was in trouble, and that only he could help him.

Dr. Cimjone's thoughts were racing... "If I could confirm that Dr. Pelceozor needed me, then Pelcozor would not have enough power to become the Supreme Ruler of the solar system without my help. Then I could pressure him to make. concessions that would enable me to have him develop more of his brother's ZYM23Ø.6 Serum. Then of course, he would pledge allegiance to me; And beyond a doubt, I alone will be the one to rule the entire solar system."

Dr. Pelcozor addressed Dr. Cimjone. "I thought you knew about the disturbance I caused on Duderyon, as a diversion for the Interplanetary Council. By my releasing the two (now transformed) Drymahords on its population, they will be too concerned with saving their lives to pay any attention to us or our plans." He was hoping that Dr. Cimjone would fall for his story, even though he was lying all the time.

"I don't understand what you mean when you say the "newly transformed" Drymahords, Doctor, said Dr. Cimjone. Anyway, transformed or not, we need those two Drymahords for our experiments because they are extremely rare."

"Rare or not, Dr. Cimjone, those two Drymahords are not in the same condition they were when you shipped them to my brother. That's what I was trying to tell you when I said 'before they were transformed'! As you know, Dr. Cimjone, they were not able to receive the necessary amount of your Reversal Antidote Agent. And too much time had elapsed without them having the correct dosage. That made them have an adverse reaction, which caused them to become bloodthirsty, deranged killer beasts!" He was still trying to convince Dr. Cimjone that he took advantage of that opportunity for their mutual benefit. Saying, with a big smile, "Now do you see why

I came to you doctor, instead of your coming to me?"

"I should have known that you had a good reason to change your plans, but I was just wondering, that is all." Now thinking to himself, Dr. Cimjone knew that he still had to be more careful than ever for Dr. Pelcozor had almost convinced him with his story. If it was all the truth or not, one thing for sure — he needed his help to work on the serum. He said to Dr. Pelcozor, "I have something I'm sure you have been waiting to see. Step this way, please, Doctor." He then led him to the room where his brother, Dr. Zuntor and Uzar were being held prisoner.

Looking through the laser-locked door at his brother Dr. Zuntor and Uzar, Dr. Pelcozor said, "At last I have the upper hand, brother!"

Dr. Zuntor remarked, "I knew that sooner or later you would go too far, Pelcozor."

Pelcozor said to his brother, "Oh, contraire, my dear brother. I'm not fool enough to let a once-in-a-lifetime opportunity pass me by and not take advantage of it. I now have a chance to be the ruler of the solar system and no one can stop me! Not even the Interplanetary Council, and least of all, you, my dear brother. How does it feel to be at my mercy?"

"Pelcozor, come to your senses. You will never get away with something like this!" stated Dr. Zuntor, trying to appeal to his brother's better judgment. But Dr. Pelcozor, looking at his brother, and his assistant, as being hopeless and helpless, felt as if all of his dreams were about to come true.

Since all the attention was not on her, Uzar recalled the plan she and Dr. Zuntor had devised that would entice Dr. Cimjone into removing her from the locked room. Then, in time, she would be able to unlock the force-field and free Dr. Zuntor. So once again, she relaxed her body and cleared her mind and began to concentrate her powers of suggestion on Dr. Cimjone. It seemed that this time she was able to send her message to him without too much difficulty.

As the two doctors were walking away, the suggestion that Uzar had sent to Dr. Cimjone began to register. He thought it was his own idea. He turned to Uzar with lust in his eyes, and said, "My dear, by now I'm sure you've realized that it is better to forget your foolish pride and capitalize on the opportunity I'm giving you. Why not be with me instead of being destroyed along with that loser, your foolish Dr. Zuntor?"

Giving him a reassuring look that conveyed she had desires for him, Uzar said to Cimjone, "I can't bear the thought of death, so tell me, what you desire from me, and if it is in my power, it's yours!"

Dr. Cimjone looked at Uzar and nodded, saying, "Consider yourself lucky, my dear." He pushed the combination to the prison-room laser and opened the door for her to walk out.

Gazing into Dr. Cimjone's eyes as if he were irresistible, Uzar said, "I only have one request to ask of you."

Feeling as if he had her under his control, Dr. Cimjone confidently replied, "Ask away, my dear one."

Then Uzar said, "If you really have any true compassion for me, please don't kill Dr. Zuntor — we have been friends and colleagues for such a very long time."

Before he could answer, Dr. Pelcozor interrupted him. "Listen, Cimjone, Zuntor is too dangerous to let live! We must eliminate him!"

Upon hearing this, Uzar, with tears running down her face, fell upon her knees and reached for Dr. Cimjone's hand. She pleaded, "Please, Dr. Cimåone! Please, I beg you — spare his life. If you do, I'll be yours in a way that you would never dream. Keep him locked up or ship him off to an uninhabited planet — or anything... but whatever you do, please don't kill him. Let him live, please, Dr. Cimjone. Please!"

Looking down at her, Dr. Cimjone knew that what Dr. Pelcozor was saying was true, but if he wanted Uzar to give herself to him completely, and of her own free will, he had to agree not to kill Dr. Zuntor. (Or at least, make her think he wouldn't.) Lifting her up from off the floor and looking down into her tear-stained face, Dr. Cimjone said (knowing he was lying), "If his life means that much to you, and you promise to be true to your word, I'll let him live. But he must be eliminated, so I'll have him shipped off to a distant uninhabited planet, far off in another solar system."

Uzar, tightly holding Dr. Cimjone'8 hand, kissed it and said, "I'll forever remember your compassionate mercifulness! I'm Yours!"

Dr. Cimjone summoned his servant from his personal harem. When she arrived, he instructed her to take Uzar to his personal quarters. There she was to be specifically groomed and dressed so she could take part in an extremely rare ritualistic ceremony.

As soon as Uzar was no longer in their presence, Dr. Pelcozor turned to Dr. Cimjone and contended, "How could you expect for us to take over the solar system if we let my brother live? And all because of a woman? What's wrong with you, Dr. Cimjone? That's not like you at all!" (Of course, neither of them realized that Cimjone was a victim of Uzar's hypnotic suggestions.)

Thinking of a reason that would balance his unusual way of thinking, but not expressing his true intentions (other than what he had said to Uzar), Dr. Cimjone calmly explains to Dr. Pelcozor, "Do you think I would let anything or anyone get in the way of our success? I'm not that foolish! Tell her anything, because we might need her in the future. Remember, she's Dr, Zuntor's assistant and she knows things about the serum that we may not know! And as for your brother, Dr. Zuntor, he is as good as dead already!"

The Duderyons are doing all they can to defend themselves from the Drymahords. Since they have sprouted wings, they have been flying all over the planet destroying everything in their path. A squadron of Duderyon defense pilots were flying on patrol, looking for the killer Drymahords. One of the officers announced over the communication network, "This is Captain Star, of the Imperial Planetary Defense."

He was acknowledged by the Communications Officer at the Command Post: "Go ahead, Captain Star."

"I'm patrolling the Nibortoz Sector in the Xeon area. There is nothing to report. It's all clear at the moment. Communicator off!"

"Very good, Captain Star. Keep us informed of any unusual activity in your area. Com Closed!" said the Command Post CO.

Making small talk with his co-pilot, Captain Star remarked, "The last time I flew to the planet Zube, it was to see a sweet little Zube girl. Let me tell you, she has the best-" He stopped before he had a chance to say the next words; something caught his eye. Then, seeing the look of terror and disbelief on his co-pilot's face, Captain Star exclaimed to the Duderyon Communications Officer: "This is Captain Star - Come in. Come In! Do you hear me? Come In!"

Answering him, the CO said, "Command Post acknowledges Captain Star - Go Ahead!"

An excited Captain Star exclaimed, "I've spotted the Drymahords flying nearby in my area! By the size of them and their speed, it's important that you send emergency backup immediately!"

Answering him, the CO replies, "Help is on the way, Captain Star!" Opening his communication lines, to all frequencies, he makes an announcement: "Attention! All Imperial Planetary Defense units in the area of the Nibortoz Sector - Code X-36! Do you read me? Code X-36! (Code X-36 means that one of their comrades is in serious trouble.)

Captain Star, thinking to himself, says, "Come on, Star, calm down! Don't let those two overgrown teddy bears cause you to panic. You are a sky warrior!" He began to sweat as he maneuvered his Space Fighter in order to intercept the newly mutated, flying, now laser—spitting, killer Drymahords. Captain Star gave orders to his co-pilot, saying, "Make ready all defense mechanisms!"

"All defense mechanisms ready, Sir!" answered the co—pilot.

"Ready to fire on command," declared the assistant gunner.

Then holding a steady course, Captain Star aligns his fighter with the killer Drymahords. Thinking about all of his training at the Imperial Planetary Defense Academy, there was nothing he could relate to concerning either an attack or defense of anything that could maneuver and change speed as these two killer Getnorite Drymahords!

"Now they are in firing range!" said Captain Star to his crew, as he sat strapped into his pilot's seat. "Fire blaster one!" Ducking the first barrage of missiles, the killer Drymahords began to prove to be more maneuverable than Captain Star had ever expected. After firing his missiles and laser systems to no avail, Captain Star, having used all of the techniques he had learned at the Academy, knew he needed help!

Being irritated by the attack upon them by Captain Star's Space Fighter, the two killer Drymahords began to fly away from the battle. "They're getting away, sir", said the copilot.

"Not if we can help it!" said Captain Star.

The copilot asked, "Are we going after them sir?"

"We will just keep up with them until help arrives. Then we will destroy those two killers", announced Captain Star, as he attempted to keep up with them. Never in his entire flying experience had he ever seen anything able to fly and maneuver as those two Drymahords!

Pacing the floor of his prison room, Dr. Zuntor was wondering what had happened to Uzar, knowing it would be just a matter of time before Dr. Cimjone and his madman brother would be back to take his life. "I hope she is all right. At least she is out of here and if I know her, if she gets half a chance, she will be back to unlock this door", he says to himself. Then another thought crossed his mind about the two Drymahords. "I wonder what happened to them and what kind of transformations they have gone through since I left my laboratory." All these things were going through his head at the same time. The realization that he was completely alone made him think that everyone he had trusted had now turned against him.

Not only the Drymahords, but he also was having a transformation. More and more as time went by, he was changing from the shy scientist into a wary warrior! Suddenly, the thought of Uzar jumped into his circle of confusion, and he realized that instead of worrying about her, he needed to calm down and meditate. By using their combined ESP energy, he might be able to contact her! He was hoping it would be possible for them to communicate telepathically. There could be no better time than now; Dr. Zuntor began to concentrate. As his mind became more under control, and he continued trying to communicate telepathically with her, he began to have flashes of his beautiful Uzar. I must communicate with her, he kept telling himself. As he wiped the perspiration from his forehead, he continued to project telepathically, hoping he could make a mental breakthrough to her: "Uzar, Free Me! Free Me!"

In Dr. Cimjone's special quarters, Uzar (not knowing what to expect) seemed very disturbed as she listened intently to a woman that knew she was unfamiliar with her new surroundings. The woman said, "I was told by Dr. Cimjone to prepare you for the fertility ritual." The woman clapped her hands three times. Uzar couldn't hide her surprise when she saw several beautiful women coming from behind hidden panels. They were walking towards her with oils, perfumes, silver and gold gowns, bubble bath solutions, make-up, and all kinds of beauty preparations.

Some of the women were also bearers of many kinds of exotic foods. Then, from a special area in the preparation room, Uzar noticed a transport beam beginning to materialize more women, playing sweet music, and filling the room with wonderful sounds. Then the light of another area in the room began to change colors. The beam was so intense, it gave off an appearance of illuminated draperies. The woman took Uzar by the hand, and led her through the beams of light that separated the pampering area from the reception area. Walking through these beams of light, Uzar saw a pool trimmed in gold, and filled with rainbow-colored water.

Standing there waiting for her to enter the pool, were three more beautiful women. They were pouring oils and a secret solution into the water. As Uzar (still held by the hand of the strange woman) slowly stepped down the golden stairs into the rainbow water, Uzar asked, "Why is it necessary for me to go through all of this? And who are you?"

The lady, still leading her into the pool, replied, Tryrenzie, I'm Dr. Cimjone's personal servant, the Supreme Provider for his harem.

Uzar continued to question her, "Who are all these women?"

"These are his wives. They are from all over the solar system", answered Tryrenzie.

Looking with amazement, Uzar said, "How many wives does he have?" Looking at Uzar, with a look of pride on her face, Tryrenzie said, "Dr. Cimjone has graciously taken only three hundred wives."

Pausing for a moment, Uzar exclaimed, "Wow!" then asked Tryrenzie, "If he has that many wives, what does he want with me? And, do all of his wives go through the same ritual you are taking me through?"

"No, my dear," said Tryrenzie, "you are the only one who has gone through this ritual in the last three hundred years."

"Three hundred years!" screamed Uzar. "How is that possible, and he has all of these wives?"

"Because Dr. Cimjone's family comes from the Gods of Elmegorly. Having many wives is something all of his ancestors have always done. But only once every hundred or so years, is one woman chosen to go through this fertility ritual, in order for her to give birth to the ultimate, most high, Supramegorloid! The Supramegorloid will be a sacrifice to the great gods of Elmegorly. Now, my dear, you must be silent!" ordered Tryrenzie.

Dr. Cimjone, trying to inform Pelcozor, explained, "Dr. Pelcozor, we've tried all the combinations of those memory retainer slides that are conserving your ZYM23Ø.6 Serum. But we have not been able to develop the right enzymes to trigger enough of a reaction from the white immunity cells. This, of course, is necessary, for us to incubate them long enough to cause the needed fusion for the ingredients to congeal and bind into a one-cell agent — without which, we will never be able to develop the ZYM23Ø.6 Serum."

In frustration, he jumped up from the lab table and knocked some of the instruments onto the floor. Dr. Cimjone then rushed to the area where he had Dr. Zuntor imprisoned. Seeing Dr. Cimjone walking toward the laser door of the prison room, Dr. Zuntor screamed as he ran toward him, "What did you do with Uzar, you no good-"

Before he could reach Cimjone or complete his statement, (and certainly without thinking), he tried to break through the laser door to attack him. He was hit with 2,500 volts. The force from the shock hit him with so much power it threw him backwards across the floor. Standing in the laser doorway laughing, Cimjone said, "I'm glad you still have so much enthusiasm concerning my affairs, Dr. Zuntor."

Lying on the floor, still in a daze, Dr. Zuntor asks, "What makes you think you and my brother are going to get away with all this madness? Where is Uzar? Tell me, or I'll-"

Cutting him off, Dr. Cimjone says, "Or you'll what? You're the one who plays the fool, Dr. Zuntor! You're under my mercy! I can do anything to you I want, any time I want! But I'm thinking about sparing your miserable life."

Stumbling to his feet, Dr. Zuntor sarcastically asks, "And just why are you going to be so merciful to me?"

With a look of innocence on his face, Cimjone replies, "I've always had a sense of fair play about my actions. And I thought I would give you one more opportunity to save your life."

Dr. Zuntor, (rubbing his arms, where he still felt the effects of the laser—lock's shock to his system) looks at Dr. Cimjone and asserts, "My life means a lot to me, but my honor means more."

At this, Dr. Cimjone begins to run out of patience. "You Fool! All you have to do is give me the right combination of the ingredients to your ZYM23Ø.6 Serum and I'll not only free you, but I'll free Uzar as well. I'll be back, and if I were you, I would change my mind!" With that, he stomped back toward his laboratory.

Once again Dr, Zuntor began trying to telepathically contact Uzar. Over and over again, he tried, but evidently she was being distracted by something much more powerful. For some reason, he was unable to 'feel' her.

Uzar, completely naked now, was being slowly led down the stairs into the pool filled with the rainbow colored water. Uzar's heart began to pound like a bass drum, almost loud enough, she thought, for it to be heard by all. She trembled with each step she took downward and felt sure her legs were going to collapse under her. Then suddenly, as her naked body descended into the rainbow colored water, she could feel a tingling sensation that relaxed her in a way she had never known before.

Slowly walking into the middle of the rainbow-filled pool, Uzar can feel hands touching her all over her body. She then sees Tryrenzie being handed a receptacle filled with a green liquid. Tryrenzie stared into Uzar's eyes as she holds the vessel over Uzar's head, and chants:

"To all witnesses hereby summoned to take part in this secret fertility ceremony, I command you to reflect on the honor bestowed upon you. The privilege of witnessing this secret fertility ritual has been denied all eyes for the past three hundred years. No other than yours in this generation, nor in generations to come, shall ever have this grand and honorable privilege granted to them."

"And now, you shall retrieve your golden daggers and at my command, you shall make a small cut on your little finger and allow only three precious blood drops to fall into the secret fertility pool." Each of the women that were standing around the pool pulled out their daggers and held the blades against their little fingers. Standing at attention, as if they were soldiers, the women waited for Tryrenzie's command. Still holding the receptacle over Uzar's head, Tryrenzie nodded her head.

The women who were surrounding Uzar inside the pool lifted the covers from some large golden incense holders.
As the smoke rose from the uncovered incense burners, the pool area began to cloud with red smoke. The smoke began to make Uzar dizzy, and her eyes began to close, but her conscious mind was trying to fight off the power of the incense smoke. She tried hard to fight off the effects of the smoke by thinking about the safety of her beloved Dr. Zuntor.

The room is now filled with smoke, and Tryrenzie, (still holding the golden cylinder filled with green liquid) continued to chant:

"Oh Mighty Gods of Elmegorly, I, Tryrenzie, your servant, am calling you. I'm calling to petition you, Mighty Gods of Elmegorly. Send down your powers of immaculate fertility into this woman. I am offering you the most highest sacrifice. To you O, Holy Ones, a sacrifice of royal virgin's blood. Blood from twelve royal Getnorite princess virgins. As I anoint this woman, I anoint her with the most high emerald oils — emerald oils from the mountains of the stars of Elmegorly. Great Gods of Elmegorly, as we give you our most precious possessions, we ask you to grant us – the House of Cimjone – your most powerful male. From out of the womb of this woman, let a male come forth! A male to be dedicated to you. O, Great Gods of Elmegorly!"

After her petition, she gave the orders for the twelve virgins (with the blades of their golden daggers still held against their little fingers) to be prepared. All twelve of them were standing around the golden fertility pool. They were all proudly waiting to simultaneously let their three drops of blood drip into the pool.

At last, the time had come for Tryrenzie to pour the Green Emerald Oil over Uzar's head. As soon as Uzar felt the hot oil running over her body, she went into shock. At the same time, the three drops of blood from the twelve princess virgins splashed into the pool. As it mixed in with the rainbow colored water, the dripping from the Emerald Oil that rolled down Uzar's body began to mix with the 36 drops of blood, and the holy rainbow water caused flames to shoot up from the pool like lightning. At this time, Uzar passed from an unconscious state into a complete coma.

Tryrenzie and the other women who were also in the water with Uzar slowly lowered her back and down until she was submersed under the flaming rainbow waters. Then, altogether, in one motion, they picked her up over their heads, and slowly walked her out of the pool. At this time, the entire fertility pool area changed from beautiful sights to beautiful sounds with fantastic, mystical music that engulfed everything.

"Captain Star, we got your code X-36", said the Commander of a small squadron of the Imperial Planetary Defense Unit. Flying along with him were six other Space Fighters, ready for action! "I'm Captain

Octzerfree. We were ordered to assist you in any way possible, and we are glad to be here! What are your orders, Sir?"

"Set your Proximetry Indication Locators toward the planet Taptuyon. The last we saw of the two killer Drymahords, they were headed that way", replied Captain Star into his helmet-mounted communicator. Speaking to his squadron, Captain Qctzerfree gave the orders and the coordinates enabling them to zero in on the planet Taptuyon. They had high hopes of tracking down the killer Drymahords.

After flying at warp speed for a short period of time, the small squadron (with Captain Star's Fleet and his Space Fighter leading the way) fortunately spots the Drymahords. They were returning from savagely destroying most of the planet Taptuyon. "There they are, Captain Star!" announced his Proximetry Indication operator. Looking at all the data on the screen, he finally sees them.

"I see them now!" And there they were — two small dots, moving very fast in their direction.

"All right you planet-jockeys, there they are! Remember, they can outfly anything in the heavens, so keep that in mind! Now! Are you ready?" asked Captain Star.

"Ready Sir!" replied each pilot of his fleet from his space fighter.

Soon they were in firing range of the killer Drymahords. BLAM! BOOM! BLAM! went the laser cannons from Captain Star's Space Fighter. But the two killer Drymahords split up in a maneuver that surprised all of the Duderyon pilots. "Wow! Did you see that!?" one of the pilots shouted over his communicator to another one of the pilots that was flying around behind the Drymahords.

"I've never seen such a maneuver as that before!" the other pilot exclaimed. All the pilots in the fleet were making these kind of incredulous remarks. They just couldn't believe their eyes.

Overhearing their comments, Captain Star spoke up, "Now you see what I was talking about!" He switched to his Repeater Blaster, and fired at them with hundreds of blasts at a time, only to miss the Drymahords as they rolled, stopped in mid-space, and sometimes reversed directions.

"Captain Octzerfree, it seems as though we can't hit them! What should we do?" implored one of the pilots.

"Try your proton torpedoes, men."

In the meantime, Captain Star maneuvered his Space Fighter into a new attack position. And all the Space Fighters in the fleet slowed down on their reversed thrusters. Then, at Captain Star's order, they opened into their famous star-burst maneuver. The entire fleet began to fire multibeam laser missiles. The firing was so intense that it looked as though two meteorites had collided. The light in the targeted area was so bright, it was absolutely blinding!

After the area had cleared, a loud cheer went up over the intercoms of all the pilots. The Carrier's entire fleet were congratulating each other. But before they were able to plan their celebration, zooming in at the speed of light, the two killer Drymahords were upon them, mounting another attack.

They attacked the squadron with moves that were straight out of the Academy books! Because of the element of surprise, and the speed with which the Drymahords attacked, the pilots became confused. The killer Drymahords were spitting an array of blue—hot lightning—type rays! So, at this point, they easily broke up the formation of the small squadron. In rapid succession the killer Drymahords flashed their rays at the elusive Space Fighter. "

"Look Out, YM-2 - Look Out! It's behind you!" one of the pilots shouted to another. But it was too late! It was hit with a blast of hot Drymahord rays. The little Space Fighter exploded into a brilliant ball of fire! Then, both of the killer Drymahords hit another spaceship. It exploded into a mushroom-like cloud! Then suddenly, they turned as if to attack the Carrier itself — but the two Drymahords turned again and flew away, leaving the Carrier and the rest of the fleet as if they were standing still.

"Did you see how those two Drymahords outmaneuvered, out-flew, and out-fought us, Captain Star?" inquired a confused Captain Octzerfree over his communicator.

"I warned you — they are unbelievable", declared Captain Star.

"I still can't believe what just happened, sir", uttered another surviving pilot.

After a moment of silence, while they all tried to gather their thoughts and calm themselves down, Captain Star said, "1f we are going to ever destroy those two killer Drymahords, we will need much more help!"

"I'm certain you are right about that, Sir", agreed Captain Octzerfree. Then the small group of Duderyon survivors flew off in formation.

"This is the last time I'm going to try any more of your combinations, Dr. Pelcozor!" a   determined Dr.   Cimjone announced. I tried everything, and nothing works!"

A puzzled Dr. Pelcozor replied, "I do not understand. It's all here on my Memory Retainer slides. There must be something I'm overlooking."

"Well, whatever it is, Dr. Pelcozor, you had better find it soon!" asserted Dr. Cimjone. He now had a look of ruthlessness in his eyes.

Feeling his hold on Dr. Cimjone was slipping away, Dr. Pelcozor knew he couldn't show any fear. With this in mind, he articulated very strongly, "What do you mean 'I Better'? You fool! I'm the one whose idea it was to take over this solar system! And so far, all my plans are working out! Wasn't I the one who released those two Drymahords on the planet Duderyon, that is now causing so much damage there... And not only on Duderyon, but they have all but completely destroyed the planet Taptuyon! All that and more was part of my plan! The rest, you already know, so don't give me that 'I Had Better', treatment, Dr. Cimjone! I'm in charge here! And don't you ever forget it!!"

After his tirade, Dr. Pelcozor continued looking into the eyes of Dr. Cimjone with an ice-cold stare. By the look in Dr, Pelcozor's eyes, Dr.

Cimjone knew it was time to make his move. He was beginning to realize that Dr. Pelcozor could not complete their work to develop more of his brother's ZYM23Ø.6 Serum. "However," he thought, "That's all right, because I still have my ace in the hole — Uzar!"

Dr. Cimjone continued to allow his thoughts to go over his plans again: "All I have to do is take my time! So, why not let him think he is in control, and that everything will work out his way? Besides, I might need him to assist Uzar later on." Thinking deeper into his plans, he knew that his entire Star Fleet was headed for Duderyon, to destroy it — especially since it had already been weakened by the Killer Drymahords! Once this feat was accomplished, it would give him all the power he needed. There would be no one who could stand up to him.

He also had Dr. Zuntor left to deal with. He had not killed him yet. He was safely locked up in case he needed him to help destroy those two killer Drymahords. Feeling satisfied within himself, he started to walk away, leaving Dr. Pelcozor in his laboratory.

He turned, with his hand extended and said, "Dr. Pelcozor, maybe I'm just a little fatigued. Of course, my laboratory is at your disposal. Use it as if it were your own. I'm going to rest for a few moments." He then walked away, smiling like the mouse that outwitted the cat.

As luck would have it, the switch for the intercom had accidentally been left on in the laboratory during the heated argument between Dr. Cimjone and his brother, Dr. Pelcozor. Zuntor was feeling better about his situation, especially since what he thought would be inevitable — that the plan for the two power-hungry doctors would soon fight over which would be the Supreme Ruler of their Solar System was actually happening. Walking around in his small prison room, Dr. Zuntor was saying to himself, "Here is my chance to take advantage of this situation; I must make my brother talk to me." He began to repeat this to himself, like a mantra, over-and-over again, "I've got to talk to Pelcozor! - I've got to talk to Pelcozor! I've got to talk to Pelcozor!"

Then out of the corner of his eye, he saw a cupful of water that he was given earlier. He thought that the laser force-field lock on his prison room might short-circuit and set off some kind of an alarm. That might get his brother's attention. Standing back away from the doorway, he threw the cup at the transparent laser-locked door. Sparks and blue fire jumped from out of the invisible doorway. This brought some of Dr. Cimjone's guards running to the prison area to see if he had escaped.

Dr. Pelcozor was still working in Dr. Cimjone 's laboratory. He notices a red light flashing on a diagram of the Getnorite Complex screen. He then noted that the light was flashing in the area of the prison room where his brother, Dr. Zuntor, was being held! Thinking it might be that he had escaped, the doctor and his assistant, Lanorque, ran down to the prison room area. They arrived at the prison area in time to see the guards slowly returning to their posts. Dr. Pelcozor, seeing through the invisible laser door, is assured that his brother is still locked safely away.

"I see you are causing trouble, as usual Zuntor!" screamed Dr. Pelcozor. "I told Dr. Cimjone to get rid of you a long time ago!" declared Dr. Pelcozor with envy in his voice and eyes.

"Well my dear brother," retorted Dr. Zuntor, trying to antagonize his evil twin, "I see you're still not able to take over the solar system yet! What's wrong?"

"It seems that by now, Zuntor, you would have learned to be more humble — knowing that your life is in our hands." He broke into loud, ridiculous laughter.

"You're a fool, Pelcozor! What makes you think that you are going to rule anything? You're in trouble yourself!" Then, Dr. Zuntor began to walk around strutting, with a put-on cocky attitude, pretending that he really knew what he was talking about. He continued, "And how do I know you are in trouble? It's because not even you, even though you have the help of Dr. Cimjone, can duplicate my ZYM23Ø.6 Serum."

Interrupting him, Dr, Pelcozor said, "Can't duplicate your serum? You Fool!" He starts raving like a madman: "I, Dr. Peloozor, have the ability to not only reproduce your serum, but I can improve it! He was smiling and shaking his head with his hands on his hips, looking over at Lanorque for confirmation. Lanorque gives Dr. Pelcozor a look of encouragement. Even though the two of them were acting as if everything was going in their favor and under control, Dr. Zuntor knew that mentally, he had his brother where he wanted him.

So, he said to Dr. Pelcozor as he was prancing around, "Pelcozor! Tell me this: if you are so in control of everything..." He slowly walked up to the transparent laser-locked door, and looked his brother directly in his standing only inches from his face, and separated only by a transparent laser beam; he gave his brother a look so cool that Pelcozor felt a chill running through his body. Zuntor paused a second, then slowly, and calmly continued, "Then, why haven't you killed me already?!"

At that moment, Dr. Pelcozor knew his brother had figured out that he and Dr. Cimjone were clashing. Not only that, he didn't have much time left. Realizing his brother knew what was happening, Dr. Pelcozor and Lanorque turned and stormed off.

"It worked! Dr. Zuntor was thinking as he sat back down on the floor. "Now I'll just wait and see what happens." He sat on the floor with his head relaxed back against the wall. He began to try once again to contact Uzar telepathically. "Concentrate, Zuntor, Concentrate! You can do it. Just relax, and you can do it!" Saying in his mind, "Uzar, I need you" over and over and over and over again.

Lying on a large couch, still unconscious, Uzar is trying to awaken herself. Her conscious mind is trying to take control of her unconscious mind. Even though she is still in a trance, she can hear voices. Someone is talking about her, or talking to her. Her conscious mind is saying, "Wake Up! Uzar, Wake Up! Take control of yourself! Wake Up!" But at the same time, her unconscious mind is faintly receiving the telepathic message that Dr. Zuntor is trying so desperately to send her. All these things were running through her brain at the same time, making her more and more confused. Instead of coming out of her trance, she fell deeper into it. Due to mental exhaustion and stress, she completely blacked out again!

"How is she, Tryrenzie?" asks Dr. Cimjone.

"She is resting well, Doctor", responds Tryrenzie, as she leans over with a sponge, bathing Uzar's head, trying to cool her down. Standing beside Tryrenzie, and looking down into Uzar's face, Dr. Cimjone is saying to himself, 'How beautiful you are my love! Of all the wives in my harem, you are absolutely the most beautiful of them all." He then said to Tryrenzie, "The moment she awakens, inform me!"

Tryrenzie agrees, "As you say, Doctor."

I also want her to be made ready for my insemination — she must be Immaculate! Do you understand? Immaculate!"

With servitude-like compliance, Tryrenzie answers, "Yes, Dr. Cimjone, I understand. Whatever you say, I will do."

"Very good, Tryrenzie, I know I can always depend on you", declared Dr. Cimjone.

Looking at Dr. Cimjone with pure adulation, Tryrenzie remarks, "I was your first wife, before all others. I live only to serve you, as it is written in our laws. This beautiful woman lying here, was chosen by you for the Gods of Elmegorly — to be the godly womb in which the Supreme Heir of the Descendants of the Most High Getnorites will grow. Therefore, Master, my life would be forever in agony, and my soul would burn in the deepest, lost pit for all time, if she is not to your desires."

With that, she bowed to the floor and said, "Master, she will be more than ready."

A very pleased Dr. Cimjone approached Tryrenzie and lifted her up by her hand and vows, "Tryrenzie, you are the wife my fathers chose for me, and again, you have shown me this day, what a wise choice they made." He then kissed her hand, and grandly walked away.

Captain Star, my Proximetry Indication Locator screen is showing something coming from the direction of the planet Getnor, headed this way — fast!"   said his Proximetry Indication Operator.

Looking at the screen, Captain Star can't believe his eyes, "Yes, I can see them. It looks as if there is at least a hundred of them!" Thinking to himself, he says, "It looks as if the entire Getnorite Space Fleet is headed for Duderyon! They are going to attack!" Captain Star addresses his pilots, "Well, you Planet-Jockeys, this is your chance to show what you can do."

"Wow! I see them too, Captain Star", exclaimed Captain Octzerfree. "What do you think we should do, Captain?"

Captain Star replies, "We have only two options: one is to veer off to another sector, in hopes they can't find us until we can get some help and regroup; or, we can intercept them, and put up a fight!"

Captain Octzerfree enjoins, "Captain Star, we don't have much of a chance, do we? The first is hoping for a miracle, and the other is just plain suicide! Are you sure those are the only options we have?"

Captain Star, curtly answers, "That's it, Captain!!"

While the two captains were trying to plot a course of action, about two dozen small battle ships zoomed in, throwing rockets at them! "Look Out - YM-7 rocket at six o'clock." Rolling out of the line of fire, YM-7 maneuvered the little space fighter away from the Getnorite rockets.

"Well, I guess they made up our minds for us, Captain Octzerfree", said Captain Star. "We'll fight our way to another sector, and communicate with the Imperial Planetary Defence's Mother-ship! Also, we must warn them that the Getnorites have launched a major attack, and are speeding in the direction of Duderyon!"

"All right, planet-jockeys, follow me!" commanded Captain Star as he thrust his Space Fighter into hyperdrive, accelerating the fighter to warp speed, followed closely by the small group of I.P.D. Space Fighters.

On the bridge of the Getnorite Mother-ship, the Chief Commander was looking at a huge Proximetry Locator Screen that was in three dimensions. His First Officer, as he was also looking at the screen, said, "Commander Boonor, are those not Imperial Planetary Defense Ships, Sir?"

"Yes, Lt. Scuff, I've been watching them for some time now", said Commander Boonor.

"I can't understand why you sent a squadron of Interceptors out of formation to their sector, Sir. Or why did you give orders for them not to pursue those I.P.D. Ships?" asked Lt. Scuff.

Looking at Lt. Scuff, with a smirk on his face, Commander Boonor explains, "Never let your left-hand know what your right-hand is doing, Lt. Scuff. By letting them get away, they can lead us to their patrol's home base."

"Very good, Sir", said Lt. Scuff.

"Captain Star, calling Imperial Planetary Defense Headquarters - Come in - Code X-36! Come in - Code X-36 Over ... Imperial Planetary Defense - Over" said the officer over the communicator. I've just seen the entire Getnorite air force headed your way and speeding fast! Believe me, they are coming with everything they've got — Over" asserted Captain Star!

"What?" exclaimed the operator. "Let me switch you over to the Chief Commander, Sir. Hold On!"

Captain Star quickly interjected, "Whatever you do, make it quick!"

After a moment, a voice said, "Commander Algor speaking — Over!"

"Commander Algor, this is Captain Star of the Imperial Planetary Defense — Over."

"Yes Captain Star, Go Ahead," said the Commander.

"I'm reporting a huge fleet of Getnorite ships that are in the Pyeeroney Sector, headed for our planet Duderyon, Sir — Over."

"I knew that they were out there some where. I've been trying to locate them since they left the Getnorite Sector," said Commander Algor.

"Well Sir, they seem to have a new Reflective Image Eliminator that provides a screen that makes them invisible at your distance. That's why you've not been able to pick them up on your Proximetry Indication Locator Screen, Sir," said Captain Star.

"How do you know that, Captain Star?" asked the Commander.

"Because we were looking for those two killer Drymahords and were scanning in a 360—degree total oval circumference, for a distance of seven—hundred—sixty million light kilometers, and didn't pick them up. But as we were cruising along, all of a sudden, there they were, right on top of us," explained Captain Star.

"Did they ever show up on your Proximetry Indication Locator Screen Captain Star?" asked Commander Alger.

"Yes Sir, they did, but only when they were extremely close to us. That's why I knew that it was the new Reflector Image Eliminator, Sir," said Captain Star.

Thinking for a moment, Commander Algor said, "Captain Star, I'm going to ask you and your squad to do something that will put you in great danger. I must also let you know, Captain, that you have the right to refuse my request."

"What is it, Commander Algor, Sir?" Captain Star inquired.

"Remember, this is not an order, Captain, this is a request. We need you to fly close to the perimeter of that Getnorite fleet so we can track you until we can get close enough for them to appear on our Proximetry Indication Locator Screen. Then we'll counter attack and destroy them," stated the Commander.

"What are our chances of coming out of this alive, Sir?" asked an anxious Captain Star.

"To be truthful, Captain, you have a very small chance of coming out alive, but without your help, our entire Star Fleet and our planet is doomed, Captain Star," answered Commander Algor.

"Well, since you put it that way, Commander, let's get it on, Sir!" With that, the two officers signed off.

Captain Star then switched back to his squadron's frequency, and directed his attention to them. "Okay, guys, you heard what the Imperial Planetary Commander of The Duderyon Defense said. You have a choice. You can go back to our home base, or follow me!"

Captain Octzerfree interrupted, "Do you think you are going to get all the glory by yourself, Captain Star? And by the way, I am also speaking for my men."

Another pilot interjected, "Then what are we waiting for, let's go!"

A very pleased Captain Star exclaimed, "Let's show those Getnorites what Imperial Star Pilots are all about! Come on, Pilot Jockeys, follow me!"

So all of them simultaneously pushed their throttles all the way down, which kicked their engines to Hyperdrive and they reached warp speed in seconds. They headed in the direction of the Getnorite Air Fleet!

In another sector of the solar system, the two killer Drymahords were headed for the planet Getnor, at warp speed. All along the solar system, they had been destroying planet after planet. Now they had made more transformations. Not only had they gained weight, sprouted wings, and could breathe laser fire, they were now able to project Sonic vibration shock waves, "SVSW". This new mutation was so powerful, nothing could survive the vibration if it were trapped in between the two of them! One Drymahord would post its position on one side of their target, and the other Drymahord would position itself on the other side. Then, like a ripple in a pool of water, when a stone is thrown into it, each Drymahord would project its Sonic Vibrating Waves, and what is trapped in between them will either explode or burst into flames. Now, indeed, they were more horrifying than ever.

Still flying in the direction of the planet Getnor, at more than the speed of light, the two killer Drymahords attacked a small asteroid. The inhabitants were helpless against these two monsters. As the Drymahords were destroying and slaughtering everything and everyone, the asteroid's small defense unit was trying to mount an attack against them. A voice from their Central Control Operation (which was being received by their orbiting air unit, that was patrolling this sector) said, "Calling all air units, all air commanders, and all pilots in the Nepheryon Sector — Code X—36! Do you read me? Code X—36 ! "

Answering his call for help, one of their patrolling pilots with his voice full of fear, says, "Nepheryon — Come In Nepheryon! — Over."

"I'm glad someone responded — Over" said the controller.

"I got your code X—36 Central Control. What is the problem — Over," said the pilot.

"We are under attack from some horrible flying beasts! They are destroying our entire habitation — over."

All units must return to home base immediately! Code X—36 !" ordered the Nepheryon Central Control Operator.

"Got you! Com Closed!" said the pilot. Then he began to head back to the Asteroid Nepheryon at warp speed.

On Nepheryon, buildings were on fire, power plants were blowing up, bodies and blood were everywhere. The two Drymahords were flying as well as walking, destroying the airships and most of the population. In a building, the Royal Nepheryon Council was holding an emergency meeting. They were trying to make plans about how to defend themselves from the Dryrnahords. Unfortunately, they were unaware that the Drymahords were already attacking their building.

The Nepheryon ground forces were firing their laser weapons at the two beasts, but their beams were just reflected off their bodies. With a blast from both Drymahords from their laser breath, using their intensely hot, blue—white laser flames (that they were spitting from out of their tightly shaped lips), they were burning up the entire ground force. Soldiers were running with their bodies on fire, screaming and rolling on the ground, trying to put out their flaming bodies.

After causing the Nepheryon Ground Forces to retreat, the Drymahords aligned themselves up as if they were bookends, standing on both sides of the building where the Royal Nepheryon counselors were meeting. They began using their newly developed sonic vibration shock waves, and beamed in on the building!

Feeling the building vibrating, the members that were attending the meeting began to run for their lives, pushing one another, and falling over each other. The heat began to melt the structure of the building as if it were hot wax! The hopeless screaming members were trapped, as debris was falling and blocking every exit.

The two killer Drymahords continued to utilize their newly acquired sonic vibration shock waves more and more on their targets. Hundreds of Nepheryons were running and screaming, trying to escape the intense heat and the tremendous vibrations, which soon caused the huge building to explode, leaving only an enormous smoke cloud.

Slowly opening her eyes, still dazed and not realizing where she was, or what was happening, Uzar sees Tryrenzie looking down at her. "Where am I?" asked Uzar, trying to lift her head.

Touching Uzar to calm her down, Tryrenzie said, "You are in the Holy Preparation Complex, my dear."

As Uzar's eyes began to focus, she could see Tryrenzie holding a lavish gown, made of pure spun gold, sprinkled with diamonds, emeralds, rubies, and many other exotic gems. Never in her life had Uzar seen anything so marvelous.

With the help of two other women, Uzar slowly rose to her feet. She then asked Tryrenzie, "Where did something as beautiful as this come from?"
Tryrenzie, still holding the gown, said, "This Royal Gown is the Sacred Gown of Fertility of the Cimjone Dynasty. It's over two thousand years old. It is handed down from the gods of Elmegorly."

After bathing Uzar in perfumes and sweet herbs, and a holy oil solution, Uzar was led to a table and gently laid upon it. There she received a sixty—finger massage from head to toe. Next, her hands and feet were manicured and pedicured. After being brushed exactly nine hundred strokes, her hair was groomed.

At last, it was time for Uzar to slide her perfectly shaped body into the sacred Gown of Fertility. Looking at her, Tryrenzie knew there had never been anyone in the entire solar system that looked more beautiful than Uzar at that moment.

Tryrenzie then clapped her hands three times, and one of the walls began to glow. The brilliancy of the glow began to reflect itself more and more, until the entire wall became one huge mirror. Uzar, looking at herself, was in total disbelief. She looked and felt so different. She was entranced by her own beauty.

Taking Uzar by the hand, Tryrenzie began to slowly lead her down a long red carpet. Then up a small flight of stairs and positioned her on a huge throne. The throne is made of one huge pearl that had been carved into the shape of a throne, trimmed in pure gold with every kind of precious gem from all over the solar system.

The thought of her being seated on such a throne, Uzar began to feel as if she were about to hyperventilate. Tryrenzie stood next to Uzar, with her chin high in the air. She then clapped her hands slowly, two times. From out of a secret panel, six women carrying a golden tray that was attached to two long golden polls on their shoulders.

They began slowly walking down the red carpet, then up the stairs, approaching her throne.

Uzar's eyes were blinking nervously in disbelief. There it was, the Holy Crown of the Cimjone Dynasty. It was about two feet in height; in two layers, molded out of pure gold, with 12 points. Each point was topped with a different gem — one from each planet in their solar system. Sprinkled with reflecting diamond dust, that gave an appearance of constant movement of the embedded gems.

Lifting the crown from the golden tray with both hands, Tryrenzie said, "To all that witness this crowning of this woman, who, through the grace of our master, Dr. Cimjone, has been chosen to be the receiver of the most holy array of the Getnorites. It is given as a reward for her sacrifice of her first male child to the gods of Elmegorly. It is an honor that only once in hundreds of years is anyone selected. Now, this woman, that we are about to honor with this crown, is about to be impregnated for the most highest of sacrifices."

Tryrenzie then slowly turned to face Uzar and placed the royal crown of the Getnorites on her head. Tryrenzie clapped her hands slowly three times. Royal music was heard as she gave Uzar a golden cupful of Emerald Fertility Oil to drink. Then Tryrenzie turned to those who witnessed the crowning of Uzar and said, "As it was written — It has been done!"

Flying through the stars, leaving the planet Nepheryon in flames, the two killer Drymahords were once again returning to their birth planet of Getnor. Picking them up on their Proximetry Indication Locator Screen, were the only three PX—16 Sky Ships left of the entire Nepheryon Air Force.

"There is something bleeping on my PIL Screen, Captain Marcy," said his co—pilot.

"Yes, and by the look of its shape and its speed, it appears to be those two monsters that destroyed our fleet and our planet!" said Captain Marcy.

"Let's pay them back, captain, for what they did to us," said one of the other three Nepheryon pilots.

After a moment another Pilot on their right wing interjected, "We haven't been able to even wound them with any of our weapons. Why do you think we can kill them now, Sir?"

"Men, all that we were sworn to protect has been destroyed, and all we have left now is our honor! So, if we can't live honorably, why live at all? Those monster beasts destroyed our civilization. I think we owe it to all the lost ones to not just let them die in vain. So what do you say men, should we go get them, or simply fly off among the stars?" expressed an angry and heartbroken Captain Marcy.

All three pilots knew what the answer would be. So they revved their engines to hyperspace, and seconds later, their PX—16 Sky Ships reached warp speed in pursuit of the two killer Drymahords!

Right at the edge of the planet Nepheryon's orbit, the three PX—16 Sky Ships navigated their small crafts into firing distance of the two Drymahords. Captain Marcy gave the command to his men: "There they are, men! Calibrate your instruments to scan their area, so our blasters can automatically keep a fix on those two monsters."

All three of the Sky Ships aimed both their blasters and their laser cannons on the targets. However, the Drymahords were also moving in on them fast!

"Fire! Fire Men! Fire!" ordered Captain Marcy. At that instant, a strong blue flame shot out of their cannons.

It was a direct hit on one of the beasts. The force of the blast threw the Drymahord about ten kilometers backwards. As it began to float motionless in space, the pilots began to gain confidence and excitedly said to each other, "We got one of them!"

But, within a few seconds, the beast shook off the effects of the blast! It then zoomed back into action, more treacherous than ever!

"Did you see that, Sir? We only stung it with that blast!" exclaimed one of the Space Ship pilots to Captain Marcy.

"Don't let that stop us men! Keep on firing!" ordered Captain Marcy.

Just as the Captain had said that, both of the Drymahords spit out a huge bolt of laser fire that hit one of the three PX—16s! "I've been hit!" screamed the pilot. He sat strapped into his pilot seat, as flames surrounded him. The automatic fire extinguisher began to spray on the pilot, but the intense heat from the laser flames was so severe that within seconds, the pilot had disintegrated into dust.

To see the inflamed PX—16 Star Ship explode with their friend on board caused the remaining pilots to fight with renewed desperation. The debris from the explosion was scattering everywhere. The other two Nepheryon pilots began to fire indiscriminately at the killer Drymahords, with everything they had. The area of the beasts was lit up as if a thousand meteorites had collided, and burst into flames.

Banking, dipping, looping at light speed, as well as firing back at the two PX—16s, the Drymahords were too much for the two remaining little Nepheryon ships. Swiveling their heads in unison, targeting both PX—16s, the Drymahords flew off in opposite directions. They then reversed their flight patterns. This maneuver placed the two PX—16s between the Drymahords! Using their newly acquired sonic vibration shock waves, the killer Drymahords began to surround them in an invisible crystal prison! They simultaneously began to telepathically vibrate the little PX—16 Sky Ships within that invisible crystal prison!

The heat inside the cockpits of the Sky Ships had Captain Marcy and his crew about to panic. The pilot in the other ship was screaming excitedly into his communicator, to Captain Marcy, "Captain! Something has jammed all of my controls and has completely shut down my computers!"

Answering him, Captain Marcy said, "I know! The same thing has happened to my ship! The way she's vibrating and overheating, it won't be long before she explodes!"

With his vision blurred, he still tried to hold onto his laser cannons. His gloved (but sweaty) hands nervously held tightly to the laser cannons' firing mechanism. Captain Marcy declared to the pilot (who was also his long—time friend) of the other PX—16 Nepheryon Star Ship, "If we have to go out like this, then let's do it as true Nepheryon Star Fighters! Let's give it all we've got!"

His friend in the other ship said, "Right! Captain Marcy! Here's to Nepheryon, and to you, Captain Marcy, and to the stars!"

Both pilots of the PX—16 Star Ships began firing indiscriminately at the two killer Drymahords! Sadly, they unfortunately became victims of their own weapons. Being enclosed in the invisible sonic crystal, their missiles and lasers were not able to penetrate the invisible sonic prison. As often as they fired their missiles and lasers, the crystal would reflect and boom—a—rang back, striking themselves! After taking a couple of reflected hits, along with the heat and vibrations from the Drymahord's shock waves, the Nepheryon Star Ships exploded into oblivion!

"Dr, Pelcozor," said Lanorque as he was about to collapse from fatigue, "How much longer are you going to work? You have been at it so long, you're about to fall asleep on your feet."

Dr. Pelcozor, stumbling against the laboratory table, said (with his eyes red and his face showing much stress), "Don't tell me what to do, you fool! I have no time to rest. We must have this serum soon, or our lives will be in the hands of that ruthless Dr. Cimjone!"

"But Dr. Pelcozor, you can't go on like this," pleaded Lanorque.

Outraged by Lanorque's being overly concerned about his condition, Pelcozor slaps him across the mouth. Falling to the floor, Lanorque, for the first time, realized he had had enough! As Pelcozor tried to kick him in the face, Lanorque grabs his leg and trips him to the floor. He crawls over to the doctor and begins to strangle him. Rolling over and over on the floor, knocking over tables and carts, the two men fought like wild animals. Finally realizing that Lanorque had unexpectantly turned on him, and was trying to kill him, Dr. Pelcozor knew that his dreams were beginning to crumble.

The two men were completely destroying Dr. Cimjone's laboratory. During the fight, the switch to the hologram scanner screen was accidentally turned on and an image of the neutral sector (in 3D) of their solar system was being displayed onto the huge screen.

Staggering back up against a wall, while Lanorque was still laying dazed on the floor, Pelcozor picked up a case full of lab tools, lifted them over his head with the intention of slamming it down on Lanorque's head and ending it all. Lanorque, with one arm extended up toward Dr. Pelcozor and scooting backwards on the floor, pleaded, "Don't! Please Dr. Pelcozor! Don't!"   Then, with his peripheral vision, Lanorque saw a large group of airships on the hologram scanner screen.

He screamed, "Wait, Dr. Pelcozor! Look! Look!" He pointed his fingers at the screen.

Dr. Pelcozor slightly glanced at the screen. Caught by surprise at the sight of all those airships, Dr. Pelcozor, with his mouth open, stopped, and slowly lowered the tool case. Then, unaware, he dropped it onto the floor.

Standing there, not believing his eyes, Dr. Pelcozor yelled to Lanorque, "Get up you fool! We've got to get the hell off this damned planet!"

"Master, she is ready," Tryrenzie speaks to Dr. Cimjone over the intercom.

"Very good! Bring her to me!" he asserts with authority. He then walked over to his personal hologram scanner screen and dialed into the room which held Dr. Zuntor prisoner. Seeing Dr. Zuntor's image on his screen, he remarks, "I see that you are still with us, Dr. Zuntor"

Dr. Zuntor asks, "How long are you going to keep playing these games, Cimjone?"

"Not much longer, Dr. Zunt.or," replies Dr. Cimjone.

"What makes you think you're going to get away with all this madness? And where is Uzar? I demand you tell me! Tell me now! Is she safe? If you've harmed a hair on her head, I'll kill you!" declared Dr. Zuntor.

Looking at Dr. Zuntor on his screen, Dr. Cimjone laughs as he says, "That's why I dialed you in on my hologram screen — so I could let you see for yourself that she is fine. In fact, she is very happy." declared Dr. Cimjone.

"You no good liar, what evil trick are you trying to pull now, Cimjone?" asked Dr. Zuntor.

Being overly sarcastic, Dr. Cimjone says, "How could you say something like that to the one who is about to impregnate your sweet Uzar?"

He begins to laugh again. Looking at Dr. Cimjone's image on the hologram screen in his prison room, Dr. Zuntor sees Dr. Cimjone laughing. This sight brings out all the hatred in his heart for him. He began to tremble as the blood rushed to his head. He also feels his eyes closing tightly as he grits his teeth and says, "You no good scum! If you do, you will never live to see it!"

"Captain Star, I know we should be close to the Pyeeroney sector, and I still can't pick them up on my Proximetry Indication Locator," said his co—pilot.

"I was just thinking the same thing," said Captain Star. He called over to Captain Octzerfree's Space Fighter (flying on his left wing), "Captain Octzerfree, this is Star. Do you copy?"

"I hear you loud and clear, Captain Star," answered Captain Octzerfree.

Star asks, "Have you seen anything of the Getnorite fleet yet?"

"No, not yet," replied Captain Octzerfree, "but I"m keeping my eyes glued to my PILScreen."

Captain Star states, "I just thought I would check in with you, and let you know that we must be very alert. With that new Reflector Image Eliminator, we could be almost in their face and smelling their breath before they show up on our PIL screen."

"Got you, Captain Star," replied Captain Octzerfree, "I'll try to stay on top of it!"

"Commander Boonor! Look! Look! On the Proximetry Locator Screen!" Lt. Scuff said as he came running up to the bridge and stood by the Commander.

"That lets me know that we are getting closer to the main Imperial Planetary Defense Fleet, Lt. Scuff," said Commander Boonor.

Lt. Scuff inquired, "Why do you think this small patrol group of IPD Ships came back, Sir?"

"I don,t. know. But I think they are a decoy. In fact, I'm almost certain of it," said the Commander.

Lt. Scuff continued to solicit information. "Why do you think that, Sir? Couldn't they be looking for those killer Drymahords, and just happened to fly back into this sector? Because, as you know, they cannot find our fleet on their Proximetry Locator Screens due to our new Reflector Image Eliminator."

Commander Boonor explained, "I must admit that what you are saying sounds reasonable, but the way they ran away from our Interceptors, they would be fools to come back into our flight space, looking for those killer Drymahords or not!"

"I never thought about it that way, Sir." replied Lt. Scuff.

As both Commander Boonor and Lt. Scuff continued to watch the small group of Imperial Planetary Defense Ships on the Locator Screen, Lt. Scuff asked Commander Boonor, "Sir, would you like for me to order a squad of Interceptors to attack them?"

The Commander acquiesced, "You might have a point, Lieutenant; if they are only decoys, it might flush out the rest of them. And, if they are not decoys, we need to get them out of the way, so they can't communicate a warning back to their mothership or their home base. So... do it, Lt. Scuff! Immediately!" ordered Commander Boonor.

"Yes Sir!" exclaimed Lt. Scuff as he turned to go and take care of business.

Very soon after the order to attack the small group of IPD Star Ships was given, the huge doors to the runway of Commander Boonor's Getnorite Mothership opened and dozens of small, triangle—shaped Interceptor Ships began to zoom out, into the Pyeeroney Sector. They headed in the direction of Captain Star's Carrier and his small group of Space Fighters.

"Captain Star, this is Captain Octzerfree. Have you seen any sign of them yet?"
Still watching his Proximetry Locator Screen for any of the massive Getnorite fleet, Captain Star replies, "I don't see any sign of them yet. But I have a feeling that they are not far away." Captain Star's instincts were giving him a feeling that it wouldn't be long before he and his small group might be in the middle of the entire Getnorite fleet!

At this point, Captain Star opened all communicator beams to his crew (as well as to Captain Octzerfree) and announced: "Okay Men! Let's not get caught unprepared! Check all of your weapons and your engine's hydrozip generators, because if we do run into them, I've got a little surprise that might keep us alive! Now, let's all go into silent mode — Communicator Closed!"

"Dr. Pelcozor — Everything is on your Sky Ship. We can leave as soon as you are ready," reported Lanorque.

Dr. Pelcozor says, "There is only one more thing I have to do before I go."

"What is that, Doctor?" inquired Lanorque.

"I've got to find out where Dr. Cimjone keeps that Reversal Antidote Agent. I'll need it, after I get where I'm going." stated Pelcozor.

"Why do you need that stuff, Dr. Pelcozor? We don't have much time — we both know that soon, Dr. Cimjone will be coming back here! And, remember, he feels as if he doesn't need us anymore, now that he has Uzar. Please, Dr. Pelcozor!" pleaded Lanorque.

Giving Lanorque an evil look, Dr. Pelcozor warned, "Haven't I told you before — Don't try to tell me what to do, you idiot! Just do as I say! Now start looking for that serum!" Both Dr. Pelcozor and Lanorque started destroying Dr. Cimjone's laboratory as they were searching for his Reverse Serum.

Slowly walking down a corridor, led by an entourage of women with Tryrenzie still leading her by the hand, Uzar can feel her body reacting to the fertility drugs that had been given her. Even though she was on her feet walking, she was still in a trance. Step—by—step her body was experiencing sensations she had never known before. With each step, Uzar felt she was on the verge of having an orgasm. The procession of women, with each slow step, was getting closer and closer to Dr. Cimjone's spacious 'Room of godly Passions.' But in Uzar's drugged mind, she was telling herself, "This is all a dream!"

Somewhere in the deep recesses of her unconscious mind, she could hear a faint voice that sounded like Dr. Zuntor saying, "Uzar, I love you — Help me!" over and over again. But the fertility drugs were so powerful, she couldn't truly comprehend that she was receiving telepathic thoughts sent to her by her beloved Dr. Zuntor.

Switching his hologram screen from area to area, Dr. Cimjone can see Uzar being brought to him in all her sensuous beauty. "How exotic and beautiful she is," he said to himself. Sitting back on his huge throne,

Cimjone switched his screen again to Dr. Zuntor's prison room. Seeing him still sitting on the floor with arms and legs folded, and his eyes closed in deep meditation.

"Well Dr. Zuntor, I see that you are making yourself comfortable," said Dr. Cimjone. Slowly opening his eyes, Dr. Zuntor can see the hologram image of Dr. Cimjone, sitting on his throne. But not wanting to break his concentration, he slowly closed his eyes again.

Thinking that Dr. Zuntor was playing games with him, Cimjone (trying to hide his reactions and his displeasure) said, "I didn't mean to disturb you, Dr. Zuntor. I thought I would do you a favor."

Even though he was in deep concentration, he could still hear and understand what Dr. Cimjone was saying. Dr. Zuntor's conscious mind is directing himself... "I must stay in control. I can't let him know that he might be able to unnerve me. As long as he knows he is not winning his mind games, the longer I will stay alive!"

"Dr. Zuntor, I know you are aware I'm here. Just open your eyes, and look at me!" commanded Dr. Cimjone.

Dr. Zuntor was thinking, "I'm not going to break my concentration; that's what he wants me to do." He didn't realize that on the hologram screen, Dr. Cimjone was in full ceremonial dress.

"Don't act as if you can't hear me, Dr. Zuntor. I know you can!" asserted Dr. Cimjone. Dr. Zuntor was still not responding to Dr. Cimjone's voice, so Cimjone became extremely antagonized and started to scream, "Who do you think you are? You are a fool! I am the ruler of this planet, and you are my prisoner! I'm not yours!" Then it came to him that he was being manipulated by Dr. Zuntor. With that realization, he suddenly calmed down, and said, (in placating tones) "How rude of me, Dr. Zuntor. I must apologize to you for losing my patience. After all, you are my guest." He then notices that Dr. Zuntor had never moved — not even an eyelid. so, he continues, "I see you are not in a talkative mood, Dr. Zuntor, so I'll just leave your hologram screen on... And since you can't come to my little party, I'm sure that Uzar will be highly disappointed that you couldn't make it. In fact, I'll also leave the sound on, so if by chance, she might want to say something to you, you will be able to hear her." He again broke out into his evil laugh.

Dr. Zuntor was so into his trance, that he didn't say a word. The only thing that was in his heart and on his mind was to get a message to Uzar. He continued saying over and over in his mind, "Uzar, don't let him touch you! I love you! Help me!"

"Sir, We've been tracking Captain Star and his squadron throughout the entire solar system, and there has been no sign of the Getnorite fleet yet," reported the Proximetry Indication Locator Operator.

"Just keep your eyes on that screen and don't let Captain Star get out of your sight! I've got a feeling it won't be long before the Getnorite fleet shows up!" said Commander Algor.

"Captain Octzerfree, have you seen any sign of them yet?" inquired Captain Star, as he nervously pressed the button on his communicator.

"No Sir, it's like we're out here all alone," replied Captain Octzerfree.

"Neither have I — that,s kinda unusual. There is always someone flying out in this sector," said Star. After a moment's reflection, Captain Star opened all beams on his communicator and warned, "Men, this is just a hunch, but I believe you had better get ready for action."

"Is something wrong Captain?" asked one of his pilots.

"I don't know, but I've got a feeling that we're right on them! — Com Closed!"

Within seconds after Captain Star had warned his men to prepare themselves, the first Getnorite Interceptors were spotted by one of the pilots. "Here they come, Captain, at 3 o'clock!"

"All right, planet jockeys, this is what we've been waiting for — let's give them a flying lessen," said Captain Star.

Now the battle was on! As soon as they saw one — then here came another one — and another one. They began to appear like bees leaving a beehive. As the Getnorite ships were flying through the protection of their Reflector Image Eliminator, they looked as if they were appearing from nowhere! They were like popcorn — popping up one by one. Then they began to pop out five or six at a time!

The first three Getnorite ships were blasted out of the air as soon as they attacked the small group of Captain Star's crew. "Look Out YM—9! Missile coming in on left wing position!" shouted Captain Octzerfree. Dipping, then rolling over into a 360-degree spin, Space Fighter YM—9 outmaneuvered the missile only for it to hit one of the Getnorite ships.

Another of Star's pilots looped his ship between three of the Getnorite Interceptor warships; firing both rockets and lasers, he took out all three of them. He continued maneuvering his ship in a figure eight motion, holding his finger down on his laser blaster. "ZAP! BOOM! BLAM!" went his laser blaster — hitting one enemy ship and then another, both of them exploding into space dust.

Taking a hit from one of the Getnorite Interceptors, one of Captain Star's ships burst into flames and began to roll out of control. "I'm hit!" shouted the pilot frantically over his communicator. As flames rushed from his spaceship, he was still able to gain enough control to ram his dying ship into one of the enemy ships, exploding them both into a big ball of fire.

Zooming past each other at light speed, the odds were getting better. Captain Star and his small group of Imperial Planetary Defense Fighters were smaller, so they managed to outmaneuver the larger Getnorite ships. They had already destroyed over a dozen Getnorite warships.

Watching this small battle from the huge Getnorite mothership, Commander Boonor sat there in disbelief, thinking, "Those pilots of the Imperial Planetary Defense are well trained — if only they were on my side." Then he gave orders to his second in command, saying, "Send out the M-13 Squadron! We must not allow those IPD ships to escape and reveal our position!"

Soon, the huge hangar-bay doors opened, releasing small M-shaped fighter ships. They began to spring through the doors! This time there were about twenty-five or more! Looking at the sight of his M-13s leaving his Mothership en route to engage in battle with what was left of Captain Star's group of Imperial Planetary Defense Space Fighters, he was thinking, "Let me see what you are going to do now!" But in his heart, he knew that even though Captain Star and his crew were few, they were of a special breed.

Still flying rings around the Getnorite pilots, Captain Star is wondering how long can we last? He knew that he, and what was left of his ships, had been lucky. Banking in and out of rocket fire, he takes out two more Getnorite Interceptors. Then both he and Captain Octzerfree saw more strange-looking ships popping out of the invisible screen.

"What kind of ships are they, Captain?" asked one of his pilots over the communicator beam.

Seeing so many strange M—shaped ships streaking toward them, Captain Star, as he was still firing his laser blaster, said, "It doesn't make any difference — they are on their way!" He then made his ship roll to the right as he kicked his engines to hyperdrive. He zoomed off in the direction of the cluster of M—shaped ships.

"Wait for us! yelled Captain Octzerfree, as he and the other two IPD space fighters followed behind Captain Star with their cannons and lasers blazing!

Commander Algor, on board the Duderyon's Mothership, watched the battle on his huge Proximetry Indication Locator Screen, and excitedly exclaimed, "Look at those pilots! Just look at those pilots! He continued shouting with admiration, "I've never seen flying like that in all my years in the Duderyon Air Force!"

"Commander Algor, those pilots can't last out there much longer without our help sir! We must do something!" said his First Lieutenant, pleading with his Commander.

"I know, Lieutenant, but I can't give our position away," responded the Commander. He was thinking to himself, "If only that Getnorite fleet would show up on the screen!"

Dr. Cimjone saw Uzar arriving with Tryrenzie in her elaborate pomp, still in a trance due to the fertility drugs. He felt as though all his biological needs were about to be fulfilled. He slowly stepped down from his throne and took Uzar by the hand. He then led her back up the stairs to sit beside him.

After he and Uzar were seated, Tryrenzie took a step forward and knelt, then prostrated herself to him. She declared, "Dr. Cimjone, with all my understanding of the laws of our gods of Elmegorly, I, Tryrenzie have done my very best. So, if I have satisfied you, please release me from my enormous obligations. And, if I have not satisfied you — here is my life!" She then raised herself and stepped up to his throne, prostrated herself again, and kissed his feet.

Looking down on her, Dr. Cimjone takes her by the hand and pulls her to her feet. He kisses her hand and sqys, "Not in all my life have any of my wives been so faithful as you!"

He takes the Royal Ring of the gods of Elmegorly off his finger. He places it on hers, and says, "Tryrenzie, you may be dismissed." With that, he takes his throne again.
Tryrenzie turns, claps her hands three times, then gives the signal for everyone to be dismissed. She then leaves and returns to her quarters in tears — thinking to herself, "If only I could have been The Chosen One!"

Back in his prison room, Dr. Zuntor is still in his self—inflicted trance. Because he had such a greatly trained mind, not only had he mastered ESP, he had concentrated so intensely that he was levitating. There he was — about three feet in the air with both his legs and arms floating, and his eyes closed as he continued his mantra, "Uzar, I love you ... Don't let him touch you ... Help me, Uzar, Help me!"
Slipping through the maze of corridors with their arms full of packages, Dr. Pelcozor and Lanorque see one of Dr. Cimjone's guards. Tipping softly behind him, Lanorque hit him on the back of his head. They continued to work their way to the hangar area, ducking and hiding

as they slowly walked through the long hallways. They nervously make their way through the many doors.

Suddenly, they see a group of Dr. Cimjone's guards talking together. Hiding behind a stack of boxes, Dr. Pelcozor picks up a small box and throws it across the room. The sound of the box hitting the floor makes the guards run over to where they heard the sound. That gave Dr. Pelcozor and Lanorque an opportunity to slip by them.

Softly running down the next maze of corridors, avoiding many of Cimjone's guards, they finally make it to the hangar.

Opening a big door to the hangar, Dr. Pelcozor saw all types of space vehicles. Feeling relieved when he saw his ship (the one Lanorque had prepared earlier,) Dr. Pelcozor said, "I can't believe that my ship is still here. I guess my luck is still holding, Lanorque."

"Yes, Dr. Pelcozor, I'm also surprised that it's still here. When I was packing away some of our things, as you had instructed me, the guards looked as though they had something up their sleeves," said Lanorque.

"Well," replied Pelcozor, "It makes no difference now! Let's get on board and get away from this planet." The two men made their way up the boarding ladders.

Flying at the speed of light, the two killer Drymahords were entering the planet Getnor's orbit. Also patrolling the intra—space of their planet were three Getnorite starships.

What's that to your left, Sir?" said one of the pilots to his squad leader.

Before their captain could answer, the two Drymahords spit laser fire, hitting the starship, which exploded on contact. The other two pilots stared in disbelief! They began to maneuver their ships, trying to attack the two Drymahords, but within seconds, they had both become tiny pieces of flaming space debris!

Lying on a huge double—king—size bed, with soft light shinning through her hair, Uzar, in her unconscious mind, was receiving a telepathic message from Dr. Zuntor. Actually, her fragile mind was at war. The voice of Dr. Zuntor is telling her "Don't!" and the power of the fertility drugs were saying "Yes!" Uzar was lying quietly on the ritual bed — dazed and very confused.

As Dr. Cimjone looked down on Uzar, and he saw her trembling body slowly move, while her eyes were partially closed, he began to feel his heart beating nervously in his chest. He stood over Uzar, and with one hand, he took his time as he removed her transparent gold and diamond studded gown, then he slowly let it drop to the floor. His lust-filled eyes were drinking in the sight of her nude, virginal, and oh so beautiful, smooth and perfectly shaped body. He began to disrobe.

Uzar had begun to feel as if her body were going to erupt with the intensity of an exploding volcano! The throbbing of her sexual parts — Oh god! the throbbing — it was maddening, and yet so pleasurable! The effects of the Getnorite fertility drugs make Uzar feel as if, at any second, she would have a compound, complex orgasm. Her psychological and her physiological systems were activated to their highest capacity. She now had absolutely no control, and her body began writhing, in a sensuous pleading for release.

With hot lust running through his mind, Dr. Cimjone softly pressed his lips against her breast. Then with his flaming hot tongue, he slowly moved down her fresh, silky body. The fragrance of her body (due to her having been bathed in the mixture of exotic oils) caused Dr. Cimjone to become erected to such a degree that it became almost painful, albeit a pleasurable pain.

He slowly licked every part of Uzar's sweet body. Then, he mounted her, and was ready to penetrate, when the alarm rang and the sounds of massive destruction were coming from everywhere!

In a state of complete disbelief, Dr. Cimjone (still nude) ran over to his huge hologram screen and began to switch from area to area. The scenes were all the same. His army was running! His servants were screaming and running. He turned the dial until he could view his laboratory; the entire structure was collapsing, fire and smoke filled the corridors, and flames were engulfing his guards. Not able to understand any of this, Dr. Cimjone switched to Tryrenzie's chambers, where his wives lived. He saw a most horrifying sight! Bodies and blood were everywhere.

He could see some of his wives running, trying to escape the falling debris from the collapsing ceiling. Some of them were committing suicide in front of his very eyes. As he stumbled around the room, he watched on the hologram screen his world being destroyed. And then, with his peripheral vision, he caught a sight that virtually hypnotized him. It was both of the killer Drymahords!

Due to so much destruction, Dr. Zuntor broke his concentration and lost all hope for a chance to escape. He saw what was happening in Dr. Cimjone's ritualistic orgy room. He knew he had to somehow save Uzar, who was still in a trance.

The two killer Drymahords had destroyed everything in their path! They were using all of their destructive powers; shooting laser flames through their mouths, but worst of all, they were using their SVSW. The vibrational shocks in Dr. Cimjone's complex made the wall in Dr. Zuntor's prison room crumble — making a big hole, making a hole big enough for him to crawl through.

He ran through the corridors and worked his way to Dr. Cimjone's orgy room. He dodged and jumped over falling debris. He stumbled over dead bodies. He fell, but still got up running. In his mind, all he could think of was saving Uzar.

At last he reached the hallway where Dr. Cimjone's orgy chambers were located. Breaking through the locks with the use of one of Cimjone's dead guard's laser pistols, he saw Dr. Cimjone trying to pick Uzar up from off the bed. He shouts, "Put her down! You space slime!" In shock and disbelief, Dr. Cimjone lays Uzar back down on his royal bed. As he stood up and turned around, he saw a face that he had never expected to see again, standing there with a laser pistol in his hand!

He says, "Well, Well, Well — Dr. Zuntor! You never seem to get enough!"

Standing in the broken doorway, with his clothes in rags, and bleeding from a small cut over his eye, Dr. Zuntor said, "You are mistaken, Cimjone. You're the one that never gets enough. But it's all over now!"

"Oh, to the contrary, Dr. Zuntor, you will never leave here alive! My guards will cut you down before you ever make it out of here!" said Dr. Cimjone.

Dr. Zuntor replies, "That well might be, but right now, I've got you! And I'm going to give you all the power that is in this laser pistol!"

He pointed the blaster at Dr. CimJone!

Tryrenzie was getting up off the floor — where she had been knocked unconscious by falling stones from the now almost destroyed complex. Looking around and seeing so many dead bodies, she knew that it was the end of their civilization. She thought Dr. Cimjone had been killed, along with everyone else. She found a Golden Ritual Dagger. She fell on her knees and said, "Oh holy gods of Elmegorly, why have you brought such destruction to our planet? All things are dying around me. Have I been so displeasing in your sight, that you spared my life only to let me see all this? I was born, and The House of my mother's mother was born in this house. Cimjone!"

"I must ask myself, was it I, Tryrenzie, that brought such calamity down on the House of Cimjone? Is it because I was the one that performed your secret fertility ceremony on that woman who was not of the Getnorite descendants? If that is true, Oh holy gods of Elmegorly, I have greatly trespassed against you. And I, Tryrenzie, of the House of Cimjone, can see no other way I can justify my actions; therefore, I will have to offer you my life."

She then took the golden Getnorite, fertility—ritual, dagger and placed it against her heart — and fell on top of it! As she lay face down, dying, one of her arms was stretched outwardly. Her hand began to tremble — and suddenly it stopped and was perfectly still. The ring of the house of Cimjone was still on her finger...

Flying right into the center of the M-13s, Captain Star and his two remaining IPD Space Fighters used every maneuver known to a starship pilot. The M-13s might have been a special elite group of ships and pilots, but they were still no match for Captain Star and his two other ships.

M-13s were being shot out of the air like fish in a barrel. Looping, diving, rolling and even reversing their engines, to cause a drag that instantly slowed their space fighters down, so the M-13s would speed past them and would find their ships in the line of fire on one or the other of the three IPD space fighters' laser blasters. They used this maneuver over and over and it worked every time.

The battle was so intense that Captain Octzerfree had to stop using his laser blaster to let it cool off. During those times, he used only his missiles and cannons. After the Getnorites had lost about nine or ten M-13s, two of them criss—crossed one of the three Imperial Planetary Defense fighters. They fired at, and hit, the space fighter so many times, it exploded. The M-13s were so close, the debris from the IPD fighter smashed the cockpit window and the vacuum sucked the pilot out through his window.

He never knew what had happened as he helplessly floated away into space.

"Captain Star, we just lost ship YM-18," reported Captain Octzerfree, as he outmaneuvered six M-13s.

"Yes, I saw that," answered Captain Star, "I've got a plan — just follow me.

"Captain Octzerfree protested, "I can't yet! I've got to get these ships off my ass!"

"Have no fear — I am here!" shouted Captain Star as his ship looped like a triangle and ended up at the rear of the M-13s that were chasing Octzerfree's ship. Boom! Zung! went his cannons, hitting two of the M-13s. One of them took a hit in the rear engine. Then he dived in between Captain Octzerfree's ship and the other M-13. They were firing all around him. Suddenly, Captain Octzerfree saw his chance to bank to the left, make a 360-degree turn, and fly down on top of them! Kaboom! Bang! Blam! went his cannons, hitting one of the M-13s. Smoke shot out of the top of the M—shaped ship. Flying out of control, the wounded M-13, still smoking, rammed into another of the M-13s! Both of them exploded!

"Here's our chance, Captain Octzerfree," Captain Star's excited voice came over the communicator beam, "Follow Me!" The two small Imperial Planetary Defense space fighters made a run for it! Both pilots slammed down on their hyperdrive, and the race was on! The two little IPD fighters were headed straight into the invisible field, full speed ahead!

Pelcozor and Lanorque were attempting to take off from Dr. Cimjone's hangar. Meanwhile, the two killer Drymahords were destroying everything around them! There were fires, wrecked starships, collapsed buildings, and the entire area was littered with dead bodies everywhere! "Dr. Pelcozor, what should we do?" asked Lanorque, as they were trying to taxi down the littered runway.

"Don't ask so many questions, Lanorque," yelled Pelcozor. "Just keep away from those two beasts!"

Suddenly, they were at the end of the runway. Their ship stopped!!

"What's wrong now, you idiot!" screamed Dr. Pelcozor!

Lanorque tried to explain, "My computer can't open the bay doors! We can't get out of this hangar!"

"Well, what the hell is keeping it closed?" screamed Pelcozor! Looking out of the cockpit windows, Lanorque could see a wreaked ship jammed between the hangar doors. It had cut the hydraulic spring cables in half. After Lanorque explains this to Dr. Pelcozor, he and the crazed doctor climbed out of their ship so they could attempt to fix the door. They just had to get it open, so they would be able to get out!

Because of the killer Drymahords, huge stones and beams were falling everywhere in Dr. Cimjone's complex! Dr. Zuntor is still standing in the room with the laser pistol in his hand, pointed at Dr.

Cimjone. He asked Cimjone, "How does it feel to have your life in someone else's hands?"

"Don't be a fool, Zuntor. We've got to get out of here and off this planet before it's too late!" charged Cimjone nervously, with his hands still up in the air.

Dr. Zuntor demanded in return, "What do you mean? 'before it' s too late?' It's already too late! Can't you see that those killer Drymahords have already destroyed your kingdom, Cimjone?"

"That's not what I'm talking about," said Dr. Cimjone.

"Whatever it is," Dr. Zuntor spoke quietly, "I am going to make you pay for all the evil you have done."

Cimjone was still shouting at Dr. Zuntor, "Don't be a fool! You must listen! I'm trying to tell you something, Zuntor! There's a huge nuclear power unit underneath this complex! It's hooked up with the same type unit, all over the planet! If one explodes, they all go!! Do you understand? Listen to me!"

Dr. Zuntor continued to speak quietly, "So — It looks as if the killer Drymahords are going to take the entire planet out. Even so, you're getting what you deserve, Cimjone. Carelessly, Dr. Zuntor started moving closer to Uzar. But as soon as he was within touching distance, a big beam fell from the wall on top of him, knocking him to the floor.

Cimjone, seeing this, jumped on top of him. Rolling over and over, the two men commenced fighting. Uzar, in the meantime, was still unconscious. Dr. Cimjone got up and kicked Dr. Zuntor in the face, rendering him confused and dazed. Once again, Dr. Cimjone jumped him. As Cimjone is trying to choke him, Dr. Zuntor attempts to crawl away to gain an advantage. Dr. Zuntor was finally able to strike him across the bridge of his nose with the side of his hand.

With his nose broken, and blood running from it, Cimjone lost his grip on Dr. Zuntor's throat. Dr. Zuntor hits Cimjone with a strong right that knocks him back against the wall. Rushing over to him, Dr. Zuntor rams his head into his stomach and knocks the wind out of him. Then, he gets him again with a left and then a right! Dr. Zuntor, (even though completely exhausted) uses all his strength, and hits Dr. Cimjone with a hard right hook, that knocks Dr. Cimjone out cold!

Glancing around, and realizing that Dr. Cimjone's entire complex is about to cave in, Dr. Zuntor rushes over to Uzar. She is lying on the bed, completely helpless, and still undressed. Dr. Zuntor picked up her gown and wraped her in it. He gathered her up into his arms and rushed into the hallway.

Dust and boulders are falling all around them as Dr. Zuntor ran (with Uzar in his arms,) through the explosions and the flames. He is, of course, terrified of all this which is going on throughout the complex!

As Zuntor is running, he is thinking, "Whatever happens, I've got Uzar back. If we don't make it, at least we will go out together!" Then, as he rushes down the corridors, he repeats over and over to himself, "Come on Zuntor! You can do this! Just a little further! Come On!!"

The killer Drymahords were still blowing up everything in sight! Fire and smoke is coming from their mouths. The heat is so intense that buildings are melting — with people still inside them, screaming! The people were running with nowhere to go! Babies were crying! There is no doubt that it is doomsday for the planet Getnor!

After destroying as much as they wanted, the two killer Drymahords took to the sky, leaving a cloud of smoke below them. It seems as though they were communicating telepathically; as soon as they were airborne, they zeroed in on Dr. Cimjone's complex. They were concentrating their sonic vibration shock waves on their target. As the shock waves grew more intense, the complex, with all its beautiful temples and living quarters, totally collapsed!

"Okay, Dr. Pelcozor! It's fixed! The doors will open now!" yelled Lanorque after he had removed enough scraps from the starship, that had been preventing the huge bay doors from opening. Covering their heads and running back to their spaceship, Dr. Pelcozor screams, "We don,t have any time left — We must hurry!"

At last both Dr. Pelcozor and Lanorque were back in their ship, getting ready for take—off through the (now open) bay doors! Dr. Pelcozor, watching the runway through the cockpit windows, saw his brother (carrying Uzar) headed for one of the few remaining Getnorite starships. He shouts at Lanorque, "Look! Look!" as he was pointing his finger toward them.

"Where Doctor?" asked Lanorque.

Dr. Pelcozor, still pointing, and shouting, "Over there! Look!" "Yes! I see them now! It's your brother! Dr. Pelcozor! It's your brother, Dr. Zuntor !" cried Lanorque with fear in his voice!

"I don't give a damn about him! Keep your eyes on the controls, stupid! Get us out of here before this damned place blows up!"

Dr. Zuntor saw his brother's ship take off, with blue fire shooting out of its rocket's exhaust. He said to himself, "Pelcozor, I'll get you this time, for what you have done to me!" The sight of his brother again, knowing he still had a chance to pay him back, gave him more stamina and more energy. Carrying Uzar in his arms, he ran, trying to find any kind of spacecraft that would help them escape this inferno!

After an exhausting effort, they were finally on a ship, starting to taxi down the runway. The hangar was vibrating; huge stones and beams were falling; fire and steam was surrounding them as they were about to take off through the big, bay doors.

As Dr. Zuntor was piloting the ship, Uzar began to awaken. But she simply couldn't believe what she saw. Her eyes opened slowly.

It was her wish come true (as she saw Dr. Zuntor at the controls). "Oh, my love — you saved me!" she murmured as she weakly threw her arms around him. She kissed him all over his face. She was rapidly coming out of her drugged state.

Smiling, Dr. Zuntor gently pushed her back as he said, "Hold it, my dear Uzar. I think we had better do this some other time." He had almost lost control of their ship.

Almost back to her old self, she looked at Dr. Zuntor, and noticed that his whole demeanor had changed. He no longer was the shy, timid, and reserved scientist. Even his body language portrayed a strong, confident, and brave hero who was on a mission!

Uzar asked him, "Who taught you to fly this starship?"

He gave her a big sexy smile, and boastfully replied, "No one had to teach me, I'm the one that designed this piece of junk!" At that instant his ship zoomed through the big bay door, and in his mind, he was thinking "I've got to catch up with Pelcozor. Knowing him, he has what I need!"

Dr. Cimjone was lying on the floor, still unconscious, with debris all around him. He still didn't know that the two killer Drymahords were about to totally destroy his planet. He started to move his fingers, and slowly his eyes started to open. He nervously stumbled to his feet. Looking around, he knew he had only one chance to save himself. He had to make it to his starship. Still dazed, he staggered to the doorway. He was almost there when the ancient stone walls collapsed on top of him. He was buried under tons of stone from "The House of Cimjone!"

They were standing at right angles, which connected the sonic waves. The sonic waves were creating a tremendous vacuum. The Drymahords increased the vibrations — more and more, until buildings were melting and exploding everywhere. The pressure of their sonic vibration shock waves began to vibrate the area where the nuclear energy reactors were housed. The pressure—meter needles were trembling in the red zone. Pressure valves were peaking; pipes were bursting, and steam was spraying into the air. People were running for their lives! But there was nowhere to go! The remaining few of the planet's population were in mass hysteria.

The Drymahords were also using simultaneously on the Cimjone complex! The heat from their laser breath, coupled with the sonic vibrations, were so intense, the nuclear energy reactors exploded, which caused a chain reaction of the other nuclear reactors throughout the planet of Getnor!

The two killer Drymahords, along with the planet Getnor, inevitably exploded into a zillion pieces.

From out in space, Dr. Zuntor could see what was once the great planet Getnor. It was now nothing but a brilliant hot ball of fire. The force from the explosion of the planet made such a ripple in space, that the shock waves made all the spaceships in the area vibrate so violently that many had to redirect or alter their course. Dr. Cimjone and his planet is no more!

Captain Star and the only pilot he had left, along with Captain Octzerfree were finally breaking through the Reflector Image Eliminator Screen of The Getnorite Royal Fleet. Seeing all the Starships headed for the planet Duderyon, Captain Octzerfree said over his communicator to Captain Star, "Wow! I never dreamed there could be so many ships out here and not be able to pick them up on our Proximetry Indication Locator Screen, Sir!"

"It's just as I thought, they were in our face all the time!" replied Captain Star.

Knowing that the only chance of staying alive was to get in touch with the Duderyon fleet and give them their location, Captain Star opened his communicator to full range. "Captain Star calling Commander Algor — Code X—36! Code X—36! If you can hear me, please reply! — Code X—36 — Code X—36!!"

Not seeing him any longer on his Proximetry Locator screen, Commander Algor knew that Captain Star had broken through to the other side of the Getnorite Image Eliminator screen. Fortunately, although faint, he could hear the X—36 call from Captain Star.

He answered, "Commander Alger here, Captain Star — continue!"

"I've found them, sir! And it's the entire air force!" reported Captain Star.

"We can't pick you up on our Proximetry Indication screen", declared the Commander.

Captain Star replied, "I know, Sir. But I can guide you in, if you can track our communicator beams."

Commander Algor excitedly announced, "WE ARE AS GOOD AS THERE! GO AHEAD, CAPTAIN!" He then turned to his navigator; "Get ready to set a new course, as soon as you hear their position!"

Captain Star gave the Commander directions: "Veer to your left 10 degrees, then head straight for the edge of the Pyeeroney sector. I'll leave our communicator beam open, then all you'11 have to do is track us! But Commander, I don't think we are going to last much longer if you don't hurry! And for God's sake, bring everything you've got!!"

Commander Algor gave the order to sound the alarm for full attack. Men and women were running and pushing buttons all over the Duderyon mothership! In the hangar, pilots were running and boarding their warships and Space Fighters!

The same activity was taking place on all of the huge Imperial Planetary Defense Transport Ships. Warships and Space Fighters of every size and shape were zooming from out of big bay doors of each Carrier in the fleet. The rocket smoke was so heavy that the section in which the Duderyon fleet was located looked like an old Ford with an overheated radiator — steam was shooting out everywhere! Soon after the orders to attack were given, the heavens were filled with Duderyon Imperial Planetary Defense Fighter Ships.

The Commander said to his Communications Officer, "Keep your fix on both Captain Star and Captain Octzerfree's ships. Until we break through their Reflector Image Eliminator Screen, our Proximetry Indication Locator Screen will do us no good. All we have is just those two little dots!"

Seeing that Captain Star and Captain Octzerfree had broken through his Invisible Reflector screen, Commander Boonor knew it was time to attack! Even though he couldn't find the Duderyon fleet, he knew they were also behind their own Reflector Eliminator screen. On second thought, not only were they out there, they were also in his fleet's face.

Slamming his fists down on the arms of his chair, Commander Boonor gave the command to attack! As the Getnorite officers and pilots were running to obey the orders of attack,

Commander Boonor was thinking, (as he continued to watch his Proximetry Indication Screen) "Who are those two pilots that are out—flying all of my Interceptors?"

"Dr. Pelcozor, there's a Getnorite ship coming up fast!" warned Lanorque, as he zoomed through the stars after leaving Dr. Cimjone's planet. He still hadn't really caught his breath after their narrow escape. He was just now beginning to realize they had gotten away just seconds before the planet was turned into space dust!

Pelcozor was sitting in the private area of his ship, holding the only cylinder of Dr. Cimjone's Reversal Antidote Serum that remained in the entire solar system. He was thinking, "With this serum, I can still control everything. There is no way anyone can acquire any of this, because Dr. Cimjone is dead — blown up with his planet! Now I have all the power right here in my hands!"

He broke out in a loud, ruthless laugh, taking pleasure in thinking about his own cleverness! Pelcozor was so lost in his own thoughts, he didn't hear Lanorque when he was trying to tell him that someone was following them. Dr. Pelcozor leaned back in his big chair and began to relax.

"There he is Uzar! It won't be long now!" exclaimed Dr. Zuntor.

"What are you going to do, Dr. Zuntor?" asked Uzar.

"I'm going to intercept his ship and force him to land on some asteroid — or even force him to go back to Duderyon!" answered Dr. Zuntor.

"What if he puts up a fight?" inquired Uzar.

Dr. Zuntor sadly and slowly, asserted, "Then, one of us will have to die."

Captain Star spoke into his communicator, "Captain Octzerfree, it's been good knowing you — cause it will be impossible for us to take on all this", indicating the entire Getnorite fleet.

"You're right, Captain Star. But I must say, I'm glad we got to work together — you're one hell—of—a pilot! And we made one hell—of—a team!"

The two pilots didn't even bother to look at their Proximetry Indication Locator screens. All they needed to do was look out of their cockpit windows. It was as if all the stars in the heavens were hiding, and in place of stars, there were Getnorite war—ships — all headed toward them!

The first wave of Getnorite ships to engage in battle with the two captains were small, Tiproll D—6s. They looked like horseshoes that fired cannons from both ends of the horseshoe. They were tiny and fast, which gave them incredible maneuverability.

Slicing in and out of the Getnorite formation, Captain Star was blasting as he maneuvered through a cluster of them.

Sizzling across the bow of Captain Octzerfree's ship were two missiles, fired from an M-13 ship, only to hit one of the Tiproll D—S's. Criss—crossing each other, and using all the firepower they had, both IPD Space Fighters managed to trap five D—s's and wipe them out! With such an impossible score, both captains became a little more confident. If only the cavalry would arrive in time! They had no time to really think about it because a second wave of Getnorite warships were upon them! Rolling and dipping, using all the maneuvers of defense they had ever known, the two pilots began to think it was over for them.

Suddenly, rockets streaked past them and knocked out six of the D—s's and three of the M-13s! Looking in their rear—view screens, what a relief! Hundreds of Imperial Planetary Defense warships were popping through the reverse side of the invisible Getnorite screen! Swirling and intercepting on—coming Getnorite ships, causing destruction with every maneuver, the IPD fleet was putting quite a dent into the overwhelming advantage the Getnorite fleet had at the beginning of this fray!

More and more D-6s and M-13s were launched from out of the belly of the enormous mothership. The battle area was blackened with space fighters, carriers, and the like. The IPD was holding its own, and fighting well against the overwhelming odds. But more reinforcements started to pop through the invisible screen. It was nothing less than a dog fight! Warships were dying each second of the brawl.

Captain Star initiated the maneuvering of his ship until he had formed a group of ten IPD ships. Captain Octzerfree did the same. These two small, newly formed squadrons of Imperial Planetary Defense Space Fighters were causing very heavy losses for the Getnorite fleet. Following the commands of both captains, the two new squadrons were displaying defenses that the captains had learned from their combined years of experience. They had picked up some of these defense tactics from the two killer Drymahords.

Their combined tactics were so unorthodox that the Getnorite warships were being completely outmaneuvered and blown out of the heavens by the dozens! However, even more Getnorite warships continued to join the conflict! There were so many destroyed ships in the arena that the floating debris were bouncing off the ships as they attacked each other.

On the bridge of both motherships, each commander was screaming orders to their pilots over their communicators. Everyone knew that this was the mother of all battles!

"Captain Octzerfree, this is Star, can you read me?"

"Yes Captain Star — go ahead!"

"Remember I said I had something special I was saving? Well, now is the time! Will you and your men follow me?"

Octzerfree declared, "We're with you Star! Lead the way!" The two small squadrons broke off from the conflict and vanished back behind the invisible Getnorite screen.

After Captain Star led the two squadrons out of the heat of battle, behind the invisible Getnorite screen, he continued to lead them to a higher geometrical orbit than where the battle was taking place. He then said to Captain Octzerfree, "I want you to align your ship alongside my ship — then, position your squad to your left, and I'll position my squad to my right. Okay? Now, it's important that we hold our pattern throughout the entire maneuver!"

"Yeah! I understand," declared Captain Octzerfree. "We will be in a triangular pattern, right?"

"You got it!" maintained Captain Star as he continued to lay out his plan.

Now, each pilot must adjust his laser cannon to a fifteen-degree angle, and his rocket blaster at a seven-degree angle. Got It?" demanded Captain Star.

Each individual pilot answered, "Got it, Sir!" "Yes, Sir!" "Right On, Sir!" until all were accounted for.

"Now, Pilots, listen closely. This maneuver can be extremely dangerous, so we can't make a single mistake!" Captain Star resumes his instructions. "Okay now! It's very important that each ship keep their distance. If one ship is lost, the next ship must move up and take its place! — Got It?" Once again, each pilot answers in the positive.

"When I give the signal, each ship must fire simultaneously, and the pattern will do the rest! So... are you ready?" asked Captain Star.

"Ready!" answered the pilots in unison.

After a wild rebel scream, Captain Star ordered his pilots! "Come on Planet-Jockeys — Follow Me!"

Then each pilot, in their newly-shaped triangle formation, revved up their engines to full throttle, and threw them into hyperdrive. This propelled them, as if they were an arrow shot from a bow, back through the invisible Getnorite force—field screen, directly into the thick of the battle!!

Following Captain Star, along with Captain Octzerfree on his right wing, the tight group of IPD Space Fighters swooped, dived, looped, rolled, and made 360-degree turns with all weapons firing at full blast. This maneuver was so effective that Captain Star's group alone destroyed more than a hundred Getnorite ships!

"Seeing Dr. Zuntor's ship banking just behind them, Lanorque shouted! "He's gaining on us Dr. Pelcozor!"

Moving into the gunner's seat, Pelcozor said, "Loop around behind them with a 360-degree loop and I'11 blast them out of existence!"

Lanorque made that 360-degree oval loop, and Pelcozor zips up behind his brother. Pelcozor was firing at them continuously!!

Realizing he had been out—maneuvered, Dr. Zuntor knew he had to use desperate means to stay alive! Rolling to the left, then banking to the right, he nonetheless rather skillfully managed his ship. He simply could not shake the fire from his brother's ship.

Suddenly, at a distance (thanks be to the gods!) he spots a meteorite storm and steers his ship directly into the middle of it! Flying, rolling from side to side, ducking huge boulders at sonic speed, both starships were taking a beating.

"Keep up with them! Don't lose them you idiot!" screamed Pelcozor.

"My first concern is I've got to be careful of these meteors, Dr. Pelcozor. If not, we'll never get out of here alive," shouted Lanorque. Beating his fists against the arms of the gunner's chair, Pelcozor is totally obsessed with only one thing — killing his brother!

Pelcozor dropped the cylinder which contained Dr. Cimjone's Reversal Antidote Agent! Seeing it rolling around on the floor, he dives out of the chair after it! He is trying desperately to seize it before the cylinder breaks. Inadvertently, he kicks Lanorque upside his head! The blow from his foot strikes him solidly, and knocks him unconscious.

With Pelcozor crawling around on the floor, and Lanorque now slumped over the controls, their ship was completely out of control. Being tossed from side—to—side, and still screaming at Lanorque, Pelcozor stumbled to the ship's controls and threw Lanorque out of the seat and onto the floor. He snatched the controls and tried desperately to fly the ship out of the meteor storm.

Of course he is now completely insane, and is rambling on—and—on to himself: "Nothing! No One! Will ever stop me! I'M

DOCTOR Pelcozor! And since I have this," (he stares intently at the serum, which he is now tightly clutching in his hand) "I can rule the entire solar system!" He starts to chuckle, then he giggles, then he laughs, and the laughter gets louder and louder!

But then, as if it were meant to be, a huge meteorite (as big as a mountain) is directly in the path of his starship. Without an opportunity to maneuver his ship away, Pelcozor covers his face and screams, as his ship slams into the huge meteorite and explodes into space dust!!

Making it to the other side of the meteorite storm and back on course to Duderyon, Dr. Zuntor and Uzar are making plans about getting married as soon as they arrive. Even after the cruelty his brother had put them through, Dr. Zuntor is still feeling the pain of losing his brother so unexpectantly. Uzar, trying to console him, said, "I know he was your brother, but he had gone mad and would have destroyed so many lives. And please, darling, don't blame yourself for his death. Karma killed him, not you, my love."

Holding her in his arms, Zuntor gazed into her sweet eyes and declared, "You are right, my love, I can't keep my mind on the past. I have to look to the future — and my future is all you!" The kiss he gave her was a long sweet one!

One thing he forgot was to put the ship on automatic pilot. So they were rudely interrupted as the ship tilted from side—to—side. Pulling away and quickly seizing the controls, Dr. Zuntor said with a smile, "We will have to continue this on automatic pilot!" He threw the switch and the little starship slowly flew back in the direction of Duderyon.

Breaking through the Getnorite's Reflector Image Eliminator Screen, the entire Duderyon IPD Air Force, followed by its enormously huge, command—mother—ship, were now all in the conflict. Each side was launching heavy attacks on the other. As soon as one side began to receive too many casualties, the commander of that mother—ship would order reinforcements sent out.

This went on until Captain Algor gave the order for his navigator to swing his vessel around and withdraw back through the Getnorite's Reflector Image Eliminator Screen. After returning back to the Pyeeroney sector, Commander Algor ordered, "I want every available craft to follow and surround me. He then had has navigator maneuver his ship in a vertical movement half way between orbits. Then he and all the ships that were not still engaged in the action, hovered in place and waited for his trap to spring.

Seeing the Duderyon mother—ship pull away from the battle, Commander Booner said to Lt. Scuff (slapping his hands together) "We got em! This is a great moment in history! All we've got to do now is destroy that big piece of junk out there!" He then turned to his navigator, saying, "Full thrust, all engines!"

Speeding as fast as his huge ship with its escort could go, and breaking through their screen feeling the thrill of victory at his fingertips, Commander Boonor could see nothing in front of him and his ship! He demands of Lt. Scuff, "Where are they! Where are they? I know they're here somewhere! Where the hell are they? "

Knowing that his prey had fallen deep into his trap, Commander Algor gave the command to his navigator to descend. As his navigator followed orders, so did his escort ships. They all descended along with him!

Now the Duderyon (IPD) fleet — all that were not engaged in the battle already — attacked the Getnor mothership and its fleet, after receiving the sommand from Commander Algor. The Imperial Planetary Defense warships were streaking out of the mothership by the hundreds. The Getnorites never knew what hit them. The IPD ships were plucking them out of space at will.

Commander Algor saw a chance to get a sharp angle on the Getnorite's mothership. He commanded his ship's gunners to zero in on the mothership's rear hyperdrive units. "Group your lasers tighter, men," he ordered as he looked at his computer target screen. "Hold it right there!" Once he had a fix on the Getnorite ship, Commander Algor gave the order to fire. At that instant, all fifty laser cannons fired simultaneously, hitting the hyperdrive units of tbe huge mothership. Upon impact, it exploded!

There was such a shockwave from that much force, it caused a chain reaction that also took out most of the fleet that were too near that immediate area. From a distance, it looked like a five—hundred megaton nuclear blast — mushroom cloud and all! The sight of the explosion filled the other Getnorite pilots with fear and confusion. They all flew off in different directions!

After all of his ships had returned aboard, Commander Alger headed back to the planet Duderyon. He then requested that Captain Star and Captain Octzerfree be brought to the bridge immediately. Not much later, the two captains were standing at attention, in front of their Commander. However, the Commander was sitting back in his chair, completely relaxed. He spoke to the two captains, "I want you to know how much we appreciate your efforts. If it weren't for your warning, we could not have won this battle. Actually, there is no doubt, if it weren't for the both of you, our fleet, as well as our planet, would have been completely destroyed."

Both Captains thanked their Commander. Then Captain Star said, "Commander Algor, Sir, I would like to say, if it weren't for Captain Octzerfree, none of it would have been possible, Sir."

Then Captain Octzerfree said, "No, Commander, that's not true! If it weren't for Captain Star, none of it would have been possible."

And Captain Star said, "He is just being modest, Sir. He knows it was him that saved the day."

And Captain Octzerfree said, "Don't listen to him, Commander. I'm telling you the truth, Sir. It was Captain Star."

This went on, back-and-forth until the Commander laughingly interrupted, with his hands over his ears. "All right! The both of you! That's Enough! It doesn't matter which one of you is responsible. All I know is that both of you are going to receive our planet's highest award — The Duderyon Imperial Planetary Defense Medal of Honor."

Both Captains knew it was the highest award that anyone could ever receive. Beaming with pride, both Captains gave their Commander a Duderyon IPD salute and stood waiting to be dismissed. Until Commander Algor, with an inquisitive look on his face, inquired, "There is only one thing I've got to know..."

Both Captains noticed the strange look on his face and said in unison, "Yes Commander?"

The Commander looked around, and checked both sides of himself; just to make sure no one could hear him, "Who in hell taught you two how to fly? I've never seen such flying in all my life! Whoever it was, I need him on my team!"

Both Captains started to giggle. Soon they were laughing. And the next thing they knew, they were roaring with laughter until the tears were rolling down their faces. Commander Algor, feeling as if he were being disrespected, shouted, "All right! What's so funny?!" After regaining their composure, both Captain Star and Captain Octzerfree (at the exact same time) announced, "YOU DID, SIR!!"

Part II: The Serum

The council meeting of the Dudery on Imperial Planetary Defence Air Force was convened to discuss the necessary disposal of Dr. Zuntor's ZYM230.6 Serum. Admiral Fitchly was saying, "My fellow Duderyons, it has been a generation since the Killer Drymahords were destroyed. As we all know, our own technology created them. It's my duty to make sure nothing like that ever happens again.

Interrupting his speech, one of the council members declared, "I thought all that was behind us. What is so important that you summoned all of us, from every planet in our solar system, to this meeting? Why, may I ask?"

"Yes, he's right," said another member of the council. At that, the entire council became unruly.

"Order! I said Order!" shouted the Chairman of the Council, as he beat his gavel on the table. Soon the huge hall, filled with people, was once again under control. Then the chairman said, "Admiral Fitchly, you may continue."

Fitchly went on to say: "Our own Dr. Zuntor, has come to a horrifying conclusion that his ZYM230.6 Serum cannot be destroyed."
Another member said, "Are you telling us that as long as that Serum's around, we are in danger of creating another creature that could be as treacherous as those Killer Drymahords?"

"I'm saying, even more horrifying!" said Admiral Fitchly.

"That's exactly what he's saying, shouted another member.

"We must come up with a way to get rid of that Serum!" a member from the planet's Green Control said.

"Why don't we just burn it up with laser rays?" asked another.

Admiral Fitchly answered, "We've already tried that, with a very small portion of the Serum, and it came back as a toxic gas. The gas accidentally got into the system of some laboratory animals, and they had to be destroyed."

"Why is that so important about them being destroyed?" asked another member.

"It would have been normal if we were trying to expose them to the gas, but it was just by chance that they were exposed. At any rate, in a gaseous form - we really have no control. It expands in volume, and we can't see it, taste it, or smell it. As of now, Dr. Zuntor tells me the remainder of the Serum is stored away in a tamper-proof cylinder. He is waiting for me to tell him what you have decided."

Jumping up, waving his hands, General Sunbird shouted, "This is all some kind of devious plot. We all know that Dr. Zuntor's Serum has been put away for his own purposes, to use at a later time! He might be just like his brother. He could be, with help of others, trying to take over the Solar System." With that statement, General Sunbird had the entire council in a panic — which was just what the general was hoping for.

The Chairman used his gavel over and over, trying to regain control of the meeting. This was probably the most important meeting in Duderyon's history, and this latest turn of events was unnerving, to say the least.

All this time, General Sunbird had been waiting for an opportunity to suggest that Dr. Zuntor was trying to use scare tactics to maintain control of his ZYM230.6 Serum. All that was important to Sunbird now, was to find a way, with the help of his men, to somehow take possession of that toxic Serum. With the confusion still at its height, General Sunbird turned to his assistant, Tufus, and stated, "Now I have them where I want them!"

"Good for you, General," responded Tufus. "Keep up the pressure..."

Smiling, General Sunbird said, "Members of the Council. it is not my intention to discredit Dr. Zuntor's good name. But we must be realistic about this matter."

Breaking in, Admiral Fitchly said, "If you've got the answers, then what do you suggest, General Sunbird?" The General couldn't help but smile as he offered, "We could form a small committee of about five of us, then, we could take the Serum on a ship to a faraway asteroid, and leave it there, so it will never again be a threat to us."
The council took a vote, and the general's advice was accepted. Admiral Fitchly said, "Well, I must admit, it's a good idea, but who do we pick to be on this important transport committee?"

Jumping up, waving his hands, General Sunbird's assistant, Tufus said, "I can't think of anyone better to lead this mission than General Sunbird. Therefore, I'm going to nominate him."

Admiral Fitchly suggested, "I think it would only be right if Dr. Zuntor goes along, since he knows more about this Serum than anyone else."

These two men were quickly approved, along with several assistants. Before the meeting was adjourned, the Admiral interjected: "One more thing before I give my stamp of approval — I'm going to demand that we designate Captain Star to be the Officer In Charge of the entire operation with all the powers of the Interplanetary Council behind him!"

With that, the council took one more vote; and with the decision being unanimous, and everyone in agreement, the meeting came to an end.

Back in his quarters, General Sunbird was pacing the floor, very upset over the fact that he had not been given total control over this mission. Saying to his assistant Tufus, "How dare those fools pick someone like that Captain Star instead of me!? I am a general! How dare they?"

Placating him, Tufus obligingly declared, "I know Sir, but to them, he is still a hero from the war with the Getnorites. Other than that Sir, they never would have even dreamed of doing something like this!"

Always scheming, General Sunbird began to smile, as he said, "Do you realize what they did? Oh well, in the end, things just might work out to be the best opportunity we could ever have hoped for."

"I don't understand Sir," said Tufus.

The General began to laugh as he explained. "Not too long ago, I got a secret message from what was left of the Getnorite Air Force. They are still out there in the old Getnor Sector! They're based on a huge asteroid. I'm going to get in touch with Commander Booner. I'm sure he will be glad to hear that he still has friends in this part of the galaxy!"

"Captain Star, wake up! Wake up!" Shaking him was his personal assistant, Jets.

"Aaah, go away Jets!" said Captain Star, with sleep still in control of his mind and body. He gently pushed Jets away.

Always persistent, Jets shook him again. "Come on Boss, you've gotta get up. It's important. Get up! Boss!!"

Captain Star, rolled over in his huge bed, and slowly opened his eyes. He pulled the red satin sheets up over his massive (and still half-naked) body, and complained, "Jets, what can be so important that you woke me so early? I feel as if I've just gone to sleep." He began to stretch.

Answering him, Jets said sarcastically, "You did just go to sleep! You partied too much and too long, Captain."

Putting his hand over his eyes, the chagrined Captain asserted, "Okay, alright, tell me why you woke me up, and it had better be good.

Pushing a beautiful woman out of his way as he sat on the side of Captain Star's bed, Jets began to show him pictures and a message he had just received. Jets said, "Not only do you have these, but, there is someone in your Galaxy Room, waiting to speak with you. You should hurry with your dressing, and you'd better make like a real person and go make some sorta intelligent talk."

It wasn't long before Captain Star entered his Galaxy Room with the pictures in his hands. Not looking up to see who his guest was, and still shuffling through the photos, he heard a voice that said, "I hope you don't make a habit of keeping people waiting, Captain Star."

Still not feeling well, and very much irritated about being awakened early, Captain Star said in a snappy tone, "You're lucky I got up at all." Before he could say "all" his eyes focused on one of the most beautiful women he had ever in his life seen. And believe me, Captain Star (being a ladies' man) had seen many women before, but never one such as this! Standing with his mouth open, he spoke slowly. "Who are you!?" He then sat down on one of his floating chairs.

"I am Lt. Tulley, she announced. I've been assigned to you, to be your new assistant." Snapping out of the surprise of such a beautiful woman with a message to the reality of her having been assigned to him, for a mission that he didn't even know he had been given, Captain Star jumped to his feet as he exclaimed, "Wait! Hold it right there, Lt. Tulley! This has to be some kind of mistake! I'm on vacation!"

Cutting him off, Lt. Tulley said, "I realize you're on vacation, but I have orders from Admiral Fitchly. As of now, I'm to brief you and bring you up to speed on your assignment."

"What assignment?" asked the incredulous Captain Star.

The Lieutenant continued to explain: "You've been ordered to head to a group – along with Dr. Zuntor – to an asteroid. Once there, you are to dispose of a cylinder of dangerous Serum, making sure that it's done thoroughly and properly. Then you are to return the group safely, back here to Duderyon."

"Any Star Pilot can do that," said Captain Star.

"It's not as easy as it sounds," asserted Lt. Tulley. "Because there are those who would like to confiscate the payload, and keep it for their own gains. Needless to say, if it gets into the wrong hands, it would cause a real problem. That's why Admiral Fitchly picked you and Dr. Zuntor to partner up and take charge of this most vital, and important mission."

"Well, I should have known it! As soon as I begin to enjoy myself, things were bound to go wrong. So, Lieutenant, when do we have to leave?"

"As soon as you meet with Dr. Zuntor, replied Lt. Tulley. "He is expecting you."

Dr. Zuntor, and his wife, Usar, were in their laboratory doing the last test on the container that will hold the ZYM230.6 Serum. The terrible, destructive Serum will be placed in this container for eternal storage on the asteroid. Dr. Zuntor spoke to his wife, "Usar, I feel sure this container will hold up under any pressure that might occur from the atmosphere, on any asteroid, in any galaxy!"

Usar, looking at. Dr. Zuntor with admiration, said, "Darling, I think you've done a great job! Now all we have to do is deposit the cylinder of Serum into this container and all of our fears will be over."

Just then, an impatient young boy came running into the laboratory, shouting: "Dad! I'm still waiting on you to come and look at my new project. Come on, Dad! You promised!" He was pulling Dr. Zuntor by the hand. It was their son, Orcal.

Orcal was born not long after Usar and Zuntor were married. Usar became pregnant the first time they mated, due to the fertility drug she received when they were prisoners of the evil Dr. Cimjone, on the planet Getnor. Now, years later, every time they looked at Orcal, they thought about how close he had come to being the royal heir of the ruthless Dr. Cimjone. Only luck, and their incredible love for each other, had made the difference.

Dr. Zuntor, with a big smile on his face, said to Usar, "Well I promised him. Besides, we're just about wrapped up here, so why not spend some fun-time with our son?" So, both Usar and Dr. Zuntor, (each holding little Orcal's hands) slowly, but, oh so proudly, walked with their son to his miniature laboratory.

When they arrived at the door of Orcal's mini-lab, he turned off the lights only to reveal an illuminated projection of their solar system on the walls and ceiling. There was a fleet of miniature Starships, flying slowly under their own power. Usar stood there, totally amazed at what a boy of his age had accomplished by himself. She was spellbound and almost speechless.

Picking him up and hugging him, Dr. Zuntor asked, "How did you ever come up with all with all of this, Orcal?"

Orcal, smiling, looked at his father's surprised face (although his eyes were filled with approval) and said, "Father, you taught me about gravitational reversal and propulsion. And, as far as the positioning of the solar system, and the battle of the star fleet, the whole scene came to me in a dream. It's a dream I've had many times."

Usar moved closer to the both of them and put her arms around them as she asked, "Orcal, why didn't you tell me you were having these dreams?"

Answering her, Orcal said, "Mother, I've been having these kind of dreams almost every time I go to sleep.

After hearing this, both Usar and Dr. Zuntor looked at each other. This was the first time they realized that little Orcal had his mother's gift of clairvoyancy and was able to foresee the future.

On an asteroid, in the ex-Getnor sector, Commander Booner had been working for years (earth time), reassembling his fleet. It was unknown to most inhabitants of their solar system that he was still alive. His Mothership had been destroyed in battle, along with the Imperial Planetary Defense Fleet under his command. Knowing his Mothership was going to explode at any second, Commander Booner and Lt. Scuff escaped in a smaller shuttle, just before the explosion. After escaping his doom, Boonor collected what was left of his old fleet and flew around to all of the outlaw planets in their solar system, and assembled a new fleet of outlaw Warships.

Now, as he was feverishly assembling a new, huge Mothership, he was saying to Lt. Scuff, "Soon I'll be able to have revenge for the loss of my fleet and our planet."

"Yes, Commander," said the Lieutenant, "It won't be long now. Sir. Our engineers are working continuously on your new Mothership." They were hidden on the dark side of their huge, newly colonized asteroid. Although it was still being constructed, it looked like a masterpiece. Commander Boonor's new Mothership was almost completed!

"Dr. Zuntor, there is a Captain Star and a Lt. Tulley here to see you, Sir", announced their assistant. Still enjoying their son's ingenious project, Dr. Zuntor ordered their assistant to show the both of them into little Orcal's mini-laboratory.

Walking into the mini-lab, Captain Star and Lt. Tulley are greeted by Usar. "We're so glad you both could come. As you see, Dr. Zuntor is completely occupied with our our son's latest project."

Looking around, both Captain Star and Lt. Tulley were totally amazed at what they saw. The more Captain Star studied the simulation of constellations and the positions of the Starships and Battleships, the more astonished he became. He could identify some of the space vessels. Leaning over to Lt. Tulley, he quietly observed, "Can you believe this? It just can't be true. This is an exact star-for-star duplication of the Plufre Sector. How could little Orcal know anything about that area? He's only a baby, how could he know?"

Since everyone in the laboratory was giving him their complete attention, little Orcal began to concentrate so intently, he started to sweat. Keeping his eyes on him, Captain Star was in total disbelief! He saw Orcal make all those Star-Warships maneuver.

As well as being amazed at the maneuvering, he was concerned about a monstrous Mothership. It had the appearance of something he had never seen before. It also had weapons that were destroying groups of other ships which seemed to have absolutely no defense against this huge, Monster-Mothership. Then, as soon as the Monster-Mothership was about to take total control of the battle, a group of smaller ships positioned themselves (in formation) and pulled a maneuver that no Starship pilot in Interplanetary Defense history had ever seen – much less than to have ever attempted – to perform. It was so confusing to the big Monster-Mothership, that it turned around and streaked off in the other direction away from the battle.

After watching this scene, Captain Star jumped up and screamed, "Yes! Yes! Yes! I love it!" He surprised everyone with his loud outbreak. Orcal lost his concentration, and everything stopped, completely motionless, frozen in place!

Usar then switched on the lights. There he was, Dr. Zuntor was holding little Orcal, who was sweating, but still like a kid, he was looking up into his father's face with a smile, as if he were waiting for his father's approval of his latest accomplishment. Pushing him up over his head, Dr. Zuntor kissed him and said "Good boy, Orcal! Good boy! You have made your father very proud of you."

Climbing down out of his father's arms, Orcal ran over to Captain Star and Lt. Tulley, and asked, "What did you think about it?"

Lt. Tulley was completely lost for words. All she could say was "Wow!" She stood there in disbelief, with her mouth open. On the other hand, Captain Star was like a kid that had just gotten a new toy. He picked Orcal up over his head, and spun them both around. He expressed his astonished, elated, delight: "Orcal! That was the most exciting battle I've ever seen! How did you do that?"

A timid, but grateful Orcal answered, "I just followed the notes on my dad's Memory Retainer Slides, and with some ideas I already had... There was nothing to it!"

"But how did you come up with the design for that monster ship?" asked Captain Star.

"I dreamed about it. And I dreamed about the battle many times!" explained Orcal.

Captain Star glanced at Dr. Zuntor. Knowing what Captain Star must be thinking, Dr. Zuntor said to him, "Captain Star, it's really good to see you again." The two men shook hands.

"Dr. Zuntor, this is a remarkable kid you've got here!" exclaimed Captain Star.

"We think so too, Captain. He's been working on this project for some time now," said Dr. Zuntor. Fearing the next question, Dr. Zuntor changed the subject. "We'll discuss Orcal's project later, but right now, let's get down to our business."

After discussing their plans, and talking about why the both of them had been assigned to the same mission, Dr. Zuntor proceeded to recount his past experiences. They agreed as to how certain people can become power-hungry and ruthless. They both sent a silent prayer that the Serum would not get into the wrong hands. Knowing that Captain Star was the hero of the Getnor war, Zuntor knew he could trust him. So, with that faith established, the doctor proceeded to relate Usar's and his own experiences while they were in captivity on the planet Getnor. Captain Star was fascinated as he listened to their fantastic story.

"That's incredible, Dr. Zuntor! I never did know the extent of how dangerous your Serum really is! I am finally beginning to understand why Admiral Fitchly insists on us being jointly in charge of this operation." Captain Star was thinking to himself, "Should I say this or not?" In his mind, he answered himself, "Why not?" So he cleared his throat and said, "But it has crossed my mind, and I wondered why they would put us in charge of this mission, instead of General Sunbird. After all, he's a Major General in the I.P.D. Air Force, and he is the Senior Officer."

Dr. Zuntor looked at Captain Star and replied, "General Sunbird — I know him well. He's one of those ambitious types, and that type will always try to take advantage of any and every opportunity to seize power! That's why Commander Fitchly (since he had no choice about letting him go - because of his influence in the I.P.D.) picked you, Captain Star. With your reputation as a hero, no one can question your leadership abilities, even over those of General Sunbird's."

"That's a real complement. Especially coming from you, Dr. Zuntor," said Captain Star. "When do you plan to get started, Doctor?

Zuntor answered, "It shouldn't take much longer, Captain. All that's left to do now, is transfer the serum-filled cylinder to my newly designed container. Then the rest is up to you, Captain." They turned, looking for Lt. Tulley, but she, along with little Orcal, had walked unnoticed to another part of the house.

"How long have you and Captain Star been working together, Lt. Tulley?" asked Usar.

"We just got together for this mission," answered Lt. Tulley.

"Oh, I thought maybe there was something special between the two of you," said Usar.

"Not only no, but never!" Lt. Tulley had a look of disgust on her face.

"Why do you say never so emphatically?"

He seems to be a very nice person," remarked Usar. "Maybe he appears to be like that to you, Usar, but to me, he's an egotistical womanizer! Did you know he's got women all over this solar system? Even when I dropped by to deliver his orders from Admiral Fitchly, he was in bed with two Tryberyon women. And we both know that Tryberyon women are the tramps of the solar system."

Looking into her eyes, Usar could tell that Lt. Tulley had a crush on Captain Star. After a hearty laugh, Usar said, "I think I had better leave that alone! Tell me a little about yourself." Having had a cup of Malturency Juice with Usar, Lt. Tulley had no problem with talking about herself.

"I went to the I.P.D. Academy. I graduated first in my class of twenty-six hundred.

I'm also an experienced geologist and an excellent navigator, as well as a pilot. I have flown at least three-hundred combat missions!"

"Does Captain Star know all this?" asked Usar.

"No, he thinks I'm just someone that is going to get in the way. But, do I ever have a surprise for him!" said Lt. Tulley.

"A surprise? What do you mean?" asked Usar.

"I was given orders from Admiral Fitchly, not to let him out of my sight until this mission is over! That means, no more wild parties, no private assignations, no nothing! Only work from here on out," declared Lt. Tulley. She and Usar began to laugh.

After a long and enjoyable time, and after confirmation of their orders, it was Captain Star that said, "Dr. Zuntor, before we part company tonight, I need to ask you about something that has been troubling me."

"Please do, Captain," answered Dr. Zuntor.

Trying to be tactful, Captain Star said, "You have a very remarkable son. The way he is able to master ESP at such a young age! Doesn't that sometimes make you wonder if he is more than just gifted?"

"Captain Star, I was hoping that you would be like most others when they noticed his uniqueness. Most folks just chalk it up as him being a bright kid. But I can tell now, that your instinct concerning Orcal is right on target." Then he took Captain Star off to another part of the house, where little Orcal was sleeping. They tipped in quietly, so as to not awaken him. Then Dr. Zuntor whispered to Captain Star, "As you see, he is sleeping, but just watch. Then, Dr. Zuntor sat in a chair next to Orcal's bed and began to meditate.

The Doctor went deeper and deeper inside his own mind, until he was in a semi-comatose state. Then, without a sound coming from his father, Orcal began to levitate, higher and higher, until Orcal had ascended nearly to the ceiling! Dr. Zuntor continued to control his levitation, moving little Orcal around his bedroom.

Captain Star could not believe what he saw. It was as if Dr. Zuntor was using his own, as well as Orcal's mind, and had interlocked them. Now, the both of them were transcending their mental powers to one another. In short, they were having a conversation by using their minds only.

After that short exhibition, little Orcal floated back over to his bed and began to descend down onto it. After Dr. Zuntor had returned his son to his bed, he slowly opened his eyes. After sitting still for just a moment, he raised to his feet. Then he and Captain Star slipped quietly out of the room.

When he and Captain Star were alone in another room, Dr. Zuntor asked Star, "Have you ever seen anything like that before in your life?"

Answering, Captain Star said, "Dr. Zuntor, not only have I never seen anything like that, but never in my life have I even dreamed that something like that was possible!" The excited Captain Star asked, "How did he get so much power? He is just a child!? And, why haven't you let the Supreme Educator know about Orcal?"

"Listen, Captain Star, Little Orcal has an I.Q. of over 250, and yes, he is just a child! Not only that, but he can communicate telepathically across the solar system. For that kind of distance, his mother and I are the only ones that can send and receive messages with each other. I suppose it is easy for him, due to the fact that that we are emotionally and genetically connected. Genes and love, Captain, that's the only way I can explain it. The Educator doesn't need to know about my son. They would think it 'in his better interest' to take him away for observation and who knows what else. But Usar and I know he should be with us, surrounded with love."

"Looking over at Dr. Zunter, and shaking his head, Captain Star said, "Wow! All this is too heavy for me, Doc! Besides, I've got to be moving — I've got to take Lt. Tulley to her home base."

As they were about to join the others, Dr. Zuntor stopped Captain Star and pleaded with him, "Captain, everything you just saw was for your eyes and ears only! We have to protect our son! It's just like my ZYM230.6 Serum — if either gets into the wrong hands, it could be very dangerous!"

"Dr. Zuntor, I know that there are some bright kids in our solar system, but Orcal is beyond belief! There's got to be some explanation for it!?"

"There is," replied Dr. Zuntor. "It's pre-conceptual."

"What?" exclaimed the incredulous Captain Star.

Dr. Zuntor continued, "Before we escaped from Dr. Cimjone, on the now extinct planet of Getnor, Usar was subjected to an ancient fertility drug. So, when we later conceived, Orcal was affected. The side effects of that drug increased his mental abilities beyond the normal! Now, as far as anyone knows, there has never been a child, exposed to that drug, that ever lived to an adult age. So, you can see, that if anyone were ever to become aware of these facts, Little Orcal would be taken away from us, and we would never see him again! So now Captain, do you understand why I'm asking you to keep this absolutely confidential?"

After looking into each other's eyes, and finding the pledge of honesty and loyalty, the two men shook hands. Star said to the Doctor, "Zuntor, you have shared with me one of the most personal secrets that one ever shared with another. I've never had anyone put that much trust in me. I feel very humble. Not only will I keep your secret, Dr. Zuntor, but you will always have a friend!"

The two men rejoined Usar and Lt. Tulley.

Not long after they departed from Dr. Zuntor's home, Captain Star asked Lt. Tulley if she would like for him to drop her off at the I.P.D. Home Base.

"What makes you think I'm going to give you a chance to get lost and get into trouble, Captain Star?" asked Lt. Tulley.

"What do you mean by you're going to stop me from getting lost or in trouble?" the annoyed Captain Star said to Lt. Tulley.

"I've got orders not to let you get out of my sight," answered Lt. Tulley.

After letting Lt. Tulley off at the base, an angry Captain Star, driving his airmobile towards his home, is thinking, "It's bad enough the Admiral cut off my vacation, but now I've got this bossy Lieutenant on my tail."

General Sunbird was in his communications room on his Hologram Scanner Screen, speaking to Commander Boonor, "Commander, it's great to see that you're still preparing your fleet to take over this solar system."

Commander Boonor, looking at his Hologram Screen, says, "General Sunbird, it's good to know that there are still some out there that know there is hope for the deliverance of our solar system from those I.P.D. fools! Even though it's my privilege to see you again, I still have to wonder what is the reason for you taking such a chance by getting in touch with me?"

Feeling justified, General Sunbird replies, "I've got great news! Soon there'll be a ship which will be in your sector, that carries a most powerful cargo."

"Powerful for whom, General?" asked an irritated Commander Boonor.

"For the welfare of our solar system, replied the General. "I have more knowledge about these things than anyone else. For instance, I happen to know you are assembling the most powerful fleet ever launched within our solar system," continued the General. "And I have some information that will be of extreme value to you."

After pausing a moment, Commander Booner demands, "Well, what is it?"

General Sunbird, knowing he must take advantage of this opportunity, quietly says, "Before I give you such crucial information, we must come to an agreement."

"What type of agreement?" asks the Commander.

"What I have is so powerful that no one will be able to stand up against us, ever again" states the General.

"Well," stammers Commander Booner, "if it's as you say, there is nothing short of my life ... well, within reason anyway ... that I wouldn't give."

"All I'm asking for, in return," continues General Sunbird, "is that you give me the planet Duderyon ... Then," he quickly adds, "build me a ship as well equipped as your Monster-Mothership!"

Feeling somewhat surprised, the Commander asks, "How do you know so much about my ship?"

"I have my ways, believe me, "stated Sunbird.

"If you know, then who else knows about my ship?" asks Commander Boonor.

"At this time, only you and I," answers General Sunbird.

Thinking to himself, Commander Boonor says, "He knows too much! So, for now, I've got to go along with him. But after I take over the solar system, I'll get rid of this bumbling idiot!" Then he said out loud to the General, "You're a brilliant person for a Duderyonite. It might be a good idea for us to join forces. Now! No more delays. What is this invaluable piece of information?!"

Feeling he had just made the deal of a lifetime, General Sunbird declared, "Before the changing of your moon, I'm going to be on an expedition that is going to hide the container holding Dr. Zuntor's ZYM230.6 Serum. Now, we both know the power this Serum can bestow on the one that possesses it! As soon as I can get more information as to which asteroid they decide to deposit it on, I'll contact you."

Realizing that that his chances of getting his hands on Zuntor's powerful Serum were much more assured now, Commander Booner boldly promised General Sunbird: "Not only will you receive all we have agreed upon, General, but you will have earned and will deserve much more!"

"Well, Commander Booner, that will be very much appreciated."

The Commander inquired of the General, "Will that be all, Sunbird? We must not speak on these communicators again."

"I've got just one more little tid-bit for you Commander. Your old friend, Captain Star, will be a part of the expedition."

Hearing this, Commander Boonor's eyes begin to burn with envy, knowing that Captain Star was the one that caused his first fleet to be destroyed. Trying to make General Sunbird think he was not impressed with this information about Captain Star, the Commander spoke very quietly... "Captain Star?" With a shrug in his voice, the Commander continued, "Well, if that's all, General Sunbird, I've got to go. I know the next time I see you, all will have gone well for us. Com Out." Both of their Scanner Screens fade out.

It was an awesomely beautiful, moonlit evening. The three lovely moons of the planet Duderyon seemed to hang loosely in the star-dotted sky. It seemed almost obscene to have this great and grand silence broken by an angry female voice.

"Admiral Fitchly, I'm telling you again, I cannot put up with that Captain Star! He's the most impossible egotistical son of a-"

The Admiral quickly cuts her off. "Hold on, Lt. Tulley, I know he's all that you say, but he is still the best damn pilot in the entire Duderyon Star Fleet. Not only that, but he knows how to make solid decisions in times of crises. So, my dear lieutenant, don't be so upset with him. Anyway, I'm sure you can handle a guy like him. And we can't do without you either, so why don't you give the whole thing more thought."

"Well, only for you Sir. I'll have to put my better judgment away for a while and follow your orders." She then turned and kissed Admiral Fitchly on his cheek and said, "Dad- Oops! I mean Admiral, Sir, you are of course, always right. Maybe I've been a little rough on the guy, but I'm going to keep my anger with him under control for the sake of this mission even if it kills me! ...SIR!" she adds, facetiously.

Smiling, Admiral Fitchly said, "That's my girl. Don't let him think he's got the best of you."

They had just arrived at her front door, so they saluted each other, and both went their own way.

As the Imperial Planetary Defense Home-Base Team was boarding with all their gear and special equipment, an anxious Dr. Zuntor admonishes the loading crew, "Be careful with that container!" It was, of course, his ZYM230.6 Serum. He then noticed Captain Star and Lt. Tulley approaching their ship.

"Is everything ready for take-off, Doctor?" asked Captain Star.

"We're just waiting for Commander Sunbird," replied Dr. Zuntor. "I wonder why he hasn't arrived yet," questioned Captain Star. "I should think he would have been the first to get here", offered Lt. Tulley.

Little did they know that General Sunbird was making plans to get the information of their departure to Commander Boonor. After several minutes, they looked up and saw him getting out of his air shuttle, accompanied by his assistant, Tufus. The General issued some last-minute orders to Tufus, "Take these cases and put them safely away, so that no one will find them."

In the cases were homing devices that would enable Commander Boonor to track them to wherever they landed within their solar system. Then he walked over to the boarding ramp of the Phantom II, I.P.D.'s new Starship.

"General Sunbird, we were wondering if you were going to make it in time for the launch", said Lt. Tulley.

"Well hello there, Lt. Tulley! It's good to see you again," replied the General. He was startled by her beauty. "If I would have known you were on this mission, I would have been here long before now! Am I the last to arrive? Is everyone else here?"

Lt. Tulley was as much in awe of General Sunbird's reputation, as he was in awe of her charm and beauty. She was actually rather flushed, as she spoke to him. "General Sunbird, it's such an honor for me to serve under a great officer as yourself. I feel as if I've been waiting for I.P.D. history to arrive."

"I thank you for the complement, Lt. Tulley, but you make me feel like I'm getting old", said General Sunbird. He was grinning like a schoolboy.

"Oh, no Sir! That's not what I meant It's your reputation, Sir," said Tulley.

"My reputation? Well indeed, I surely hope it's a good one," said the General.

Before she could answer, Dr. Zuntor came out of the ship, having just taken a load of equipment aboard. He waved as he made his way down the boarding ramp. When he approached the group, he turned his attention to the General, and said, "General Sunbird! It's so good to see you Sir." He had known the General for many years, and was an admirer of his. "Welcome aboard, Sir!"

The General reluctantly turned his attention away from Lt. Tulley, and focused on the Doctor. "Dr. Zuntor, it's always a pleasure seeing you again. When I heard you were part of this mission, I just knew I had to come and take part in this endeavor. I wouldn't have missed this for the world."

The three of them were standing on the boarding ramp, greeting each other, when a voice came from out of the ship saying, "Hey! I hate to break up this little party, but if we are going to hit our trajectory, we'd better get started!"

Everyone turned to see to whom the voice belonged, and there he was, looking directly into the eyes of General Sunbird. Both men knew this was not going to be a pleasant trip.

"If we don't get a move on, we won't be in orbit in time to align with the coordinates of our assigned destination" said Captain Star. His instinct was telling him that General Sunbird wasn't too happy about him giving orders. However, the General was the first to verbally comply, and said, "Come on people, let's not keep Captain Star waiting any longer.

Working more feverishly than he ever had (even on his Monster-Mothership) Commander Boonor was saying to his engineers, "You must hurry — I have a rendezvous with destiny." Pacing the floor, and thinking about how surprised the entire solar system was going to be when they found out that he had possession of Dr. Zuntor's ZYM Serum.

Still pacing, he thought to himself, "I'll be able to hold the entire solar system hostage once I have the Serum.

They all know what it would be like if I were to use it to turn their household pets into monsters — at will! No one has forgotten how those two Killer Drymahords, alone, had almost destroyed them. With the thought of my being able to create many such monsters — if I choose — WHEN I choose — and WHERE I choose! There'll be no one that will have the nerve to stand up against me! And, if someone were fool enough to try, when they see and feel the sting of my new Monster-Mothership!... No doubt about it, fear will turn them around. No one will be able to stop me!" Again, he screamed into his loud speaker, "Hurry up men! We have to finish this NOW!"

Taking off from I.P.D.'s Home Base, the Phantom II breaks through the Duderyon atmosphere. Captain Star accelerates his ship to warp speed. Looking through windows, they can see the stars streaking by as dots turning into white lines. Then there is total darkness as space swallows them up.

"Here are your secret orders, Captain," Lt. Tulley says as she hands Captain Star a tube containing a memory retainer slide. "I was instructed by Admiral Fitchly to give them to you as soon as we were out of the Duderyon sector."

Captain Star accepts the tube and inserts it into his Hologram Scanner Screen. In seconds, an image of Admiral Fitchly is speaking to Captain Star, saying, "By the time you receive these orders, you'll be well on your way to a sector which has been classified as top secret from all parties on your ship. It was very important that there would be no chance of anyone on this mission inadvertently divulging your destination. We all know the importance of being discreet about the location of the indestructible ZYM230.6 Serum... Captain Star, there has never been a mission of such importance in all interplanetary history! You and everyone on board your ship could be in extreme danger if anyone discovers your destination before you complete your mission and return home to Duderyon."

"I'm entrusting you with full authority over the entire mission. We of the Duderyon Imperial Planetary Defense Council are putting all of our confidence in you, Captain Star."

"Dr. Zuntor is our planet's most brilliant scientist. He knows all there is to know about the Serum. When you reach your destination, he will be the one in charge of disposal. All parties are ordered to assist him in every way. It is your job, Captain Star, to make sure he has full cooperation from everyone."

"As far as Lt. Tulley is concerned, she is more qualified than anyone on our planet in the field of geology. Her expertise will be of great benefit to Dr. Zuntor. Also, if by chance, there is a need for another pilot, she is not only qualified, but she has experience as a Star-Fighter pilot as well. But most of all, Captain Star, she can be absolutely trusted, since she is my daughter."

After hearing this, it took a moment for the Captain to get over his shock and settle down to receive the rest of his orders. He switched the hologram screen back on, and continued listening to his instructions from Admiral Fitchly...

"Last of all, there's General Sunbird. My advice to you is to stay out of his way as much as possible. He's a very ambitious person. But he is also one of the finest Generals that the Duderyon I.P.D. Airforce has ever had. From the start, this mission was his idea. Knowing him, he might appear not be concerned with your being in command. But in his heart, he has an enormous ego. It might be best that you keep an eye on him at all times... You might be asking yourself if he is going to be a problem, and if I were aware of his frailties, then why was he assigned to such an important mission. The thing is, I had no choice. It was after all, his idea; and he is a senior member of our council. He has the right to go, if for no other reason than to satisfy his constituency. But once again, I warn you always be on your guard! Remember, your real concern is not to let him, or anyone else, stop you and Doctor Zuntor from completing your mission..."

"Now, here are your coordinates, Captain; There is an ancient asteroid that is 975 thousand kilometers from where the old destroyed Getnor planet was. This asteroid is now orbiting in that sector. It only moved into that particular orbit because of the vacuum that occurred due to the explosion caused by the Killer Drymahords on the planet Getnor. Very few astronomers are aware of its existence. It has been given a name by our committee. We call this asteroid Plufre..."

"Orbit your ship around it until you have made enough revolutions to decrease its gravitational pull. Then, you are to land 130 degrees longitude and 349 degrees latitude. That should put you on its dark side. Now, with the help of Lt. Tulley, you will find the proper geological formation in which to deposit the container. Once you have reached the correct area, Dr. Zuntor will take it from there. After you have accomplished all these tasks, immediately return to Duderyon. I need not tell you the importance of confidentiality regarding your orders. You have permission to destroy this Memory Retainer Slide, as soon as you reach your destination."

"Once again, Captain Star, this is Admiral Fitchly saying, Good luck to you and everyone with you. May God take care of all of you come home safely!"

The scanner screen fizzled out along with the image of Admiral Fitchly. Captain Star took the memory slide and put it into his pocket.

"Tufus, did you put that special equipment away safely?" asked General Sunbird. "Yes, General, it's with the rest of your gear," said Tufus. "I've been looking at the star formation and it looks familiar," said General Sunbird.

Tufus inquired of the General, "What do you think are the secret orders Captain Star received?"

"If I know Admiral Fitchly," responded General Sunbird, "They're just ordinary briefings on our mission. But it will have the coordinates of the exact area where the Serum is to be deposited. If we don't get that information, and soon, it could get lost and never be found again. And, if that happens, all of our plans will be of no use.

"How do you plan to get those orders from him, Sir?" asked Tufus.

"I'm sure he'll have them in his possession at all times. We'll just have to wait until we reach our destination, then at the first opportunity, we'll take them, and get rid of everyone. That's why I had you bring along my communication equipment. If we need help, I can get in touch with Commander Boonor, and you know the rest!" said General Sunbird.

As the Phantom II was zooming through space at 6.4 warp speed, Lt. Tulley and Captain Star were going over some charts. Confirming the position of the stars, Lt. Tulley said to Captain Star, "According to the alignment of those five moons orbiting around the planet Anebular, we should be entering the Magnor sector soon."

"I thought these star formations were familiar," stated Captain Star. In his mind, he was wondering why the directions given him in his orders were sending him on such an unusual route pattern. He already knew the course he usually took to go to the Getnor sector.

Then Lt. Tulley stated, "I can't understand why we are flying such a confusing pattern. It's as if we were trying to lose someone that might be trying to follow us."

"It's not my doing, Lt. Tulley. I'm just following orders." Then, it came to him that the intentional, but unusual pattern, was designed to keep his passengers from being able to recognize the constellation formations.

Therefore, they would be unable to anticipate their destination. But why did they route his ship through the Magnor Sector? Everyone knows that the Magnorites are some of the most bloodthirsty and ruthless creatures in this solar system.

"Captain Star?! Captain Star!! Are you all right?" Lt. Tulley was shaking him, in an effort to wake him from his deep thoughts.

"Oh Wow! Forgive me, I was just thinking, that's all," replied Captain Star.

"I'm sorry to interrupt your dreams, Captain, but I was just wondering about us flying

through the Magnor Sector ... I'm kinda concerned about that", stated Lt. Tulley.

"Funny, I was just thinking the same thing, said Captain Star. "Maybe we'll be lucky and not have to deal with them. After all, they know that this is an I.P.D. Ship."

"I really hope So, Captain," said Lt. Tulley. "Well, Captain Star, whatever happens, our orders say this is the course they want us to fly. So, Magnorite or not, I'm going to follow my orders."

The I.P.D. Ship, Phantom II, with Captain Star and his passengers, were almost out of the Magnor Sector when Lt. Tulley picked up (on their Proximetry Locator Screen) the first sign of two Magnorite Star-Warships approaching fast! "Captain Star! It looks as though we've got company, Sir!" exclaimed Lt. Tulley.

Looking at the screen, he saw two small dots that were flying in attack position. Captain Star observed, "Yep, I believe we've picked up a couple of Magnorite Star Fighters, and I don't think they are inviting to a space disco!" "We better try to run for it, Sir," advised Lt. Tulley.

"No, I don't think that's possible. By the time we can get this big, untested junk-heap up to light-speed, they'll be there too, so it looks as if we are going to have to fight! Hit the alarm, Tulley!" ordered Captain Star!

"Got you, Captain!" Lt. Tulley hit the emergency alarm. The I.P.D. Phantom II came alive with crew members running to man their posts. Within seconds, the crew was in place and waiting — ready for action.

"I was in my cabin when I heard the alarm", said General Sunbird, as he joined Captain Star on the Phantom II bridge.

"It's the Magnorites, General", directs Captain Star. "Take a look at the Proximetry Screen."

"It looks as if they're preparing for an attack, Captain", said General Sunbird.

"I was thinking the same thing. That's why I sounded the alarm," said Captain Star.

"I know it's your command, Captain, but let me get into the action," requested General Sunbird.

"It's a pleasure, Sir. If you really want action, take that mini-cluster cannon. On the port side, Sir," said Captain Star.

"That's great! I helped design that weapon. I'll have Tufus feed my switches." With that, he and his assistant hurried to their positions.

Dr. Zuntor knew what to do when he first heard the battle alarm. Calling Captain Star on the communication beam, he announced, "Captain, it's Dr. Zuntor. I need the controls engineer to remove the rear gunner's flaps and switch on my laser cannon's cluster systems."

"Done!" asserted Captain Star. He then ordered Lt. Tulley to keep the course of their ships accurate, no matter what happened. He knew that he, himself, might have to do all kinds of maneuvering in order to prevent his ship from being damaged.

Soon, all stations were manned and all that was left to do was wait. "Captain, do you want me to put up our force field, Sir?" asked his Control's Engineer.

"Not yet, Mr. Pep. I've got a little plan for those Magnorite ships." Mr. Pep answered, "Let me know when, Sir."

Thinking of a way to outwit the two Magnorite Semi-Motherships, Captain Star began to devise a strategy that wouldn't jeopardize his mission. "I'll just play with them a little," he thought. "Maybe I can get them so upset and confused that they might get careless, and then, perhaps I will be able to reverse the attack."

He then called out over his Com-Beam, "Mr. Pep!"

Answering him, Mr. Pep said, "Here, Sir!"

"Pep, you know more about the Phantom II than any of us. Tell me something: does it have the Reflective Image Eliminator?"

"Yes Sir," replied Mr. Pep, "The Phantom II is the first of our new hyperspace Starships to have that unit installed, Sir."

"Good, Mr. Pep. Now, I have an idea: as soon as we are within firing distance, switch on the R.I. Eliminator to half power, on command" ordered Captain Star.

"Why half power, Sir?" asked Mr. Pep.

"With half power, it will allow the enemy ship to get closer before they break through our invisible screen. That's also why I said to not turn on our force field yet. Because, with the force field on, their radar can pick up magnetic energy on its screen and even though we are invisible, they will be able to pick up our waves," explained Captain Star.

"I've got you, Sir!" answered Mr. Pep. "Ready when you are! Just give the order, Sir!"

"Good man, Mr. Pep!" said the enthusiastic Captain Star.

Now the trap was set! Captain Star and his crew were ready, willing, and able, to take care of the Magnorite Warships!

Speaking in the Magnorite tongue, their captain switched on his universal language translator as he simultaneously switched on his hologram scanner screen. The scanner screen picked up the Phantom II as he spoke, "Captain Icpek calling Phantom II, come in Phantom II."

On his Proximetry Locator screen, Captain Icpek can see the Phantom II looking helpless. In the meantime, he is waiting for an image of its captain to appear on his Hologram Scanner screen. He also said to his first in command, "We need to take that Phantom II ship for our fleet! By the looks of it, it's probably lost — because no ship flies through our sector without an escort, and everyone in the solar system knows not to come through our sector without advance notification. They know if they do enter, it's at their own risk!"

The two Magnorite Mini-Motherships were only waiting for their orders to attack. Once again, Captain Icpek sent out his message, and once again, he received no response. He became disgruntled with their actions. He slammed his hands down on the arms of his command chair. Captain Icpek, along with the other Magnorites on board are becoming upset, and can't wait for action. Feeling completely disrespected, after having his communications ignored, Icpek gave the orders for his men to prepare to strike.

"Captain, are you going to answer that Magnorite ship, Sir?" asked Lt. Tulley. Looking at his Proximetry Locator, he can see that it won't be long before the rat falls into the trap. So, replying, Captain Star says, "I wouldn't answer them for all the stars in the heavens. I've got them just where I want them!"

"Attack! Now! Attack!" shouts Captain Icpek. He felt prepared and capable of taking possession of the I.P.D.'s Phantom II Warship. His order to attack released a squadron of fighter interceptors from out of each Mini-Motherships. As Icpek watched his squadron heading for the Phantom II, he said, "Now, let's see if their captain will still think he is so important, after he feels the sting of Magnorite power!"

He took a grandstand seat as he sat back in his Captain's chair.

"O.K., Mr. Pep! Get ready!" Captain Star alerted his Control's Engineer.

"Just say when, Captain," answered Mr. Pep.

Captain Star, looking somewhat amused, calmly watched the Magnorite squadron on their attack, with his ship as their prey.

"Come on!" pleaded Star, "just a little closer."

He was impatiently waiting for them to get into the range of his trap. Like a kid in a game of tag, he shouts as he snaps his fingers, "Got you!" Then He called out over his Com-Beam, "All right, Mr. Pep!

Responding immediately to Captain Star's orders, Mr. Pep hit his switches! Then, like a puff of smoke, the Phantom II vanished out of the sky.

"What!? What's going on here?!" screamed Captain Icpek. He stood up, and ran over to his huge hologram scanner screen, then over to his Proximetry Locator Screen. Then he turned with his back leaning against the huge screen, and with his arms stretched out, he shouted, "Where is it? I know it's out there! Where is it!?"

At the vanishing of the Phantom II, the Magnorite squadron lost the focus of their attack, although they were directly in the face of their invisible victim.

The squadron leader called back to his Captain; "Squadron Leader F-5-6, to Captain Icpek, Icpek, Come Come In." Acknowledging him, Icpek said, "Captain Icpek here, F-5-6, go ahead!"

"What's going on, Sir? They just vanished! Can you pick them up on your Proximetry Screen, Sir?"

As he continued to look at his screen in disbelief, Captain Icpek shouted, "Keep looking! They're out there somewhere!" Icpek began to reason with himself: "Maybe if I pull my ship closer to where they were last located, I might be able to pick up their force field on my radar." He gave orders to move his ship closer to the area where they were last seen.

"Mr. Pep, get ready to switch off our Reflective Image Eliminators, and simultaneously give me our full force field on my command," ordered Captain Star.

"Just say the word, Captain," replied Mr. Pep.

"All gunners get ready but wait for my orders before fire!" commanded Captain Star. Looking at the two Magnorite Mini-Motherships foolishly move back into firing range, Captain Star softly coaxes, "Come on, just a little closer..."

"Now! Mr. Pep!" shouts Star. On his command, Mr. Pep switched off the R.I.E, then quickly turned and switched on the force field. All the attacking Magnorite ship-pilots were caught off guard! They were frozen in complete disbelief! Within seconds, Captain Star gave the command to fire.

In the first volley, the Phantom II shot down six Interceptors and had three hits on one of the Mini-Motherships.

"Mr. Pep - all engines to hyperdrive!" ordered Captain Star.

"Gotcha! Captain, Sir!" answered Mr. Pep. After the Phantom II went into hyperdrive, it was like a runaway train speeding down a hill, streaking between the remaining Magnorite Warships. Also, as the

Phantom II was distancing itself from them, Dr. Zuntor was firing from the rear of the ship and destroyed the enemy ships as they were attempting to escape.

After seeing that his plan had worked, Captain Star gave orders to Mr. Pep to slow the Phantom II down. He then ordered Lt. Tulley to confirm their coordinates.

General Sunbird came running over to Captain Star's Command Bridge and exclaimed, "Where did you get that maneuver from, Captain? I haven't had this much fun since the Getnorite war!"

"Yep, we did have a little luck," replied the spirited and smiling Captain Star.

Noticing that everyone except Dr. Zuntor had gathered around him, Captain Star switched his Hologram Scanner to the where Dr. Zuntor had been firing a cannon. After he scanned the area, to no avail, he switched over to the storage area. There, he observed Dr. Zuntor trying to strap down the case where the ZYM230.6 Serum was stored.

"Dr. Zuntor, is everything all right back there?" asked Captain Star. Still strapping down the case, Dr. Zuntor charged, "Someone has cut the straps on this case, and if it would have broken open, there's no telling what might have happened!"

The incredulous Captain Star demanded, "Did you say, 'cut the straps?!'"

"Yes, Captain. That is exactly what I said!" declared Dr. Zuntor.

"When you finish securing that case," ordered Captain Star, "Report to me!"

"You got it, Captain! answered Zuntor.

Back in General Sunbird's quarters, the General was slapping Tufus around, as he screeched, "How could you be so stupid as to make a foolish move like that!? Cutting the straps on that Serum case was dumb! Dumb!"

A quivering Tufus attempted to explain. "I thought I could replace the cylinder with another one during the battle, while no one was paying any attention to it. If that battle would have lasted only a little longer, I would have had enough time." Tufus sort of folded down onto the floor with his hands over his face. He actually feared for his life.

Standing over him, in a quiet, threatening tone, General Sunbird was saying, "If you've blown up my plans, there's only one thing left for me to do. I'll have to turn you over to Captain Star with your head blown off, and tell him that you were overcome by your greed, and that I had to get rid of you.

"Oh no, please, General," pleaded Tufus. "You won't have to do that. You'll need me when we get to where we're going. I can show you what to do. If you just give me one more chance. Please just give me another chance!"

"O.K. Show me!" whispered a smiling General Sunbird. Just then, a still terrified Tufus happened to glance out of their cabin door, and saw a crew member walking down the corridor. Without speaking, he slipped up behind the crewman and hit him over the head. He dragged him into the cabin.

Sunbird, his face unable to conceal his frustration, still spoke in a quiet, deliberate, voice, "Don't you think you've gotten us into enough trouble without something like this?!"

"Don't be upset, General. Please — I know what I'm doing." Tufus then ripped off the crewman's I.D. badge. He then sneaked his way back to the area where the case of Serum had been strapped down. He dropped the I.D. badge where it could easily be discovered, and then he slipped unnoticed, back to their cabin.

"Tell me what you're doing now, Tufus. Now! I want to know right now, Tufus!" demanded the agitated, but emotionally drained General.

Tufus, still frightened of the General's mood, implored, "I don't have time right now. Time is of the essence so please, let me take care of this first!"

Knowing something had to be done about such a mistake, General Sunbird decided to give Tufus a little more time. Picking the crewman up, he threw him over his shoulder in fireman's carry, and slipped back to the storage area. There, Tufus dropped him down by the doorway. Nervously, he looked around to see if anyone was coming; seeing no one, he ripped the crewman's flight jacket sleeve. He screamed for help, as he pulled his laser pistol, and shot the man.

Soon other crewmen, along with Lt. Tulley and General Sunbird, came running into the storage area. Seeing the dead crewman lying on the floor with Tufus still holding the laser gun in his hand, Lt. Tulley asked, "What happened?"

Looking stunned, Tufus stammered, "He ... he jumped me when I caught him trying to steal something out of the storage room."

"But you didn't have to to kill him," objected Lt. Tulley.

"I didn't have much choice. He was trying to keep me from telling anyone what I had seen, so he jumped me! We began to fight over my pistol. And that's what happened!" explained Tufus as he pointed to the dead crewman. In the middle of all this confusion, another crewman was looking around the area where the cylinder containing Dr. Zuntor's Serum was stored. He spotted the dead crewman's I.D. badge laying on the floor, between some boxes, near the strapped-down case of Dr. Zuntor's cylinder. Picking up the badge, he ran over to Lt. Tulley and handed it to her.

He said, "I found this over between those cases, Ma'am."

She examined it and said, "I'll have to show this to Captain Star. He has to know what's been going on."

"You're right," agreed General Sunbird. "We must let him know that someone has been trying to steal Dr. Zuntor's Serum. I should let him know it's time for us to be more cautious, so I'll go with you," stated the nervous General. They made their way to Captain Star and Dr. Zuntor; they were busy on the top-side of the Phantom II.

Steam was still shooting out of the pipes in the damaged area of the Mini-Mothership. Alarms were sounding, and the signs that were displaying "DANGER!" were flashing off and on, as steam and flames were making this wounded Mini-Mothership almost helpless.

Crew members were frantically running in all directions and small ships were being transferred to the other Mini-Mothership. Knowing that the ship was was doomed, and being a true Magnorite commander, he knew he had to go down with his War-Starship. After all men, equipment, and records had been transferred to it's sister ship, he sat back in his command chair. He switched on his hologram scanner screen to his sister ship's frequency, and spoke to Captain Icpek, saying: "In the tradition of a Magnorite commander, I will not abandon my ship. I've had all the ship's men and equipment, that is still in fighting condition, transferred over to you, Captain Icpek, my brother... As you know, I was next in line to become our planet's Air Force High Admiral, but now, by losing my ship, I'm no longer worthy. Therefore, my brother, I turn all of that, and it's power, over to you."

As soon as he said these words, his ship exploded into a hot ball of fire. Captain Icpek jumped out of his seat and covered his eyes as he saw his brother's ship scattered throughout the entire sector.

"I know the Captain of the I.P.D.'s Phantom II thinks he has gotten away with this, but he is, Oh! so wrong!

I'll get him, if I have to fly back and forth throughout this solar system a thousand times! Oh Yes, he is going to pay," promised Captain Icpek, with tears flowing from all three of his eyes.

As Lt. Tulley was filling him and Captain Star in on what had happened, Dr. Zuntor observed, "I know that crewman was not acting on his own. He had to be working with someone else."

"I was just thinking the same thing," said General Sunbird. He said this, of course, to throw suspicion off Tufus and himself.

"What do you you think, Captain Star?" Dr. Zuntor asked.

Acting as if he didn't have any idea, Captain Star said, "I don't see it any other way, unless he was acting alone. His plan might have been to try and get his hands on it, and then steal one of the Phantom's shuttles and slip off the ship. Then, of course, he could make a deal on some other planet or asteroid."

Again, the obsequious General Sunbird agreed. "I was thinking the same thing, Captain Star. It's good that Tufus stopped him before he could pull it off!"

However, in his mind, Star was still remembering what Admiral Fitchly had said about everybody on the mission. He knew what was going on, but didn't want to give his secret away, so he played naive. "Well, it's all over now, but I'm still going to put extra guards on our cargo until our mission is over," said Captain Star. All parties agreed, that this was the thing to do, and went back to their duties.

Flying along, trouble-free, the Phantom II was streaking on course, at 7-warp speed. Then Mr. Pep called over the Communication-Beam, "Mr. Pep calling Captain Star. Come in, Captain Star!"

Pressing down his Com-Beam button, Star answers, "Captain Star here. What is it, Mr. Pep?"

"Look at your Proximetry Locator, Captain. Tell me if I'm seeing things."

Switching over to his Proximetry screen, Captain Star saw a huge, glowing, cluster of dots speeding their way. In order to have a better look, and hoping he was wrong, Star switched over to his huge Hologram Scanner Screen. But there it was in three dimensions — a meteor storm! An enormous cloud of meteors as wide as an ocean, was headed their way!

"Mr. Pep, this is Captain Star. What are our chances of avoiding it?"

"We have two possibilities, Captain," Mr. Pep promptly replied. The first one is none, and the second one is the same as the first one — Absolutely None!!

"In that case, there is only one thing left for us to do. And that is to fly this thing manually," said Captain Star. With that, he literally ran down to the cockpit area and as he strapped himself into his Captain's Chair, he exclaimed, "Mr: Pep, I'm going to fly through this crap myself! Switch all operations to manual; all engines everything! Also, put up our force field. Oh! And, don't forget to put our pilot's laser cannons on manual too! STAT!"

"Yes Sir!" confirmed Pep. "I got you!!"

Star then used the Com-Beam and announced to the entire ship: "All stations! Listen up! This is your Captain speaking! We are entering a meteor storm! Secure your stations and man all laser guns! Gunners, as we fly through this storm, keep a sharp eye! If you see any meteor that looks as if it's going to collide with our ship, shoot it before it does! Use your laser cannons! And, don't wait for orders! Use your own good judgement!"

He turned away from the ship Intercom-Beam, and directed his attention to Mr. Pep. "O.K. Pep you heard my orders, now sound the emergency alarm!"

Acknowledging him, Mr. Pep simultaneously reached for the alarm switch, and snapped, "Yes Sir!!"

Within seconds, everyone was waiting nervously at their stations. He had seen ships smashed like eggshells by even small meteorites! But that wasn't the main problem! If his ship was smashed, the gas might escape into outer space and settle on an inhabited planet. It could cause a chain reaction throughout the solar system. Monsters like the Killer Drymahords might pop up on every planet in the cosmos. Star knew he was in a hell of a predicament he had no room for mistakes!

He was thinking to himself, "I'm gonna have to fly this ship better than I've ever in my life flown before!" The Phantom II began to shake and tremble as it plunged deeper into the storm. Upon seeing meteors approaching his ship, Captain Star swerved to the left and then to the right, firing his laser cannons, which were blowing the incoming meteors into dust.

All of his gunners were shooting them as fast as they would appear. The force field was doing its job well; its rays would repel the huge meteors away from the ship. From side-to-side, the Phantom II was making its way deeper and deeper into the storm.

A meteor, as big as a house, broke through the force field and glanced off the side of the ship! This disrupted Star's control of the Phantom II. However, the powers that be seemed to protect the ship while it was in free fall, through the spaces between the meteors. The Captain was quickly able to regain control and get back on course. Up- and-down, side-to-side, he piloted the Phantom II and made his way through the storm.

Mr. Pep called Captain Star over the Intercom-Beam: "Captain, our left rear engines are shorting out. They must have taken the brunt of that hit! We have no choice, I'll have to shut them down until I can get them fixed! If not, they will set the ship on fire!"

"This is bad!" thought Captain Star. "This means it'll take longer to fly through this damnable storm!" Slowing the ship down meant the meteors hit the force field more often, causing it to use extra energy. Star looked at the power meter. With two rear engines shut down, the Phantom II slowed down even more. Now it became almost impossible for the meteors not to hit their ship again and again!

Captain Star knew he had to do something right away. Thinking out loud, he said, "If only I could cause a back-fire that would repel the flow of those oncoming meteors. I need something like a screen in front of my ship." Even though he was still firing his laser cannon at the huge meteors, he began to really concentrate on the problem. Suddenly, it came to him!

"Mr. Pep! I need you to reroute the force field from 360 degrees to 120 degrees. Put all the power of that 120 degrees into the front of the ship! Got it?"

Answering, Mr. Pep said, "Captain, that means over half of our ship will be exposed and open to a direct hit by the meteors from behind."

"I know, Mr. Pep, but I've got to take that chance." Then Star turned his attention to the ship's Intercom-Beam. "All gunners, this is Captain Star. I want all laser cannons set to remote control. "And I want all weapons balanced in twenty degree angles, starting at 120 degrees. Go from left to right, and work your way around until they reach 120 degrees. Remember, one group of guns at 20 degrees, then 40, then 60, etc., until the last group is at 120 degrees, Got It? I'll tell you when to fire!"

In no time, all orders were carried out and every one was ready to go. He gave the order to go! Instantly, the force field was switched from 360 to 120 degrees and pushed to its limit. All laser cannons began to fire at the same time. Mr. Pep stepped up the engines as much as possible, and the Phantom II was now fighting back!

Since the entire force field power was being pushed into this 120 degree position, it had formed an invisible, protruding, concave repellent, which made ripples that preceded their ship. This created a current that forced the meteors to move around each side of their ship, like a speed boat makes waves in water. The laser cannon fire was pulverizing the huge meteors with its concentrated fire, which turned them to space dust. With this method, the Phantom II flew safely through that monster of a meteor storm.

Looking at Captain Star with admiration, Lt. Tulley said, "Captain, I've got to give it to you, to tell the truth, I didn't think we were going to make it!"

Smiling, Captain Star said, "I never had any doubt." But in his mind, he was saying, "I didn't think We were going to make it either!"

Then he called over the Intercom-Beam: "Mr. Pep, what's the damage?"

Answering, Mr. Pep said, "I'm making an inventory as we speak, Captain. I'll be letting you know as soon as all the reports are in."

Shortly things returned to normal, but Star had a feeling that the worst was yet to come. He asked Lt. Tulley, "Do you have any idea yet regarding how far off course that storm has put us?"

Lt. Tulley replied, "Looking at my charts, it shows by the positioning of the Eurca Constellation, we must be off by 38.6 degrees or we are approximately two hundred thousand kilometers off course, Sir."

"If that's the case, Tulley," he conferred with his Lieutenant "In order to swing back on course, we'll have to fly through the Planet Toplyron's Sector, and that means more trouble."

"What kind of trouble, Captain?" asked Tulley.

With a tone of shame in his voice, he cleared his throat and said, "Nothing I can't handle."

As the Phantom II came closer to the Planet Toplyron, Captain Star began thinking back to a time long ago, when he was vacationing on Planet Toplyron. He was in a club having a Ziptor cocktail, when he saw them — twin sisters that were also on vacation. Each of them flew a huge War-Starship for the Toplyron Air Force. He played, they played, and circumstances played, until he realized he had promised to marry the both of them. After playing for a week or two, he sneaked away, and had been ducking and dodging them ever since. Actually, this was one of his youthful adventures he found rather amusing. While he was reminiscing, a voice came over the audio of the Hologram Scanner. Star switched the scanner to full screen in order to pick up the image. He beheld two, beautiful, green women that looked identical. The Twins!!

"Calling the Phantom II - Come in Phantom II - This is the Toplyron Air Defence Muzly V3 - Calling Phantom II - Come in Phantom II" Star reached over and switched off the visual block on his hologram screen, allowing the twins to see their own Captain Star.

Speaking simultaneously with each word, the twins said, "It's You! Do you mean you have the audacity to come back through our sector after what you did to us?"

Gazing at the two beautiful women, Captain Star says, "The loves of my life! I finally see you again. How long I've been hoping for an opportunity to apologize to the both of you. And, here you are! Do you know, I was just thinking about you two when I knew I was going to be flying this way." (In his mind, he knew he was lying like a rug.)

Still speaking simultaneously, the green twins said, "You must think we are nothing but fools to believe anything you say. You space scumball! Do you think we're going to let you get away? After lying your way into our beds — with all those promises of marriage. We know you've done others like that and gotten away with it. But not with us!"
They faded, then vanished from his Hologram Scanner Screen. Know-

ing he was in trouble, Captain Star called Mr. Pep on the Intercom-Beam, saying, "Mr. Pep, how are those rear engines coming along?"

Mr. Pep replied, "It wont be long now, Captain."

"Well I think you'd think you'd better hurry," warned the Captain.

"Is there an emergency, Captain?" asked Mr. Pep.

"It's all in how you look at it," murmured Captain Star.

Looking at him, Lt. Tulley said, "You are just like I thought. A real space sex-animal. Doing anyone the way you did those two women — how could you!?"

Seeing her with his peripheral vision, he turned to look directly at her, and yes, she was rolling her eyes at him. He knew he was in trouble, from yet another place! Following his instinct, Star ordered Mr. Pep to put up their mini-force field. Not long after it was in place, the Phantom II took a light hit on the starboard side, causing it to rock back and forth.

Dr. Zuntor called up to Star on the Intercom-Beam. "I've been looking at my Proximetry Locator, and there is a ship coming up on us fast! Also, I've noticed we have our force field up. I don't understand. Are we not in the Toplyron Sector? They are one of the oldest members of the I.P.D. in our solar system. What's wrong, Captain Star?
Should I fire when they get within range?"

"No, Dr. Zuntor, it's just a little personal problem. I'll take care of it."

"Then, what do you want me to do, Captain?" asked Dr. Zuntor.

"Just lay back and enjoy the ride," replied Captain Star.

"Fire!" said the Toplyron twins simultaneously.

Seeing the blast coming on his P.L.S. screen, Captain Star rolled his ship away from the flash — just in time! As the beam went sizzling past the Phantom II, the chase was on! Rolling over and over, up and down, looping, ducking each and every blast. The Phantom II was flying rings around the Toplyron twin's ship. Suddenly he got the word from Mr.

Pep that the engines were back to normal. This little fun game of tag was over!

Making a gesture of goodbye, by throwing them a kiss, Captain Star jammed his engines into hyperdrive. The Phantom II skipped a beat, then zoomed out of sight!

Back on course, the Phantom II was zipping along at 8.6 warp speed. The stars were shooting past so fast, they looked like hot, white, lines. To the crew it seemed as if they would never get to their destination. But, as with all trips, theirs would come to its long-awaited end. And, at last, they were in orbit around the asteroid named Plufre.

"Captain Star," reported Lt. Tulley, "We can make our landing with our small shuttle as soon as you are ready, Sir."

"Very good, Lieutenant. You will be staying on board the Phantom II, to keep her in orbit," stated the Captain. "Have you gone crazy!? There's no way I'm staying here! Remember, my orders were to not let you out of my sight, and that is exactly what I mean to do! ...Sir!" snapped Lt. Tulley.

"All right! All right!" replied the Captain. I can't win for losing, thought Star. So he called to Mr. Pep, "Mr. Pep, you are in charge of the ship until we return."

"As you say, Sir." answered Mr. Pep.

After landing on the asteroid, the small team set about looking for the best spot to store the cask containing the ZYM230.6 Serum. It looked as if this job was not going to be an easy one. The asteroid was foggy, and its surface was full of pot holes. Heat and steam were spraying from out of the ground. It was like being in the pits of hell.

Walking in formation, the small group was struggling over hills and down into valleys. Lt. Tulley was studying rock formations, looking for the best place to store this dangerous canister of Serum. Clouds were covering the light coming from the asteroid's moons, which made it even more difficult to move without stumbling or falling over boulders. After a long, debilitating walk, Dr. Zuntor suggested they make camp until the exhausted team could regain its energy.

It wasn't long before they had set up camp. Looking up at the sky, Dr. Zuntor knew by the look of the red and green clouds that the asteroid's atmosphere was unusual. He looked at the horizon and to his dismay he saw a huge storm headed their way. Calling out to Captain Star, as the wind began to blow stronger, he yelled, "It looks as if we're going to have to button everything down! I know you are aware that there is a monster of a storm coming!"

Looking at the debris blowing all around them, Captain Star said, "We might be in luck! I saw a cave over there just over that hill!"

"Well, I think we had better not wait much longer, warned Dr. Zuntor, "or we won't be able to make it in time!"

The wind had stirred up an enormous amount of dust. Without delay, Captain Star ordered everyone to make their way into the cave with as much equipment as they could possibly manage.

Star shouted, "This way, everyone! Follow me!"

They were stumbling as they ran, as fast as they could, to reach the inside of the cave. Then, as long as they were able, they ran in and out, again and again, trying to get as much of their equipment and supplies as possible safely inside, away from the fierce elements! The wind had gotten so high that rocks and boulders were flying through the air like frisbees.

As Lt. Tulley was climbing up to the mouth of the cave, she slipped and fell! As she started to roll down the steep hill, Captain Star dove in front of her, stopping her from rolling off the shear cliff. In that instant, he grabbed her by the hand, and was desperately holding on to her as she was swinging from side-to-side.

"Hold on Tulley! It'll be O.K.," Captain Star assured her.

In her panic, she was kicking and screaming. Suddenly, she became quiet. Her strength was gone, and she gave up convinced within herself that she simply could not hold on to his hand any longer. In that instant, she realized her panic was only making things more difficult.

She just had never lost it like this, but being So completely exhausted, her usual sensibilities abandoned her. When she realized she had panicked, she became quite embarrassed.

Star sensed her collapse, and with one last giant effort, he pulled her up to safety. Soon both of them were standing, with their feet on solid ground. The wind was blowing through her hair, and their eyes made contact. In that instant, just before she gratefully threw her arms around him that eye contact revealed a great deal to both of them! My God! They were falling in love!

They slowly started to kiss, but before their lips could touch, General Sunbird ran over to them inquiring, "Is everything all right? I saw the whole thing. It was lucky for you Lt. Tulley, that the Good Captain was there for you."

Then the three of them, fighting the fierce wind, made their way into the cave. The interior of the cave was slightly illuminated by the small lamps placed at strategic locations. The small group was bedding down.

After everyone had fallen asleep, General Sunbird tipped over to where Tufus was sleeping. Shaking him, and whispering, "Wake up!" He then put his hand over his mouth in order to keep him quiet and said in a low voice, "Get up! Get that homing device and follow me."

Slowly creeping through the cave with their equipment, General Sunbird located an ideal spot to set up the homing device. Opening the case, Sunbird took out the device and activated it. Smiling, he said, "That should do it. Now all we have to do is wait for Commander Booner to pick up the signal and follow it."

Tufus, looked around at the spooky surroundings, and said, "General, I don't like this place. If we are finished, let's go back." Feeling good about his plans, and thinking evil thoughts, the General paid no attention to a big, brown, mud-filled hole.

Not only was there a huge, muddy hole, but peeping its head out from it, was a Gyberoake, a cross between a snake and an alligator. It is as wide as a horse, and about fifty feet long. Its mouth had razor sharp teeth. When it's mouth was open, the Gyberoake could easily bite a man in half.

Slowly making their way back to the area where the others were sleeping, neither of the two men noticed when the Gyberoake slid out of its muddy hole. As they were carefully walking across a rock-formed bridge, the Gyberoake sprang out of the hole and bit off one of Tufus' legs up to his knee. As he screamed for help, Tufus was frantically kicking the beast with his other leg, trying to stop it from eating the rest of his body.

General Sunbird was completely horrified. He began to run, stumbling and falling down, getting up, and in and in terror trying to run again.

Tufus, still screaming, was fighting with everything he had. But the Gyberoake was too much for him. It was eating him up, bit by bit. Blood was running down the Gyberoake's mouth as Tufus' arm and half of his head was laying on the floor of the cave.

Then, it began to slither after General Sunbird.

Although it was a huge beast, it could move very fast, and could easily gain on him. Screaming, his heart about to burst, The General could only run for his life!

Back at the mouth of the cave, Captain Star was just completing his communication with Phantom II, ordering Mr. Pep to send down an additional hundred persons to help them complete their mission. He could vaguely hear General Sunbird screaming for help. He ran back to the sleeping area; he grabbed his laser gun and woke Dr. Zuntor. "I think I heard someone screaming. It sounds like it's coming from over there", as he pointed in the direction of the screams. Dr. Zuntor grabbed his laser gun and they both took off in that direction.

As the two men ran, they met the hysterical General running toward them. As he got closer, he fell onto the ground and pointed his finger in the direction of the Gyberoake. Unable to speak, he could only point, as the snot and tears rolled down his bloody face. When the Gyberoake

attacked, Tufus' blood had splattered in all all directions,
covering the General with the last of his life force.

Captain Star was trying to ask him what had happened, and suddenly, there it was, raising up to a springing position! Within its opened mouth, fragments of Tufus' body, (some parts appeared to to still be moving) were dangling from its teeth, as the blood poured from the monster's half opened mouth!!

Knowing they didn't have much time, both Captain Star and Dr. Zuntor opened fire with their laser guns. Zing! Zing! Zing! went the lasers! The huge Gybercake was hit with hot rays, time and time again. It seemed like every time the lasers would blast it, a hole would pop open and blue blood would gush out. The force of the guns would knock the thing down, but it would just get back up from the ground and keep on coming after them!

Dr. Zuntor shouted, "We're slowing it down, but it's not stopping!"

"I know," Star yelled back, "Just keep firing!

The two men continued firing their lasers over and over, until the Gyberoake began to weaken. But it was still trying to fight! Realizing that it would soon be necessary to recharge their weapons, they both knew it was only a matter of time before their guns would be totally useless!

Looking around, while he was trying to come up with a plan, Dr. Zuntor saw a huge group of rocks located just above the head of the Gyberoake. He exclaimed to Star, "Look up! See those boulders up there?!"

"Yeah! I see them!" replied Star.

No need to say any more, with one accord both men began to fire at the boulders! Zing! Zing! Zing! The lasers hit the boulders, and down they came! They landed on top of the gigantic Gyberoake, and crushed it to death!

Star and Zuntor walked around the huge, dead beast, examining it with amazement. "What the devil is it?" Star asked the doctor.

"I don't know for sure, but it looks like something I've seen on other asteroids that have been orbited. But never one this big!" The Doctor got up close and personal to the thing. He looked into its eyes. He then turned to Captain Star and stated, "If I'm not mistaken, this is a Gyberoake! And believe it or not, we are extremely lucky!"
"How is that?" asked the incredulous Captain Star.

Dr. Zuntor, looking intently at Star, replied, "We are lucky, because this one is only a baby!"

"A baby?!" shouted Captain Star, "If this is only a baby, then let's get the hell out of here, before Mama shows up!" The two men picked General Sunbird up by his arms, and carried him back to their camp.

When they arrived, the entire camp was awake. Lt. Tulley, spotted both Captain Star and Dr. Zuntor as they helped the General back into camp. She ran over to meet them, asking "What happened?"

Putting Sunbird down, Star replied, "It's a long story. But first, I've got something I need to know. General Sunbird, what were you doing out there at this hour and that deep inside the cave?"

Knowing he couldn't tell the truth, he answered them, saying, "I woke up and saw Tufus walking in that direction, so I thought I had better follow him."
Dr. Zuntor inquired, "So What was he doing?"

Sunbird, still in shock, tried to think what he could say that would hide his evil plot. After a short pause, he stammered, "I never had a chance to find out, because he was still walking, when that ... that thing got hold of him! Oh God! It was so horrible I can't talk about it."

Lt. Tulley broke in, "Don't you think he's gone through enough? Leave him alone let him rest."

Dr. Zuntor, in support of Lt. Tulley, said, "Well, she might have a point. We all need some rest, because we're gonna need a fresh start in the morning, and the additional troops will be arriving soon. As for myself, I'm going to turn in." After Star appointed a guard to keep watch for the rest of the night, everyone returned to their sleeping containers.

As things settled down, and everyone had gone back to sleep, Captain Star was still thinking about what Admiral Fitchly had said regarding General Sunbird. Now, without a doubt, he knew he had to keep an eye on him.

Picking up the homing device signal, Commander Booner knew it was time to make his move. Calling to his Communication's Officer, he said, "Make ready all ships! Our invasion of the Planet Duderyon is about to begin!!"

From out of underground hangers, ships were taking off and getting into formation as soon as they hit the atmosphere. All kinds of strange looking ships from all over the solar system, every outlaw ship that had made a commitment to Commander Booner, was ready for action!

Slowly moving to the front of the formations was the powerful, new, Monster-Mothership. Feeling like a god, Commander Booner gave his newly formed fleet a grand speech: "I have never seen a fleet as powerful as this one I have just assembled! No one will be able to stand up against us! How long I have waited for this moment, when the I.P.D. would be at my mercy. I'm sure we all have one reason or another to pay them back for all of the wrong they have done us. As you can see, I have built an unstoppable Mothership. It has every conceivable weapon that has ever been invented! So, if you are ready... follow me and let's take over our solar system!"

Soon after his speech, Commander Booner called Lt. Scuff to give him his immediate orders: "There is an asteroid named Plafre. It's close to us. As a matter of fact, our fleet will have to pass by it on our way to destroy the Planet Duderyon. I want you to take a small shuttle and a crew down to it. There is a Duderyon by the name of General Sunbird; he is on our side. And, he has in his possession a very special Serum. I want you to take it from him. Then, when you get your hands on it kill him and all who are with him! Now, when you have done all this, meet us in the Magnor Sector. I'll be waiting for you there."

"Yes Sir, Commander Booner! I'll do just as you say", declared Lt. Scuff!

Then, Commander Booner handed him a small black box as he explained, "This is the receiver for a homing device. When you land on that asteroid, just read its computer. It will guide you to the very spot you need to be, so that you can find General Sunbird and he will have the Serum. All right! Do as I say you can go now!"

"Dr. Zuntor, we've been all over this asteroid looking at rocks and testing them. What are you and Lt. Tulley looking for?" asked General Sunbird.

Instead of Dr. Zuntor answering, Lt. Tulley interjected: "It's a certain certain kind of rock formation that has a rich lead component called Laperzin.

"What makes it so different from all the others?" General Sunbird persisted.

Tulley tried to explain. "The rocks that have more than a sixty-percent Laperzin content are ideal for storing anything toxic. If it's barricaded behind that kind of rock formation, with that much lead content, the rocks will form a natural, protective, casing around it. Then, the gravitational pull will seal it tightly. The more gravity, the tighter it will seal. Also, the lead in the Laperzin will stop radiation from escaping; and it will prevent erosion, which will keep the ingredients from deteriorating. Sooo... the longer the deadly toxin is stored in that kind of rock formation, the safer it will become."

"Well, whatever is in those rocks you're looking for, be it lead, laperzin, or ice cream, I'm exhausted, and I'm going back to camp!" declared the General. He walked away from the others, going in the direction of the camp.

Watching him walk away, Lt. Tulley remarked, "He needs to get some rest. He must still be upset about the death of his assistant, Lt. Tufus." "Yes, of course you're right." stated Dr. Zuntor, as they continued looking for the Laperzin rock formation.

Back at the camp-site, Sunbird was trying to figure out some way to get his hands on Dr. Zuntor's Serum. Walking around the camp, he was snooping into everything, looking for the Serum. Talking to himself, he said, "Where can it be? I've got to have it! I know it's not with Dr. Zuntor." Then, it came to him. "It must be with Captain Star!" So, he started looking around, trying to find the Captain. He asked some of the crew if they had seen Captain Star.

Pointing his finger in the direction of the cave, a crew member responded, "I last saw him going into that cave, Sir."

As he walked over to the cave, Sunbird was wondering, "What would he be doing inside the cave?" With trepidation, he entered the cave, and followed Captain Star's tracks. After a short distance, he spotted Captain Star. So, he ducked behind a big boulder. As he watched, he could see Star covering something up, and then stacking a bunch of rocks on top of it. Star straightened up and looked around apparently checking to see if anyone had seen him.

Satisfied that everything was cool, he walked away back toward the mouth of the cave. When he knew it was safe, Sunbird ran over to the spot where Captain Star had been so busy. Hurriedly, he removed the stones. There it was!! Dr. Zuntor's ZYM230.6 Serum!

"Wow! Am I ever in luck!", he said to himself, "I think I'll just leave it here until Commander Booner comes for me. Then I can dig it up. As for Captain Star and Dr. Zuntor, just leave them to that Gyberoake mother. I know she's around here someplace." Feeling jubilant, he quickly (though carefully) made his way back to the campsite.

Commander Booner and his fleet had finally made it to the old Getnor sector, and hovered in the area of the Plufre asteroid. Booner received a communication from Lt. Scuff, who was in his shuttle, ready for take-off from the hanger of the Monster-Mothership. He heard Lt. Scuff calling "Come in, Commander Booner - Over."

Answering him, Commander Booner said, "I'm here, Lt. Scuff, - Over"

"We're ready to follow your orders, Sir," offered the Lieutenant.

Commander Booner announced, "Remember, I'm depending on you to follow us to our rendezvous as soon as possible, so don't fail me. Do you understand me? Lt. Scuff!?"

"Leave it to me, Sir!" declared the Lieutenant. "Com-Beam Closed!" Then he and his crew through the huge, bay-doors took off into the heavens.

Lt. Scuff, orbiting around the Plufre asteroid, was trying to pick up the signal from the homing device that General Sunbird had activated. As he finished briefing his men, he said, "Those are your orders. As soon as we land on this asteroid! Now! I want each man to take his personal, Mini-Reflective Image Eliminator Unit with him. Also, make damn sure you take a pair of neutralizing glasses."

One of his men inquired, "Sir? We have never used this new equipment before. What does it do? And how does it work?"

Lt. Scuff, (thinking to himself) "This is a fine time to try to show these guys how these things work, but I'll just have to give them a demonstration." All eyes were on him, as he strapped on the Mini-Reflective Unit. Then he showed them the "ON" and "OFF" switch. As they were all intently watching him, he pushed a button and snapped a switch. In that instant, in front of their very eyes, he became invisible!

The astonished crew could not believe what they had just seen — or not seen! They were looking at each other, and searching the area where the Lieutenant had been standing.

Suddenly, one of the men found himself lying on the floor! He'd been knocked down! The rest of the crew saw him hit the floor, and thought he must be playing some kind of a joke.

Then Lt. Scuff knocked another man down. When they saw that, they began to examine their R.I.E. Units - they realized this unit had something to do with the disappearance of their Lieutenant. Even though he was completely invisible, they could still hear his voice when he spoke: "I'm going to ask all of you to put on your neutralizing glasses.

They followed his orders, and as soon as they had the glasses there he was, actually standing directly in front of them!

The crew became as excited as kids in a a toy store. They couldn't resist turning on the R.I.E. units "OFF" and "ON"! Confident that his crew fully understood how the equipment worked, Lt. Scuff interrupted their play. "All right we have no more time to waste. It's time to go to work!"

They found a place to land and were soon on the trail of Captain Star and the Serum.

Lt. Scuff and crew were walking slowly, following the directional computer on the receiver of their homing device. After a while, the Lieutenant ordered his men to put on their neutralizing glasses, and switch their R.I.E. Units to "ON".

Knowing they couldn't be seen, they felt very secure, and very brave. They knew they were on the right track when they spotted one of Captain Star's men, who was guarding the perimeter of the camp. Walking up to him, Lt. Scuff looked the man in his face, and hit him in the mouth knocking him down! Scuff's crew was watching this through their neutralizing glasses. The confused guard got up off the ground; looked around, and not seeing anyone, he took his hand and wiped the blood off his mouth, and looked at it. Now he was really confused!

Lt. Scuff didn't kill him on the spot because he wanted his men to realize that the R.I.E. Unit really worked on the enemy. He wanted his men to have complete confidence in this new equipment. With that accomplished, he grabbed the guard and broke his neck. Once again, they made their way toward Captain Star's camp.

Spotting two more of Star's men, Lt. Scuff sent two of his own men to take them out. Walking up to them, Scuff's men beat them to death! After observing this, all of Scuff's crew were eager to kill, because in their hearts, they felt invincible and unstoppable!

Meanwhile, back at the campsite, most everyone was about to bed down for the night. Everyone, that is, except General Sunbird. He was nervously waiting to hear from Commander Booner. All kinds of thoughts were going through his mind: "I wonder if he's picking up my transmissions, or has he changed his mind and is making his own way? Or, maybe he is already here?"

Lt. Tulley and Dr. Zuntor were going over samples of rocks, trying to test as many as they could before they turned in. Captain Star was still walking around, trying to understand how a man like General Sunbird could betray his own planet for power and what would be his next move. He also realized the General would have to make that move soon.

Looking down from a hill, Lt. Scuff saw Captain Star's small camp. He said to himself, "This is going to be an easy job." He then turned to his men, and declared. "It looks as if our luck is holding. There they are, all together, in a neat little group! Get your weapons ready, men!" His crew made a final check of their laser guns and other equipment.

Scuff gave the order to move in on them. Still unaware that they were being invaded, Captain Star's camp was totally unprepared for what hit them! Lt. Scuff's men were running through the camp, firing their laser guns, and killing everyone in sight, while they searched for General Sunbird!

The I.P.D. group could not understand what was going on. All they knew was that they were being slaughtered! Men were screaming and running with their laser guns in their hands, but there was no one in sight to shoot!

Dr. Zuntor knew the best thing for him to do at the time – seeing men dying all around him, but not understanding where the enemy was located – was to seize Lt. Tulley's hand and run for the safety of the cave!

As they were running, hot rays from laser guns were hitting all around them. Ducking behind a boulder, Dr. Zuntor inspected the scene in the camp and could see flashes coming from what looked like laser guns. They were all over the place, but no one was there! After thinking for a second, it came to him! They were being invaded by men who somehow had become invisible!

Zoom! Zoom! went a flash just missing his head. Firing his laser gun into the midst of the flashing laser lights, he hit someone. The invisible killer hit the ground. As he landed on his R.I.E. Unit, it was by chance, switched to the "OFF" position, and there he was! Dead but visible!

Dr. Zuntor then knew he was right about the enemy somehow being invisible. At least, now they had a chance!

Running over and diving behind the boulder where Dr. Zuntor was hiding, Captain Star inquired, "What the hell is going on?"

Lt. Tulley, still not knowing what was happening, asked, "Where have you been? We thought you were dead!"

He replied, "I was out of camp, just doing some thinking. I heard a racket, and screaming; I knew it was coming from -" As soon as he said "camp", a flash zoomed over his head! Peeking around the boulder, he could see nothing except his crew running and dying.

He asked Dr. Zuntor again, "What is going on?" He simply couldn't understand why he couldn't see anything or anyone except his own men. Zoom! Zoom! went went more flashes over their heads. Dr. Zuntor explained to him. Now understanding everything, the three of them began to open fire.

Soon, some of Lt. Scuff's men were being randomly hit. Rushing into one of the camp's shuttles, Lt. Scuff saw General Sunbird lying on the floor with his head covered up. When he saw his uniform, he knew that it was General Sunbird. Grabbing him by his hands, they dragged him with them as they began to retreat. They had no other choice after seeing some of their men killed.

Lt. Scuff rushed back into the hills. General Sunbird, still not knowing what was happening, could not believe he was being taken away by something he couldn't see. His memories of the Gyberoake, and his imagination, caused him to go kicking and screaming with his rescuers. He was a nervous wreck!

Soon, Lt. Scuff and his remaining crew (along with General Sunbird) were in a safe place. Looking around, the General could hear voices, but he still could not see anything. He was trembling with trepidation; indeed, he was absolutely terrified!

Then, Lt. Scuff gave the order for his men to switch their R.I.E. Units to the "OFF" position. Popping up, one by one, the men suddenly became visible. Seeing this, General Sunbird began to feel more confident, and decided he had made the right decision by teaming up with Commander Boonor.

Introducing himself to General Sunbird, Lt. Scuff said, "You look surprised, General. Did you think Commander Booner would go back on his word?" Still wearing a silly, nervous grin, the General maintained, "Seeing is believing. I had hopes that he would be able to send me some help to complete my mission, but I never never thought it would be something elaborate as this!"

Looking as if he were unstoppable, Lt. Scuff proudly announced, "This is just a small representation of Commander Booner's powers." He knew that by now, his mission had been discovered; and he knew that by now, Captain Star was aware of the fact that General Sunbird had defected to the other side. He also knew he had to keep the pressure up. So, he said, "General Sunbird, we can't waste anymore time. We must move on Star, and get that Serum now! Do you have it? If so, where is it?"

Trying not to look incompetent, General Sunbird quickly replied, "I have it put away in a cave on the other side of the camp. I'll have to take you there, so I can show you."
But, he was thinking to himself, "I hope Captain Star hasn't moved it without my knowledge."

Knowing he had to move fast because of the rendezvous with Commander Booner, Lt. Scuff regrouped and gave everyone their orders. He then picked up one of his R.I.E. Units and a pair of neutralizing glasses.

It didn't take long for General Sunbird to learn how to operate this new equipment. Then they were off headed for the cave, in hopes of removing Dr. Zuntor's ZYM230.6 Serum before anyone anyone knew knew what had happened.

Walking around their camp, looking at all the destruction and all the dead bodies, Captain Star, Lt. Tulley, and Dr. Zuntor (along with the remainder of their crew) were still trying to figure out how the killers were able to find them and the asteroid they were on so soon.

There was no doubt that General Sunbird had something to do with all this devastation. "It seems like all this killing was so they could get their hands on him", declared Dr. Zuntor.

"It's not only that he's on their side, but he knows all of our plans as well," enjoined Lt. Tulley. "Let's not forget that they also have the ability of making themselves invisible!" exclaimed Captain Star. Dr. Zuntor said quietly. And that troubles me the most," Zuntor went on to say, "Those guys could be standing next to us as we speak, and none of us would know it!" Then, as a normal reaction, all three of them began to look around suspiciously.

The thought came to Dr. Zuntor to ask Captain Star, "What did you do with the ZYM Serum?"

Star answered, "I put it in a safe place in the cave."

Lt. Tulley advised, "I think we should pick it up and keep it with us." They all agreed that this might be a good idea.

Dr. Zuntor said, "First, we need to find a safe place to put it, outside the camp, because I believe they're coming back. I'm sure Sunbird told them it might be in the cave, and if by chance they get by us, and find out it's not there, they'll tear this camp apart looking for it!"

Lt. Tulley enquired, "How about those rock samples we found over there?" pointing her finger to the area on their left.

Answering her, Dr. Zuntor said, "The full results of the testing is not conclusive, but so far, they appear to have a sufficient amount of

Laperzin, so it might be safe to store it. But, to make sure, I'll run a few more tests before we pick it up and bring it out of the cave."

"That sounds like a good idea," said Captain Star. He continued, "In the meantime, I'll just take a look around and see if I can spot them. I'll meet both of you back here as soon as I think you've completed your testing." He left the area.

As he was walking through the debris that was laying around his trashed camp, his foot happened to kick something lying on the ground. Looking down at it; he saw a pair of glasses. He stopped and picked them up, and examined them. He said to himself, "I wonder where these came from?" He tried them on. As he looked around through the glasses, he couldn't believe what he saw. There were dead bodies laying around that he hadn't been able to see before. He took the magic glasses off, and put them back on, again and again.

It came to him that the guys who had attacked his camp were wearing these glasses along with some strange-looking apparatus they had strapped to their bodies. As he was still looking through the neutralizing glasses, he noticed something else: The dead men who belonged to the invaders were wearing Getnor Air Force uniforms.

"Well now", Star said to himself, "things are beginning to make sense; the pieces are finally coming together — all of this is the work of Commander Booner! I thought I had gotten rid of him in the Getnor war. He must have gotten away! Now I understand what Admiral Fitchly meant when he said that General Sunbird was too ambitious!"

Putting two and two together, Captain Star knew he had better let his commanding officer know they should be on the alert for an attack on Duderyon by Commander Booner's new fleet! "I've got to make it to my shuttle and tell Admiral Fitchly that General Sunbird has joined Commander Booner. I should ask him if he still wants us to store that ZYM230.6 Serum out here, or bring it back to Duderyon..." He made his way to the area where his shuttle was waiting.

"There's the cave over there," said General Sunbird, pointing his finger in that direction.

"Well, let's move out!" ordered Lt. Scuff. As they made their way over the rough territory, Lt. Scuff was giving his men orders not to make any hostile moves against anyone. "Just stand ready since we are invisible until we come out of the cave with the Serum. Then, once we get out of the cave, we can kill everyone in Star's crew!"

Star, in his shuttle, was transmitting to the Phantom II. "This is Captain Star calling Mr. Pep! - Come in, Mr. Pep!"

Answering him, Mr. Pep replied, "Mr. Pep here Sir! What can I do for you?"

"Mr. Pep," orders Star, "I want you to contact I.P.D. Headquarters and hook me up with Admiral Fitchly! Over!"

"Got you, Sir," said Mr. Pep.

Within seconds, Admiral Fitchly was on the Hologram Scanner Screen: "Yes, Captain Star I'm here. Go Ahead!"

"Admiral, you were right about General Sunbird. He's gone over to Commander Booner's side."

"Commander Booner?! I thought he was dead!" said Admiral Fitchly.

"I did too, Sir, but he's not! As we speak, he is more than likely headed your way with a newly formed fleet. And, he has also left some of his men staked out on this asteroid! He is trying to snatch the Serum! Sunbird has gone with them! I know they are coming back soon to try and get the Serum. My question now is, what do you want me to do with it, Sir?" asked Captain Star.

"No matter what happens, Star, you must guard it with your life! If you find it necessary, bring it back here! As for Commander Booner, we'll take care of him," said Admiral Fitchly.

"Thanks, Admiral. I thought it would be best to let you know what was going on. I've got to get back to camp and follow your orders. Com-Beam Closed!" He began to make his way back to his camp.

Just as he reached the summit of a hill that overlooked the camp, he began to have a strange feeling. Everything looked normal, but somehow he knew something was wrong. Then he remembered those glasses he had found lying on the ground at the camp. He retrieved them from his pocket and put them on.

There they were standing around with the drop on everyone in camp. Because they were invisible, no one knew they were even there. Looking over at the cave, he could see a group of men entering, with General Sunbird leading the way.

Looking further, he could see Dr. Zuntor and Lt. Tulley working on their experiments. They had no idea that they were surrounded! "Somehow, I've got to stop them from getting that Serum, he said to himself, as he began to work his way closer to camp. Peaking from around and behind boulders, running a little here and a little there, he was soon behind some boxes where Dr. Zuntor and Lt. Tulley were working.

Still wearing the glasses, he was able to keep his eyes on Lt. Scuff's men. Speaking in a whisper, he said, "Dr. Zuntor, don't move! It's only me. Don't turn around! Act normal! You're surrounded by those invisible men. Here — take these glasses!"

Slowly, Dr. Zuntor reached behind his back so that Star could put the glasses into his hand. He slowly put them on, and finally, he could see the men that were once invisible as plain as day. He slowly returned the glasses to Captain Star.

Then he saw a chance to get under cover of some rocks. Seizing Tulley by her hand, they nonchalantly walked to a stack of rocks, as if they were gathering more samples. Once there, they quickly ducked behind them! Making his way to the big boulder where Dr. Zuntor and Lt. Tulley were hiding, Captain Star said, "Dr. Zuntor, come with me. We're going to stop them from taking the Serum out of the cave."

"Lt. Tulley," Star said, "You must stay behind." An upset Tulley quietly exclaimed, "Stay Here?! Not on your life!"

Looking at her determined face, Star knew there was no sense in arguing with her about it, so he said, "All right! Come on, but you have to stay close to me!"

The three of them continued ducking and dodging, trying to keep hidden as they made their way to the mouth of the cave. They finally found themselves inside and moving toward the area where Captain Star had hidden the case with the Serum. They were peering over a huge boulder, and Captain Star, using the glasses, could see Lt. Scuff and General Sunbird. They were accompanied by several of their troops. All of them were busy digging, looking for Captain Star's case.

The Lieutenant, unable to see them without the special glasses, asked Captain Star if she could look through his. Putting them on, for the first time, she could see the men. To her amazement, she saw Sunbird with them. She said, with a sad voice, "I would never have believed it, if I hadn't seen it with my own eyes! Why? General Sunbird? Why?!" She gave the glasses back to Captain Star. But she became angrier and angrier. It took a real effort to control her voice, but she kept herself under control and whispered, "We have to stop them!"

Dr. Zuntor asked Captain Star if he had a plan. Star replied, Since this location gives us an advantage, I think we just need to let them go ahead and dig it up, and then jump them when they pass by us here!"

"But we cant see them," objected Lt. Tulley.

"I'll take care of that," declared Star.

After telling them to wait for his return, he took off, back to the mouth of the cave. Standing guard at the mouth of the cave were two of Lt. Scuff's men. Thinking they couldn't be seen, they had become very relaxed. Climbing to the top of some rocks behind them, Captain Star dived onto the two men, knocking them to the ground. He leaped up like a cat, and with a left and a right, one man was down and out! Kicking the other guy in the face with a round-house, down he went in an unconscious heap!

Moving fast, before any of the enemy could see them, he pulled them inside the cave. Taking the glasses from the two unconscious men, Captain Star made his way back to Lt. Tulley and Dr. Zuntor. "Here, put these on!" said Captain Star. Now that Dr. Zuntor could see all of them, he dedicated a facetious little poem to General Sunbird: "Now we'll show you what we can do. Not only can you see me, but I can see you."

"Come on, men Dig! We don't have much time," Lt. Scuffsnarled He knew if he were going to be on time to rendezvous with Commander Booner, every second counted, and they would have to hurry more than any of them ever had hurried before. Soon they hit something with their shovels. One of the men looked out of the hole, and shouted, "We found it, Sir!" Not long after that, the men were handing it up and over to Lt. Scuff and General Sunbird.

The case was about the size of a footlocker. Falling on top of it, and throwing his arms around it, General Sunbird, feeling elated, exclaimed, "At last! It's mine!" Now that I have it, no one can stop me!"

Observing General Sunbird's face, brought back sad memories to Dr. Zuntor. That look of madness was on Sunbird's face. Seeing his eyes turn red, and foam gathering around the corners of his mouth, made Dr. Zuntor think about his brother, Dr. Pelcozor — how mad he had become over the same Serum. At that moment, he knew he had to stop them, no matter what it took!

Looking at Sunbird laying on top of the case, Lt. Scuff remembered what Commander Booner had ordered him to do when he got his hands on the Serum. Pulling his laser gun, he kicked the General in the face and said, "You're not going to have a chance to take over anything! What a stupid man, talking about 'No one can stop you'!"
Lying on the floor of the cave and trembling from fear, General Sunbird said, "Have you gone mad? You fool! Commander Booner and I have a deal!"

Laughing, Lt. Scuff said, "Do you think my commander would trust you after you crossed your own people?" Scuff pointed his laser gun at the General's head.

"No! No!" screamed General Sunbird, but it was too late. Lt. Scuff blew his body away with his laser gun! All that was left of the General was hot, bubbling, red mud.

"All right men, grab that case and let's get out of here!"

Two of his men picked up the case and the five of them began to make the trip back toward the mouth of the cave.

"Here they come!" whispered Captain Star. "I'm ready!" answered Dr. Zuntor. As the five invisible men were slowly walking across a natural rock bridge that spanned over a huge pool of hot, bubbling, brown, mud, an enormous size Gyberoake ten times bigger than the first one rose up out of the hot mud, with its mouth open! It thrust out a fifteen-foot tongue, and slapped one of the men into the boiling mud!

Screaming as he fell, he splashed into the hot mud, and as soon as his body hit the bubbling pool, it went up in flames! Seeing what had happened, the other three men and Lt. Scuff began to run — only to be followed by the vengeful mother of the first Gyberoake!

A frightened Dr. Zuntor, seeing the huge Gyberoake gaining on Lt. Scuff and his men, and knowing it was about to eat them alive, exclaimed to Captain Star, "We must get that Serum! Now! Remember the Drymahords! If that thing swallows it, no telling what might happen!"

"What can we do?" asked Lt. Tulley.

"I really don't know, but first things first! We'll have to take it from those men! And, the only way we can do that is to stop that Gyberoake!"

Star's quick mind came up with a plan. "Lt. Tulley, keep firing your laser gun at the beast! Maybe that will get its attention long enough for Dr. Zuntor and me to take the Serum away from those men!"

Screaming and running, Lt. Scuff and the two men carrying the case with the Serum made it to the other side of the bridge. But the man in the back — his luck ran out! The huge Gyberoake, with one big bite, snapped the top half of his body off as his legs were still running! At the sight of this happening, Lt. Tulley fired her laser gun and the flash hit the monster in her face. The shock of the blast hitting her made the Gyberoake stop and look around as if to see where it had come from. Then she continued to follow after the three men!

The delay was enough time for Lt. Scuff and the men carrying the case to get a small distance away from the beast. They continued running and falling down the steep hills inside the cave. At last, they could see daylight shining in from the mouth of the cave.

Making it to the edge of a boulder, and looking down on the three men, as they had worked their way under them, Captain Star and Dr. Zuntor jumped down on top of the men, knocking them to the ground.

The blow from their bodies colliding caused the case to fall down to fall down a small incline! The case broke open! The cylinder rolled out onto the ground!

Dr. Zuntor quickly got up and threw a fast right hand, hitting Lt. Scuff, who lost his balance, fell, and rolled down another incline. Zuntor then quickly hit another man with a left and a right, which knocked him to the ground. Then with a round-house kick to the face, he knocked the other guy down. As he hit the ground, his glasses fell off! He struggled up, but he couldn't see Captain Star when he was hit with a long, right cross that put him to sleep!

Jumping down the incline on top of Lt. Scuff, Dr. Zuntor hit him again and again. Scuff fell down onto a big rock he turned, picked up the rock, and threw it at Dr. Zuntor, hitting him in the stomach. Dr. Zuntor fell to the ground in pain. With only his incredible will to stop them, Zuntor gets up and kicks Lt. Scuff in the balls. Scuff, grabbing at the pain, falls and rolls up into a fetal position on the floor of the cave.

Captain Star, as he was having a give-and-take battle with the other guy, sees the cylinder lying on the ground next to the broken case. However, Lt. Scuff, lying on the ground in pain, also saw the cylinder at the same time.

Both of them made a dive for it! Suddenly, like something from out of hell, the Gyberoake picked up the man that Captain Star had been fighting by the head. She swung him like a rag doll, until she had bitten his head off of his body! As he lay on the ground, the man's body was still kicking! It soon stopped.

Realizing that the Gyberoake was closing in on Dr. Zuntor, Lt. Tulley fired at it again it again with her laser gun. Zing! Zing! Hitting it over and over again.

Being hit by the flash only seemed to madden the beast! It began to go wild, slamming its tail against the side of the cave. The shock of so much force against the wall of the cave caused an avalanche of rocks to fall everywhere! Running over to Dr. Zuntor, Tulley helped him up and they ran toward the mouth of the cave.

A knee to his face knocked Captain Star up against a big boulder. As he lay there, out of breath, Lt. Scuff picked up the cylinder and ran. Seeing him trying to get away, Captain Star, with a last burst of energy, ran to catch up with him. When he got close enough, Star made a dive and tackled him. Down to the ground they went! Rolling over and over, until Scuff's grasp on the cylinder failed, and it fell out of his hands!

Watching the cylinder roll and seeing it about to fall off the edge of a cliff, Captain Star made a dive for it — just in time! Getting up off the ground, Lt. Scuff picked up a big rock and was about to smash Captain Star's head in. That's when the mother Gyberoake slapped him down with her tongue. The force from this tongue slap knocked Lt. Scuff across the cave and up against the wall. While Lt. Scuff lay there dazed, the Gyberoake leaned over and slowly ate him!

Captain Star, almost unconscious, crawled away. Through his fear-filled and hazy brain, he realized he had to put some distance between himself and that extremely huge, and insanely angry Gyberoake! As soon as he could, he got up and stumbled out of the cave. Meeting him at the mouth of the cave was Lt. Tulley. She carefully helped him down the side of the rocks.

Still holding onto the cylinder, Captain Star told Dr. Zuntor and Lt. Tulley that the Gyberoake was on her way out of the cave and somehow, they had to get their men together and get off this blasted asteroid! They quickly made their way back to the camp.

As they approached the camp, they could see Lt. Scuff's men. One-by-one they were reappearing!? By some strange coincidence, the camp itself had been set up on a huge deposit of Laperzin, with its high lead content. The Laperzin had drained the power packs on their R.I.E. Units. Since they had been standing around in the same spot for so long, their units were going dead. Seeing the once invisible men reappear, Captain Star's crew began pulling their laser guns and firing. The two groups of men fired at each other and fought until almost all of Lt. Scuff's men were dead. The remaining few gave themselves up. Captain Star ordered his men to disarm the remainder of Scuff's crew.

"Hurry men! Back to the shuttle!" Still holding onto the cylinder, he didn't have to repeat this order, because the men were already headed in that direction! They were more than anxious to return to the shuttle. After all, there was an enormous Mother Gyberoake – over ninety feet long, and over 25,000 pounds – with human flesh and blood drooling from her mouth, that was quickly moving toward them! She was at the mouth of the cave, and headed their way!

Each person began to fire their lasers at her and running for their lives! Even Star, while holding onto the cylinder, was firing his laser, and rushing for his shuttle. Even though she was being hit hundreds of times, the mother Gyberoake continued coming for them! The more she was hit by the lasers, the wilder she became! In her befuddled brain, she was still protecting her baby.

Soon they were at the I.P.D. shuttle. They rushed on board and took off — just in time! The Mother Gyberoake leaped up and bit off an insignificant part of the shuttle, just as it was taking off.

Back on board Phantom II, just after the shuttle had docked, Captain Star asked Mr. Pep if the ship's engines could take 12.4 warp speed.

And if so, how far could it go before he would have to brake the speed down? Answering the Captain, Mr. Pep falteringly said, "That's a lot of work for her, Sir, and I don't know about that much stress.
But I'll see what we can do."

Impatiently, Star repeated: "How far?"

As he snapped to attention, Mr. Pep answered, "Maybe as far as the Magnor Sector, SIR!"

Lt. Tulley inquired, "Isn't that where we had a battle with those Icpek brothers, Captain?"

"Yes, I know, but it's halfway between here and Duderyon. Anyway, it really doesn't matter, because I have a rendezvous with destiny!" predicted Captain Star.

"Captain Icpek, Sir, we have been picking up transmissions of a fleet of ships headed this way from out of the Getnor Sector," said Icpek's Communication's Officer.
"Tune them in on my Proximetry Locator Screen, and my Hologram Scanner Screen," said Captain Icpek.

Seconds later, he was looking at his P.L.S., and saw hundreds of small dots and one big dot — moving at warp speed, and headed for his sector! He switched over to his giant Hologram Scanner, which showed (on a huge 4D screen) a close-up of Commander Booner's Monster-Mothership.

Looking at it, Icpek knew it had to be stopped. Having never seen any ship that huge before, there was no doubt it was a planet destroyer. And, his small planet would surely be destroyed unless he gave in to them, or made a stand and fought. Everyone in their solar system knows that a Magnorite never gives up! So, he had no other choice — they would fight!

Captain Icpek sounded the alarm, which called up reinforcements. Captain Icpek's entire War-Starfleet was always prepared for war. Sitting back in his Captain's Chair, and looking at his P.L.S. screen, he felt proud as he watched his huge fleet being assembled.

"Commander Booner, I don't see any sign of Lt. Scuff's ship on our Proximetry Locator screen! We've picked up another machine on the Locator, but it looks like an I.P.D. Ship! The only thing is, it's speeding faster than I've ever seen one of them fly before, Sir!" reported his Communications Officer.

"Can you identify her with a name?" asked Commander Booner.

"I'll have to wait until she gets a little closer, Sir." answered the officer. "But there is also a fleet of ships massing in battle formation in the Magnor Sector! Com-Beam Closed!"

Changing the direction of his P.L.S. over to the Magnor Sector, Commander Booner saw about three hundred Magnorite ships, flying in his direction! Knowing all the Captains that lead each planet's Star-Warships by name, Commander Booner said, "It looks like Captain Icpek has a greeting committee on its way to meet us!" He began to laugh!

Admiral Fitchly himself was the commander of his Own huge, I.P.D. Mother-Starship of war; along with the largest I.P.D. fleet, ever assembled. He was speeding through the Toplyron Sector, on his way to the Magnor Sector, where he was to meet Captain Star's Phantom II.

"Do you think we'll be there in time, Admiral?" asked his First Lieutenant, Mazerbe.

"We're pushing it as best we can — I just pray we'll make it", said Admiral Fitchly.

The Admiral walked over to his P.L.S. screen. The upper corner of the screen measures distance in light-years; it is now indicating fifteen light-years away. He could see the massing of two groups of Star-Warships gathering in battle formation. Calling to his Communications Officer, he said, "Zero in on this section, so we can pull them up closer. Then, I might be able to identify them."

Seconds later, he was told that they would not be able to isolate this for him, at this time, because of a meteor storm. The Admiral said, "Let me know then, as soon as things clear up!"

The officer replied, "Will do, Sir!"

It was only a short time later when his Communications Officer interrupted his thoughts and announced, "Commander Booner! It's close enough to identify now, and it's an I.P.D. Ship The Phantom II — it's coming this way fast!" Thinking out loud, Booner said, "The Phantom II — that's that treacherous Captain Star! He should have been dead, back on Plufre! If it is him, Lt. Scuff must be in trouble or maybe dead. Either way, I don't see Lt. Scuff coming, so we might as well continue on our mission."

He then gave the orders to speed up his ship to 2.7 light-speed. Moving much faster than before, it wasn't long before the two fleets were within firing distance of one another!

"I thought that fool Captain Icpek would see us and turn around, knowing we were too powerful for them, remarked Commander Booner. "Oh well, there's only one thing left for us to do and that is — destroy them!"

After giving the order to attack, Commander Booner switched on his Hologram Scanner screen, and sat back so he could see the battle in close-up mode.

"Commander Booner, do you need to use our Reflective Image Eliminator for your ship only, or for our entire fleet, Sir?" asked his Operational Officer.

Feeling as if he had the superior air force, Booner egotistically replied, "No! I want to kick him out of the heavens fair and square! No tricks!" So instead of attacking his enemy in the invisible mode, he chose a straight-forward attack!

Sending out his first squadrons, Captain Icpek, in his heart believed that his decision to go into battle against the Getnorite forces, was justi-

fied. After all, they had trespassed into his planet's sector, with a mighty force, and without his permission! So Icpek was motivated to strike first, fast, and viciously! Captain Icpek ordered his fleet to attack!
Each fleet's advance squadrons exchanged rocket and laser cannon fire, most enthusiastically! Soon they both needed reinforcements.

"Send out my ZP-7s," ordered Captain Icpek. They opened the big, bay-doors, and springing from out of the Mothership came two dozen or more W-shaped Warships. They revolved around and around like a spinning top, firing laser cannons from both sides! The ZP.7s were zipping in and out of the older, dissipated, Warships of the Getnorite's Air Force. The ZP.7s were blowing them out of the sky at will, and it was impossible for the older ships of the Getnorites to target and hit them!

Seeing that he was losing too many ships from his "outlaw-acquired" fleet, Commander Booner ordered his own special squadrons from out of his own Mothership, saying, "Those W-shaped ships of Icpek's have got a little something.

Now I want to see what they can do against my D-6s!" Springing from out of the bay door of his Mothership, the D.6s flew out as if they were raindrops! The battle between Icpek's ZP.7s and Booner's D.6s was nothing less than a dog fight! Zooming in and out, rolling over and over each other, as both of them were firing thousands of rounds-per-second!

Somehow, the D.6s seemed to be getting an edge on the ZP.7s, until Captain Icpek ordered fifty or more ZP.7s to intercept the oncoming fleet and to attack Commander Booner's Monster-Mothership!

Thinking he should take this opportunity to instigate a one-two-punch, Captain Icpek ordered his group of ZP.7s to fly with the thought of not coming back — A suicide mission! The idea was to take two (or maybe even three) enemy ships out with you, because it was a sure thing you were going to die!

Their pride in their fleet and planet, not to mention history's portrayal of "the incredible bravery of the Magnorite Pilots" made this order seem like a simple request. This wave of Magnorite pilots were so effective that they had fought their way up to Commander Booner's Mothership. They were killing every enemy ship (including the D-6's) every step of the way.

As we know, every dog has its day, but some dogs keep a trick or two up their nostrils. Commander Booner, as he slams his fists down onto both arms of his chair, yells to his First Officer, "Enough is enough! I've got to put a stop to this!" He forced himself to calm down. After a few seconds, he continued speaking to his officer: "We have a 'real' war coming up with the Duderyon I.P.D.. I simply must complete my mission to destroy the Duderyon planet. So, we have to show Icpek and show him NOW, that he is nothing but a fool — how can he possibly think he has any kind of a chance?!"

Then, not wanting to continue wasting war power on such a useless battle, he decided to get it over with quickly, once and for all! Calling his co-strategists, he asked if it would take much time to ready one of his new war-toys. He had been trying to save these weapons until he could use them on the Duderyon's I.P.D. Star-Warships, but he decided that now was the time.

"Commander, it wont take long for our engineers to set the computers, which will prepare the firing mechanism arms, Sir," explained his officer.

" O.K., Whatever it takes. I need it, and I need it now! So Move!"

Not much longer than "Now", the officer called back, "Commander Booner, It's ready, Sir."

Checking his Hologram Scanner screen for the battle, he said to himself, "I'll see if Captain Icpek likes the taste of my new Swirling-Cluster Laser Cannons! As a matter of fact, I think I'll use all three of them, and put a quick stop to this little game!"

The "Swirling-Cluster" is a laser cannon, which has been mounted to the Mothership. There is one on each side of the ship, and the third one is mounted to the top. Each cannon swings from side-to-side at a 120-degree angle. Each cannon has a huge barrel that can fire up to fifty missiles at a time! When the missiles are projected, before they reach their targets, they explode, so that hundreds of smaller laser rays spread out in enormous clusters. These clusters spin out laser rays indiscriminately, and any ship that is hit by these hot laser rays explodes on contact!

"Put. me in contact with all my fighting units", he orders. Seconds later, Commander Booner is speaking to his pilots, "This is Commander Booner. I am ordering all ships to retreat! Do you read me?! Retreat! Now!"

Not understanding the order, since they they were holding their own, the Getnor pilots, brave fighting men all, reluctantly followed their Commander's orders, and returned to their Mothership.

Seeing the sudden change in tactics, Captain Icpek began to feel that he was winning the battle. So, at that time, he ordered his reserve ships to attack!

Captain Star had been orbiting around the battle, and watching from a distance long enough to know that Commander Booner was up to something.

When he saw him withdraw his ships away from the battle, it looked as though they were running away. But Star knew Captain Icpek was no match for Commander Booner. Captain Star said to Dr. Zuntor, "Can you believe what we're seeing here?! Booner certainly is up to something!"

Dr. Zuntor replied, "It looks like a trap to me! And, that dumb Captain Icpek seems to be falling into it!"

"I wonder what it is?" Then — a Sudden Flashback! He remembered when he was in little Orcal's mini-laboratory. He remembered how the boy seemed to have the gift of clairvoyance. Captain Star could again see little Orcal's small-scale model of this entire battle! As he was watching the battle develop, both in his mind's memory, and in present time reality, it was accurate — tactic by tactic, down to the last laser shot, including the Monster-Mothership!

"WOW!" said Captain Star, as he watched his screen, "Idon't have to guess now! I know what's going to happen!" He reminded both Lt. Tulley and Dr. Zuntor of little Orcal's original model of his dream.

"You're right! Now I remember!" exclaimed Dr. Zuntor. "And if that's the case, Captain Icpek is in for the surprise of his life!"

"What are we going to do about it, Captain?" asked Lt. Tulley.

"Well," replied Star, "As for me, I'm just going to lie back, kick my heels up, and watch the entire thing!" And so, he did just that with a smile on his face!

"I got you! I got you!" shouted Captain Icpek as he jumped for joy, watching Commander Booner's Warships retreating! "Now we'll see just how much of a coward he is! I knew he couldn't stand up to me! Just look at how those fools are running away from me back to their Mothership like a baby to its mother's teats! Not only have I spanked the baby, but now, I'm going to destroy the Mother ... ship!"

He then ordered more ships to attack. In seconds, three hundred of Captain Icpek's Star-Warships were headed for Commander Booner's Monster-Mothership, and his fleet! (This gave the appearance that they were about to run!)

"Admiral Fitchly," reported his Navigational Officer, "we are just entering the Plufre Sector. Very soon, we should be within firing range, Sir."

Fitchly gave his orders: "Make ready all I.P.D. Warships! I want my P13-Zs to lead the assault, followed by my Looper SP-9s, with full Laser Reflectors. Then all of my Stingers (Double X-2s) are to follow for mop-up! Do you read me!?"

"Yes Sir! We'll have everything ready, Sir!" replied the Air-Attack Officer.

NOTE on I.P.D. Warships:

The P13-Zs are special squadrons that exercise complex maneuvers as they simultaneously spray groups of laser fire.

The SP.9s are sometimes called Loopers. These ships fly in a stop-and-go pattern, using a reflective laser shield, with the use of electromagnetic pulses. These electromagnetic pulses create a reflecting hot glow from laser flashes that bounce off the shield and back to their origin. Their stop-and-go action prevents them from being hit by these reflections, allowing a clear path to the enemy ship.

The Double X-2s (XX-2), sometimes called Stingers, are little one-man ships that are extremely fast and flexible. They are so small that instead of a Mothership carrying a few hundred, regular-sized fighter ships, she is able to accommodate two or sometimes three thousand of the smaller ships. When they are on the attack, they swarm around their victims like bees. With their speed, flexibility, and almost uncountable numbers, they are almost unstoppable!

"Here they come! I knew he would fall for it!" shouted Commander Booner. After making sure that all of his own ships were safely out of the range of his Swirling-Cluster Laser Cannons, he gave the orders to fire! At once, they began to spit rockets! Rapidly, one after another, they were swirling vertically on both sides of his Monster-Mothership and swirling horizontally on top of it.

As soon as its missiles were in the target area, they began to explode, dispersing hundreds upon hundreds of small laser rays. There were so many clusters of hot laser rays, spewing indiscriminately, that there was no way for Captain Icpek's enormous fleet of attacking Star-Warships to escape.

Exploding ships were flying out of control, smashing into one another. Yet they still continued to come, even though they were being shot out of the sky by the hundreds. They kept on coming! Seeing all the action on his H.S. Screen, Commander Booner began to laugh wildly! He laughed louder and louder at the sight of Icpek's fleet being destroyed.

Captain Star, also, at his H.S Screen, amused at the sight of his two enemies destroying each other, said to Dr. Zuntor and Lt. Tulley, "Isn't it nice, letting someone else do a nasty job like this for you? Now all we have to do is wait for Admiral Fitchly to arrive, and then we can take on the winner!"

"Now all I have to do is send my fighters back into the fray! Then I can mop up the mess of Captain Icpek's Air Force! The next thing is, I can proceed on to destroy the I.P.D. Fleet. And then it's on to the Planet Duderyon, to destroy it! No holds barred! No one can stop me now! The solar system will soon be mine!" He gave the order to attack! "I want to show that foolish Captain Icpek which one of us really has the power, and who really is The Master of the Solar System! Send out all ships! Everything!!"
Soon wave upon wave of Star-Warships were on the attack.

Watching his entire fleet being destroyed, Captain Captain Icpek couldn't believe it. He screamed, "NO! NO! This can't be!" He ordered his navigator to fly his own ship into the heart of the battle. Once there, Captain Icpek showed his pilots that he was a brave leader — exploding one ship, then another, at will. No one could say he wasn't a real Star-Fighter!
In his heart he knew the days of his glory were over. Seeing his entire fleet dying around him, he realized there was only one thing left to do. He must run for his life! In order to fight another time, he sadly gave the orders to his pilot: "Take me out of the action." Then, as he had done

only once before in his life, he wiped all three of his eyes, as he began to cry!

Still watching the battle, Captain Star saw Captain Icpek's ship turn away from the battle and head his way. Captain Star, knowing Captain Icpek was unaware that he was headed in his direction, announced to Dr. Zuntor, "At long last! It looks as if we're going to get a chance to surprise our old friend, Captain Icpek!" Pointing his finger at his H.S. Screen, he said with disdain, "Look at him running away and leaving his command to die for nothing! But, we will be right here, waiting for him! Dr. Zuntor, you and Lt. Tulley make things ready for action. I think I'm going to fly the Phantom II myself."

After removing his pilot from his seat, Captain Star takes over the controls. He ordered his cannons and missiles to be switched over to manual. Then he asserted, with deep anger showing in his voice and eyes, "Captain Icpek - This time you won't get away! This time you die!!"

Reporting that all of the officers of his I.P.D. Star-Warships were waiting for his command to to attack, his Air Attack Officer said, "All things are ready, Sir." Looking at his Hologram Scanner Screen, Admiral Fitchly was thinking, "Now would be a great time to attack. Since they are fighting each other, and it is so confusing out there, they won't know who to fire on. Therefore, we now have the advantage, because my fighters know that every ship that is not an I.P.D. Ship is open game."

He then said, over the ship's intercom-beam, "Attention all Imperial Planetary Defence War-Starship Squadrons: This is Admiral Fitchly. We are going to engage in battle with two of the most evil and treacherous star fleets in our solar system! Be brave, and remember your training. You are the best pilots that have ever been assembled! Your orders are to kill and destroy anything out there that is not an I.P.D. Ship! Some of you may not be coming back, but with God's help, most of you will. You have no reason to fear! And remember, I'll be out there with you!

"Now – for personal reasons – I want to personally take out Commander Booner's Monster-Mothership! So, I, myself, personally take on that responsibility! O.K. Pilots. That will be all."

He paused for the count of two, then shouted "ATTACK!!"

Upon his command to attack, the first wave of P13-Zs sprang out of the huge I.P.D. Mothership. Flying in perfect tactical formations, they were rolling and dipping, wing-to-wing, spraying laser fire into groups of enemy Star-Warships. Balls of fire and debris were everywhere. Confused and not knowing who to draw down on, all the pilots – other than the P13-Zs – were in deep trouble.

Seeing this, Commander Booner said to his communications officer, "Have all my ships remove themselves from out of the action. That way, I can use my Swirling-Cluster, Laser Cannons on these fools!"

Not long after Booner's orders, his ship had cleared the battle area. Having used that maneuver once before, they already knew what to do. Seeing that it was now feasible to use his Swirling-Cluster Laser Cannons, Booner called for their use.

BAZOOM! BAZOOM! went the huge S.C.L. Cannons, firing over and over again. Still not knowing what to do, Icpek's War-Starship's fleet, (and some of the I.P.D.'s, P13- Zs) were being destroyed every time his missiles exploded and the clusters of hot, lasers were spinning and shooting blue-white laser rays that were eating out sections of all the battling Star-Warships.

Not waiting a second longer after he realized this, Admiral Fitchly ordered his SP-9s into action. Before the battle could turn to Commander Booner's favor, the SP-9s were busy looping over one another with their stop-and-go pattern. With their reflector laser shields glowing, as well as firing their own cannons, the cluster laser missiles were being reflected back onto all the enemy ships that were within its reflective area. What was left of Captain Icpek's and many of Commander

Booner's Star-Warships were being slaughtered by his own Swirling-Cluster, Laser Missiles.

"I don't believe it! This can't be!" the incredulous Commander Booner was saying, as he watched his own missiles killing everything flying except the I.P.D. Warships! There was only one thing left to do — stop firing the cannons and release all fighting ships on board his Monster-Mothership, and then, join the battle himself.

"It's working! I knew it would!" exclaimed Admiral Fitchly. Seeing his SP-9s doing a perfect job. He knew his timing was right, so he said, "It's time I release my Double X-2s."

As he was about to give the order for the Stinger attack, he saw Commander Booner's Monster-Mothership begin to move in the direction of the battle. The big, bay-doors opened, making it look like a huge dragon. Then a long runway extended out of it as if it were a huge tongue. Taking off from the runway were so many ships, it looked as though the runway-tongue was spitting fire! Ships were taking off and rushing to the area of the battle by the hundreds. There were so many, the heavens were almost black with them.

Fitchly, still watching his H. S. Screen said to himself, "I almost made my move too soon! I bet he thinks that's all I've got, just those ships that are out there now. Well, I've got a surprise for him! Calling down to his chief engineer, he said, "You will have to follow these orders to the letter! I want you to set your computers so so that that they will be coordinated with my XX-2 computers. I want to control our Reflective Image Eliminator from our ship. I want the power switch in my hands, so that I can turn it 'OFF' and 'ON' in an instant! Now, Hurry! We have no time to waste!"

Within seconds, the engineer was returning the call to his Admiral, telling him that the Reflective Image Eliminator was ready. Seeing that the battle area was filled with Commander Booner's ships, he ordered his Double X-2s to attack. He then switched "ON" the computers that connected with the computers on each of the XX-2's. Then, he switched "ON" the Reflective Image Eliminator. In two seconds, each double-X2 became invisible! Thousands of the invisible XX-2s were attacking the enormous fleet of the enemy Star-Warships!

Not seeing what was coming to destroy his fleet, Booner was sure he had the upper hand. He had no idea that his own "old tricks" were about to turn on him. Still more and more of his ships were entering into the battle. Seeing this on his Hologram Scanner Screen, he was filled with joy! Giving orders and laughing wildly, he said, "I'm taking on the best the I.P.D. has, and it still is not good enough to stop me! Now, I'm going to move in on the kill!"

"Captain Icpek! Captain Icpek! Check out your Proximetry Locator! There's a ship on our tail, Sir!" exclaimed one of his officers.

"Switch frequency on my Hologram Scanner so I can see who it is," ordered Captain Icpek. Seconds later he was able to see a close-up of the Phantom II. Not believing his eyes, in a low voice, he said, "It's Captain Star! How the devil did he find me?"

Another one of his officers, his voice full of fear, said, "If it's him, we're doomed! What are we gonna do Captain?"

Slapping the frightened officer across the face, Icpek announced in desperation: "We are going to turn around and fight!"

"Looks like he's spotted us, Captain," remarked Lt. Tulley.

"Good! That's just just what I wanted him to do," declared Star. "I've got to let him know that the time has come for law and order to rule in this sector. The days of his killing and destroying small ships and planets are over! Besides that, I want to find out if this Phantom II is the fighting machine I've been told she is!"

Zooming past the Phantom II with lasers firing, Captain Icpek made his pass. Rolling away from the angle of his fire, Captain Star looped the Phantom II and came up behind him.

BaZoom! went the Phantom's cannons. They missed Icpek's ship. Instead of the expected distance between them, the two ships were face-to-face, firing cannons at each other at this close range, ironically missing each other by only a few feet.

"I'll show him what flying is all about", said Captain Star. Revving up his engines to hyperdrive, he took off as if he were running away from the fight. Seeing this, Captain Icpek took off after him with his ship also in hyperdrive. Noticing that Icpek's ship was about to about to catch up with him, Captain Star dropped his rockets into drag speed this slowed his ship down by half.

Not expecting a maneuver like this, Captain Icpek's ship flew right over the top of Captain Star's Phantom II. Within seconds, after some adjustments, Captain Star was behind his enemy's ship. BaZoom! went his cannons. Rockets were zooming all around Captain Icpek's ship! Both Captain's Star-Warships were rolling, dipping, and looping together as if they were on a roller-coaster, with Captain Star firing at the back of Captain Icpek's ship.

Spotting a small meteor storm, Icpek headed into it to evade Captain Star's Phantom II. Captain Star followed!

Rolling from side-to-side, up-and-down, doing whatever it took to shake Captain Star off his tail, Icpek was soon out of the meteor storm and well on his way. Seconds later, Captain Star had also made it to the other side of the storm, only to see Captain Icpek's ship high-tailing it deeper into the Solar System, getting away, to maybe fight again another time. But to Star's crew, it seemed he had cowardly run away.

"He got away," said Lt. Tulley, "We almost had him!

"Yes, I know," said Star, "But sooner or later, we'll see him again. Next time, he won't be so lucky.

Then Dr. Zuntor said, "Captain, we must not forget about Admiral Fitchly. He might still need our help with Commander Booner's fleet."

"You're absolutely right!" agreed Captain Star, "We had best get back and do what we can to help him!"

So the Phantom II turned around and at warp speed and they hurried back to join their Admiral.

Flying deeper out into space with his ship smoking and fire streaming out of its tail section, swaying from side to side, Captain Icpek was working nervously, trying to put out some of the fires caused by Captain Star's cannons. He was muttering as he declared, "Damn that Captain Star! He and that I.P.D Command have not seen the last of me! I'll be back! And when I do come back, I'll have so many ships, the galaxy will be black with my laser dust. I promise you Captain Star: I'll be back!" He then wiped all three of his crying eyes again, and flew off into deep space.

Shooting missile and laser rays by the thousands, Commander Booner's ships greatly out-numbered the I.P.D.'s Star-Warships but the I.P.D. still held their own.

"Attack! Attack!" Commander Booner was screaming as his ship got closer to the battle area. As he checked his H.S. Screen, he realized no one was out there fighting except a few ships. Then it came to him that he could no longer see Admiral Fitchly's I.P.D. Mothership! He looked at his Proximetry Locator Screen. It wasn't there either.

"Something's wrong! I know that something is wrong!" he declared. Soon enough, he realized that Admiral Fitchly had used his Reflective Image Eliminator trick on him. He screamed, "NO!!!"

At that very instant, Admiral Fitchly switched off the Image Eliminator, and there they were! Thousands of double X-2s!! Not only the Stingers, but there also was Admiral Fitchly's I.P.D. Mothership!

Like bees, the little XX-2's were buzzing around everything in the sky. It was like trying to blow away a fly from off the end of your own nose. Zip! Zip! went these small laser cannons, almost never missing their target. Commander Booner's over-sized Warships were just too slow for these flexible little XX-2s. His outdated Star-Warships were being killed by the dozens. It was nothing less than a complete slaughter!

Satisfied with the job his little double X-2's were doing, Admiral Fitchly said, "Now it's my turn! Commander Booner, ready or not, here I come!" Giving the order for his Mothership to step up its speed to hyperdrive-plus, the big ship took off on the attack! He ordered his force fields up, and all laser cannons trained on Commander Booner's Monster-Mothership. He knew it was just a matter of time before it would all be over.

BOOOOM!! It was the sound of a huge hole being blown through the lower part of Commander Booner's ship! Steam and smoke, along with hot sparks, were swirling through the corridors. BOOOOM!! another hit! This time, an enormous hole was blown out of the left side of the hanger area.

"Fire!" ordered Commander Booner to all of his gunners. His ship was firing all the laser and missiles it had, trying to fight off Admiral Fitchly's Mothership, but nothing seemed to work.

Speeding back to the battle zone, Captain Star saw all the action, and said, "Well, Dr. Zuntor, it looks as if we made it just in time! Man your cannons, and let's give the Admiral a hand!"

Soon, the Phantom II was smack in the middle of the battle. Ba ZOOM! went Dr. Zuntor's cannons, hitting two or three ships, as they were making their way closer to Admiral Fitchly's Mothership.

The double X-2 Squad Leaders, seeing the Phantom II making its way to assist their Admiral's Mothership, began to group around it. Seconds later, the Phantom II was surrounded by hundreds of XX-2s. Knowing this was going to be another historical battle, Captain Star had Lt. Tulley switch his communication frequency so he could speak with the XX-2s.

Letting Star know that the communication frequency was ready, she said, "All right, Captain, it's show-time and it's all yours!"

Star announced, "This is Captain Star of the I.P.D. Phantom II. Let me explain how we're going to do this. Now this is my plan. I'm going to position my ship on the opposite side of Commander Booner's Monster-Mothership about the same angle as Admiral Fitchly's ship, so Booner will be trapped between us. And, all you XX-2 pilots join up in a 360-degree formation around that Getnor Mothership. On my command, close in on him. Now, as you continue to circle around him, you must keep your lasers firing, because we don't know where the ship's vulnerable section is. However, with this maneuver, there will not be any section that won't be hit by our lasers or our cannon missiles. So – if you are ready – come on you planet-jockeys, Follow Me!" Then, off they all went!

The battle between Admiral Fitchly and Commander Booner was getting pretty bloody! Each ship had taken some good hits, but the Monster-Mothership was not in danger of being destroyed, because it had all of its nuclear mechanisms built internally. That way, no weapon could penetrate deep enough to seriously damage it. However, there was one small section that was vulnerable. If a missile or a laser ray hit that particular section, it would cause a chain reaction that would blow it to smithereens. Yet, the chances of hitting it were a million to one.

Captain Star believed it must be something like this, because it had taken so many hits from their Mothership, yet seemed impervious to damage. Any other ship would have exploded long before now. With each hit he became more convinced that it had to have been constructed differently. That's why he ordered all of the XX-2s to form such an unusual formation of attack. He was hoping they might get lucky and hit something.

"Admiral Fitchly Look! Here comes the Phantom II and hundreds of those double X-2s! They're coming to help us Sir!" exclaimed his Communication's Officer.

"Great!" shouted the Admiral. "Now there is absolutely no doubt about it — Commander Booner is through!"

"What do they think they're doing? All of those I.P.D. ships gathering around my craft? Well, I've got a huge surprise for them! They don't seem to understand that it's impossible to destroy this ship! They might hit it now and then, but they will never be able to destroy it!"

Commander Booner then gave orders to his Chief Weapon's Officer, saying, "Fire everything we have at them! Even fire our Swirling-Cluster, Cannons!!"

The officer said, "Sir. You mean you're going to use the S.C.L. Cannons? We still have a lot of ships out ships out there fighting! That Swirling-Cluster will kill everything out there, Sir!"

"I don't give a damn! Just follow my orders!" shouted Commander Booner. "Now Move!"

"All right, you Planet Jockeys Come On! Let's give it to him!" ordered Captain Star to all the XX-2 pilots. Closing the circle tighter and tighter, flying around and around the Monster-Mothership, like the rings around Saturn. Firing their small laser cannons, they were hitting Commander Booner's ship with thousands of missiles and laser rays. There wasn't a a spot on it that wasn't being hit simultaneously by the little Stingers.

Not only that, but Admiral Fitchly's I.P.D. Mothership and the Phantom II, were also giving it hell with huge laser rays! Blue sparks and fire were leaping from the enormous Monster-Mothership. Even though all this was being done to his ship, Commander Booner was still fighting back.

Then it happened!! He began using his Swirling-Cluster Laser Cannons!

Seeing this, Captain Star knew what the S.C.L. Cannons were able to do to their XX-2s. But, he also knew what the I.P.D.'s Looper SP-9s could do to Booner's S.C.L. Missiles!

Captain Star, who had been communicating with Admiral Fitchly throughout the battle, said, "Admiral, send out our SP-9s that you still have in the hanger on-board your ship. Have them replace the XX-2 formations around Booner's ship. I'll retreat with the replaced Stingers and pick up the battle from the rear of the SP-9's circular perimeter. When the timing is right, we'll attack!"

Knowing this was a great idea, Admiral Fitchly said, "Captain, whatever fuels your rocket! You call it, you got it! I'll back you up all the way!"

Firing his S.C.L. Cannons, Commander Booner's Monster-Mothership was killing ships by the dozens. Everything that was in the arena of its exploding missiles, even his own ships, were being zapped out of the sky.

Standing in front of his H.S. Screen, looking at the effectiveness of his S.C.L. Cannons, he began to laugh like the mad fool he was. His eyes were red and looked hot as fire. All he could say, over and over, was "Fire! Fire! Fire!" There was so much fire power coming from his ship, and it was vibrating so violently, it looked as if it were about to spring itself out of orbit.

He was SO involved with the action in his immediate vicinity, he didn't notice, on his hologram screen, that Captain Star's War-Starship rotation maneuver had been completed. The only ships that were being blasted out of the sky from S.C.L. Missiles, were his own, since the XX-2s had been replaced with the I.P.D. SP-9s! The SP-9s, using their stop-and-go flight pattern, along with their reflecting laser shields, were reflecting the laser rays from Booner's exploding missiles! The reflected rays also began destroying his own ships! Even though the XX-2s had been replaced by the SP-9s, the consistent firing upon Commander Booner never let up!

Orbiting around the outside perimeter of the action, Captain Star and the XX-2s were waiting for their opportunity to join Admiral Fitchly's Mothership and his SP-9s. Dr. Zuntor commented, "Now I'm beginning to understand why you rotated our ship and ordered this

unusual formation around the entire battle. At first I didn't understand, until I saw Commander Booner slaughtering all of his own ships. I've got to give it to you! This indeed was a smart move!
But tell me, where did you get this ingenious idea?"

Smiling, as he looked at him, Star replied, "I got it from little Orcal!" Then seeing the timing was right, and that most of the enemy ships had been destroyed, Captain Star ordered, "Come on Planet-Jockeys! Follow me!" Then he and about five hundred XX-2s, along with Admiral Fitchly and his SP-9s, began to attack Commander Booner's huge Monster-Mothership!

This time, there were so many I.P.D. ships firing laser cannons and missiles at Commander Booner, that that his ship's force field broke down. There wasn't anything he could do to stop his ship from being hit. Every section took a hit. After tons of missiles and millions of hits from laser rays, a large section of the Monster-Mothership broke off into exploding flames.

Seeing the huge opening in Booner's ship, Captain Star and the XX-2s, along with Admiral Fitchly's ship, began to fire directly into the opening of the enemy ship!

Seeing his Monster-Mothership exploding all around him, Booner knew it was just a matter of time. All of his dreams were about to crumble. The few remaining smaller ships with members of his crew were abandoning the doomed Captain Booner. Falling from side to side, he was yelling, "Come back, you cowards! We must fight! Don't you understand? Gunners, keep firing! Fight you fools! Fight!"

Soon, everyone except himself had flown off, and away from, the Monster-Mothership. Now he was all alone, surrounded only by dead bodies. Fire and smoke filled the interior of his ship. His actions at this time left no doubt that Commander Booner had gone totally mad.

Still yelling out commands: "Fire! They can't stand up to us! Fire! They know who I am! They know they can't win! Fire! Who do they think they are, coming up against me? Keep Firing!" But no one answered, because he was all alone. His crazed mind convinced him he could still win, indeed, convinced him that he was winning! He walked slowly to his Commander's Chair and proudly took his seat. He then looked around and began to laugh louder than ever in his life. The smoke and flames were intense. He took about three deep breaths. They were his last; it was over.

The explosions from Commander Booner's Monster-Mothership were so great, they were like giant asteroids slamming into each other. The flash from the final explosion was so bright it could be seen three planets away.

"Captain Star This is Admiral Fitchly. Come In Captain Star."

"Captain Star here Sir," came the reply. "Captain, I've got to tell you what a magnificent job you just did. By the look of things, there might be peace in our solar system after all," asserted the proud Admiral.

"Sir," Star was anxious to express his deep-felt emotions, adrenalin was still coursing through his blood, "Dr. Zuntor and Lt. Tulley, as well as myself, would like to be the first to congratulate you on your victory. We can't think of any other Admiral that would have come out here personally to take charge of a battle such as this one. Believe me Sir, this was the mother of all battles!"

Flying back to their planet, Lt. Tulley stood looking out of one of the huge windows, watching the millions of stars streaking by at the speed of light. She was daydreaming, thinking about how much compassion she was feeling for Captain Star. In her heart, she knew he was the man for her. But, how could she let him know... and could she dare hope?

All these things were running through her head as she continued to speak privately with herself. "I can't tell him how I really feel. I'm too proud ... and too scared to take a chance on him thinking he can treat me the same way he does all the others that are weak for him. But I'm different — I refuse to be 'just another girl' ... even though he plays around from planet to planet and he has a reputation as a space-bed-jockey. Oh well ... I still think I'm in love with him."

She then began to look at him sitting over by Dr. Zuntor. They were discussing what should be their next move concerning the ZYM230.6 Serum. "I know I should be thinking about anything other than him, but I've never felt this way about anyone before!" She tried to snap out of it and said to herself, "Come on, Tulley, what is happening to you? He's nothing but an egotistical bed-jumper!" But, nothing seemed to work.

She tried to examine some rock samples that they had gathered from the asteroid Plufre when they first arrived there, but she simply couldn't keep her mind on them. So she tried to reason with herself about why she felt this way about him, asking herself other questions, trying to find some excuse or explanation about why she was falling deeper in love with him.

In her private conversation with herself, she answered, "Maybe it's because he is so brave or could it be that he is not running after me like the other pilots in the I.P.D. sex-chase?!" After thinking about that for awhile, she adamantly said to herself, "No! That's not it, exactly, but whatever it is, some way, or somehow, soon, he's going to jump into my bed, and he's never going to leave!"

Ironically. the same thoughts were running through Captain Star's mind. As hard as he tried, he couldn't keep his mind on the conversation he and Dr. Zuntor were having about what to do with the Serum. He was saying to himself, "Look at her, sitting over there looking out of that window. She's always thinking about everything except me. If I could only let her know how I feel about her ... but why should I make a fool of myself, since I know she can't stand me. I know she hasn't forgotten about the first time we met. I still remember how she looked at me when Jets introduced her to me at my home. I can never forget her face when she saw those two women from the Rocket Streakers Club leaving my bed. Wow! If nothing else, she'll think that's all I want from her. But that's not so. If I had her, I wouldn't need anyone else! - Ever!"

Then it came to him that the only way he could be at peace with himself was to get it off his chest. In his private speech, he said, "All right, Star, what are you going to do? Just keep thinking about her, or go, and do something about it?"

Dr. Zuntor tried to break into his trend of thought. He was shaking him and shouting, "Star! Captain Star! Are you O.K.?"

Looking surprised and blinking his eyes, Captain Star answered, "Oh! Yeah! Yes! I'm fine! I just kinda wandered off a little."

Knowing he still didn't have all of his attention, Dr. Zuntor said, "I don't know what to say, but I know you well enough by now to know something's troubling you. Come on, Star, I'm your friend! Star, tell me about it. Maybe I can help you."

Captain Star looked at him and said, "I'm fine, I've just got to do some thinking. I have some things I have to figure out for myself." He then politely got up and walked away.

Thinking to himself, Dr. Zuntor said, "I can't figure out what's wrong with both Captain Star and Lt. Tulley. It seems as if everyone should be happy! The war is over! The Admiral is happy. We're still in possession of my ZYM230.6 Serum, and we are able to take it safely back to Duderyon. The Phantom II proved out to be a great ship. I just don't understand??"

He scratched his head in confusion and said to himself, "Well, whatever it is, I'm not going to spend any more time worrying about it. Unless they tell me what it's about, I certainly can't do anything to help. And since I can't help, I'm tired, and I'm going to get some sleep." He walked slowly to his quarters and went to bed.

On the Phantom II, everyone was bedded down for a much-deserved rest. Admiral Fitchly's I.P.D. War-Starship's fleet was leisurely cruising on its way to Duderyon. Lt. Tulley was still sitting at the window, still searching her mind as she watched their solar system's constellation and star formations zipping by. Over and over again, she tried to sleep, but it only made her feel more stressed out. All she could think about was Captain Star. She did know this could go on no longer, she simply had to do something about her situation.

Then something happened. She felt a gentle tapping on her shoulder; she turned around, only to find her desire standing there, looking down into her eyes. His smooth, deep, gentle voice saying, "The rings around Septor are absolutely exquisite don't you agree?"

To her delight, she slowly came to realize he was real! He was really standing there, speaking to her! Almost unable to answer, all she could do as she looked up into his eyes was utter a soft, breathless, "Yes".

He slowly moved his face near to hers, as he whispered, "And those two green moons around Zetraper, they are more beautiful now than ever, aren't they?"

Once again, as her face slowly moved closer to his, (she was still unable to breathe) all she could say was, "Yes." He continued, "But not as green and beautiful as your eyes." Now their lips were only centimeters apart from one another.

At that moment, she knew she was helpless. There was nothing left for her to do but surrender. Without thinking, Tulley threw her arms around his neck. Cautiously, and oh-so-gently, their lips pressed against each other. Never in her life had she experienced such a feeling. Her legs began to tremble, her heart began to beat faster and faster, as he continued to kiss her more and more passionately!

Her body began to feel as if her sexual organs were about to explode. He looked into her eyes once again, and with her arms still around his neck, she could hear him say, "I knew the first moment I saw you, there would never be anyone else but you in my life. Tulley, I'm in love with you — only you, and I need you! Oh my God, Tulley, please tell me you will be my wife."

Still trembling, and at the verge of orgasm, Tulley, sweetly and softly said, "Yes! Oh, yes my Love! Yes! Yes! Yes!"

Their lips touched once again in a strong, gentle kiss of promise; the Phantom II zoomed, at light speed, back to the Back to the planet Duderyon ... back to Dudetyon, with it's crew and cargo – the ZYM230.6 Serum – for the time being at least, all safe and sound.

Part III: The Black Hole

Back home on Duderyon, after all the pomp and ceremony had subsided, and the fanfare concerning their victory over Commander Booner's outlaw fleet had played itself out, it was once again back to the business of what to do with Dr. Zuntor's ZYM239.6 Serum. The council was in an uproar. Members were shouting at one another. The Chairman was once again banging his gavel on the podium, trying to regain order.

Sitting side-by-side we find: Admiral Fitchly; Captain Star, with his new bride, Lt. Talley; Dr Zuntor, with his wife, Dr. Usar; and their very young son, Little Orcal. All were shaking their heads from side-to-side, in the universal mime language, meaning "no". Captain Star leaned over to Admiral Fitchly and said, "Things never seem to change, do they Sir?"

Smiling, the Admiral replied, "I think it was safer when we were out there in the thick of battle, than it is in here, with these guys!"

There was so much confusion going on, concerning the Serum, that little Orcal had his hands over his ears. Things must have gotten to be too much for him, because he turned to his father, Dr. Zuntor, and asked, "Dad, is it always like this at these meetings?"

It seemed that every member of the council had their own opinion on what to do with the Serum. At one point, things got so heated between two of the oldest members, they actually started throwing blows at one another. The two members were so old, as soon as they were separated, they both needed to be given medical attention. The Med

Techs gave them an intravenous shot of Zilapoo, followed with two large glasses of water. Even considering these minor injuries, the sight was absolutely hilarious. Captain Star and little Orcal were laughing so hard, tears were rolling down their faces. Dr. Zuntor had to calm them down, because they were having an uncontrollable fit of the giggles — highly inappropriate since this august body was convened for such a serious matter.

After they had settled down, little Orcal tapped his father on his arm and declared, "Dad, I've got a good idea about what to do with the Serum!" Not being at all surprised at him having a good idea, Dr. Zuntor gave an attentive ear to his teenage son. After hearing Little Orcal's idea, Dr. Zuntor's eyes blinked and he gathered everyone within their special little group into a huddle. He whispered something, and seconds later, everyone turned, looked at Orcal, and concurred — "Why Not!"

Admiral Fitchly stood up and addressed the Chair. He requested the floor. The Chairman of the Council recognized him, so the Admiral proceeded, "I have just received a great idea from one of our most brilliant, up-and-coming, young, scientists. If he agrees, I would like for him to present his plan for what we should do with this Serum. Fellow Imperial Planetary Defense Council Members: I am proud to introduce to you, the son of our own Dr. Zuntor ... I would like to add, that he too, will soon to be addressed as Dr. Orcal!"

With that introduction, Little Orcal shyly stood up and walked to the front of the council and began to explain. All eyes were upon him. Some faces were unable to hide their distrust and dislike of Dr. Zuntor and/or his son. But, like a real leader, he held his head up and paused long enough to get their attention. "We all are aware that the greatest minds in our solar system have grappled with this problem, and have come up with ideas about how to get rid of my father's- uhh, that is ... Dr. Zuntor's ZYM230.6 Serum. I think everyone has more than likely overlooked the answer, because it is so simple and straightforward.

When he said this, everyone began to murmur and look around at each other. Little Orcal continued: "I think if we use my calculations –

because if I remember what my father- uhh ... Dr. Zuntor, has taught me about astronomy – then soon, our planet will be aligned with another distant solar system. Not only is this solar system quite similar to ours, but it's only three planets away from us, on the other side of a black hole, called Bassera. Now, if we could send a ship to the edge of that black hole, we could launch a missile from one of our motherships and fire it into the middle of that destructive abyss!"

Suddenly, there was an outburst of applause. Then one of the members declared, "We all know about the black hole and where it is, but let's get real! How could a ship fly that close to its gravitational force and not be pulled into it?" Then everyone began murmuring again, saying, "That's right, who would take a chance like that?"

Another member shouted, "This child is crazy! This is not a simple thing! black holes are the most dangerous and least understood of anything in our (or any other) solar system!" Someone else interjected: "It's a good way to lose a mothership and crew! The force of gravity will crush anything, including stars!"

"You're right! and I for one have more sense than to go anywhere near that bitch, Bassera — or any of her kind!"

After letting the group blow off steam, Little Orcal continued to explain. "I'm aware that the gravity of a black hole could crush any ship into nothing. And, there is nothing it won't pull into its center. But, I've got a theory. With the help of my father, and my godfather, Captain Star, it could work!"

Then another member demanded, "What kind of theory are you talking about that could stop a ship from being lost after it has been sucked into a black hole?" We all know, without any doubt, the escape velocity would be impossible to attain — let alone maintain!"

Little Orcal knew his theory was not only possible, but highly probable, because he had seen it in his "dream mind". Little Orcal's parents, Dr. Zuntor and Dr. Usar, both had highly developed psychic abilities, with a strong forte for seeing into the future and reading each other's minds. Little Orcal has inherited these mental strengths from them.

(Hence his name, "Orcal" which was taken from a very ancient Greek word, "oracle".)

With the diligence of youth, together with much practice and concentration, Little Orcal exercised his mental muscles — which strengthened his ESP and mind-reading skills. His mind became like a finely tuned violin. The amazing experiences he had undergone with his "dream mind" led him to totally believe in it. He had no doubts that his "dream mind" revelations were not mere intuitions, but were absolutely true! His family and friends concurred.

Little Orcal continued speaking to the irate group, "My father and I have been playing around with a device that we call the "Gravity Equivalent Reversal Power Unit."

"And what, may I ask is that!?" demanded the amazed Chairman of the Council, as he leaned over the podium and looked over the top of his glasses at little Orcal.

"Well Sir," replied little Orcal, "It's an old theory that my father has had for some time. We only play with it, in my mini-laboratory, when he has some extra time."

"What it does, is reverse whatever the gravitational force of gravity is. It is able to reverse its force from pull to thrust. With one little finger on a switch, a ship could have power in its thrust, that would be equivalent to the pull of the black hole."

Then, one of the members, from the planet nearest to the black hole, said, "Let me see if I understand ... because, if your theory can be proven, our planet needs this kind of technology. With something like this, we will be able to explore new solar systems and maybe even fly into a black hole. Now, if I understand you, you are saying that if this Gravity Equivalent Reversal gadget can be adapted to our I.P.D. Ships, we would be able to control gravity and use it as an alternative, or an additional, power source — even inside a black hole?"

"Yes! You're correct, Sir! The more gravity pulling force, the more power and controlled energy our ship will have. So, as you can see, it's not all that complicated," said Little Orcal. After a round of applause,

Little Orcal reached into his pocket and pulled out a piece of Gorga (candy). He popped the Gorga into his smiling mouth, and walked to his seat.

After little Orcal had been praised by his father and other members of the group, the Chairman of the Council stated, "Dr. Zuntor, you have an extremely bright son there."

Standing up, Dr. Zuntor acknowledged, "Thank you — You're right, of course." Then smiling he said, "By the way, he taught me everything I know." That statement broke the tension, and caused everyone in the room to laugh.

With the tension broken, they discussed the matter of the huge amounts of money that would be needed to rush the research and development of this project. Of course, they couldn't agree on the money subject, but at least they were in agreement on going "full speed ahead" with this important invention!

This monstrous black hole was constantly consuming everything around it! And, the agonizing fear of this "Bitch Bassera", had been growing within them all for quite some time! Indeed, they were more than willing to try anything that might stop this ever-hungry black hole, which they had nicknamed "The Bitch!"

Sometime later, back in Dr. Zuntor's lab, he and little Orcal were still working on their Gravity Equivalent Reversal Power Unit. Usar walked into the lab saying, "You two guys never seem to get enough of working on that thing. It's time for Orcal to go to bed anyway."
"Oh Mom, I've just got to help Dad. Please ... don't make me."
"Well," said Dr. Zuntor, "we have been at it for some time now. I think we best give it up for now, and get some rest. We'll think more clearly in the morning."

Then like every kid in every solar system, little Orcal slowly walked to his bedroom saying, "I'll be glad when I grow up; then I can stay up all night if I want to."

Picking him up and giving him a big hug, Dr. Zuntor said, "Son, you are a very bright boy. And it's only for a little while that you are a kid. But you will be a man for a long time. After this project is finished, we'll take a long trip to some faraway planet. Just the three of us. You, Mommy, and I are going to have a great time!"

This made little Orcal's face light up with a big smile. Then he said, "Oh Dad, I can't wait." He gave his dad a big hug. Then he lay down in his bed and went to sleep.

Not long after that, there was a surprise visit from Captain Star and Lt. Tulley. They were smiling as they accepted Zuntor and Usar's invitation to enter and have a seat. Dr. Zuntor said, "Well, if it's not my two favorite people. Tell me, how do you like being married?"

The smiling couple answered at the same time, saying, "Great!" Then Usar asked, "What brings you by? I would have thought that you would be on a honeymoon or something?"

Captain Star answered saying, "We just got back."

Then Lt. Tulley said, "Usar, let me tell you, it was lovely." Then the two women, talking and laughing, walked away to another part of the house.

"Dr. Zuntor, there is no doubt that I'm glad to see you again. But the most important thing that brings me by, is to see how you are coming with that Gravity Equivalent Reversal Power Unit?"

"It's coming along, Actually, to tell you the truth, it's moving along on schedule," answered Dr. Zuntor.

By the look on Captain Star's face, he could tell that something was troubling him. So he asked, "Do you have anything you wanted to tell me?"

"I've just gotten word from Admiral Fitchly, that there's been a lot of trouble on the inside perimeter of the planet Vertex. And, as you know, Vertex is only a few light-years away from that black hole we were considering for disposal of your ZYM230 Serum."

"What kind of trouble?" asked Dr. Zuntor.

Captain Star, walking by the bar, fixed himself a drink, and answered, "It's our old friend, Captain Icpek."

"Captain Icpek!?" shouted Dr. Zuntor.

Star replied, "Yes, that's what I said, Captain Icpek! Somehow, he made it to some asteroid and regrouped his forces. At last report, he now has over a thousand War-Starships!"

A stunned Dr. Zuntor remarked, "How could a mad killer like him get so much help, so soon, to do so much harm?"

"Well, it's not only him; it's that evil, ruthless, Dr. Poolong that's backing him. And, as you know, we've been trying to bring him to justice for what seems like an eternity!"

"Well I'll be a son of a space egg," said Dr. Zuntor. "If it really is Dr. Poolong that's backing him, we certainly are in big trouble! I remember him from the Supreme Intelligence Council. He was the chief scientist over the Advance Physics Department at the time when my brother Dr. Pelcozor and I were in Development. I can never forget him ... he was one of the reasons why my brother went bad."

"How was that?" asked Star.

"He knew Pelcozor was weak and needed to have power so he could feel like he was in control. He was always filling his head with foolishness. But he would never try it on me, because he knew, that I knew, he was just looking for someone to carry out his evil schemes for him.

Now, what the Admiral had said to him made more sense. Every time Captain Icpek and his outlaw ships were discovered, doing some of their traitorous deeds, they were never captured by our I.P.D. Air Force. Not only that, but every ship in that sector, that ever pursued them, were never heard from again. Dr. Zuntor looked at Star and said, "Are you thinking what I'm thinking?"

"I'm afraid so," said the Captain. "After looking at all the facts, and knowing that Dr. Poolong is in the middle of all this, I'm inclined to believe that they might already have their own type of Gravity Equivalent Reversal Power Unit! I also believe that's probably why our I.P.D. ships were never heard from again."

A devastated Dr. Zuntor, who was deep in thought, mused, "Then that's what has been happening to our ships — they have been pulled into that damned black hole, trying to follow Captain Icpek! And because they didn't know that he had this unit, it would be easy for him to trick them into following him. All Icpek had to do was pop in and out of Bassera, and they would fly after him to their doom! Never to be seen again!"

He then walked over to his bar alongside Captain Star and said, "You are right, we don't have any time to waste!" That's when Usar and Lt. Tulley came back into the room and announced, "That's enough shop-talk, fellows. We need some relaxation time." So they all kicked back and enjoyed each other's company; they laughed about some of the silly things that happen in ordinary life, and remembered some of the crazy things they had done in their younger days. Actually, they had a great time socializing. But in the back of their minds, they all knew that sooner or later, they would have to deal with the problem.

Some time later, back at I.P.D. Headquarters, Admiral Fitchly was giving both Captain Star and Dr. Zuntor their orders: "I'm glad to hear that you managed to get that Gravity Equivalent Reversal Power Unit (G.E.R.P. Unit) into operation as soon as you did, Dr. Zuntor. Now we can go ahead with our plans to dispose of that ZYM Serum. No need to tell you to be careful and to stay on guard. Knowing that you have the Serum on board, every outlaw starship in the solar system will be on the lookout for the Phantom II!

"You will be completely on your own once you reach the sector of the planet Vertex. From there on, you're in the danger zone of the black hole. Even our Astronomers are calling it the "Bitch". It is absolutely insatiable! However, on the other hand, we have added some new features to the Phantom II that might give you an extra advantage if you happen to get into a jam.

Dr. Zuntor, I'm giving you a list and the instructions on how the new features work. Go over them with Captain Star. I'm sure you'll be able to explain them to him much better than I could. As for that Captain Icpek, I've got only one order concerning him, and his cohort, Dr. Poolong: don't take any chances with them. They're both sick from greed and power. If it comes down to it, and you have to fight, don't hesitate to kill the both of them! But whatever you do, don't let them get their hands on that Serum. Because if they do, our entire solar system will be at their ruthless mercy. So, if either of you has any questions, now is the time to ask."

Both Captain Star and Dr. Zuntor looked at each other, then at Admiral Fitchly. After a slight pause, Star replied, "I think we understand you very clearly, Sir." They soon boarded the Phantom II and were off on their new adventure to the black hole named "Bassera"!

As the Phantom II was speeding through the heavens, Captain Star reflected, "You know, Doctor, it sure feels good to be back in the sky again! Just look at all those stars out there!

Everything was serene and going well, until a voice came from the audio portion of their Hologram Scanner screen saying, "Calling Phantom II — this is Captain Sumoon. You are illegally flying through our sector! We're ordering you to pay the toll for unlawful entry into our sector."

Switching to "video" on his scanner, Captain Star tuned in the image of the voice they heard. Instantly recognizing the image of Captain Sumoon, Star knew what he was up against. Speaking over his In-Beam, Captain Star spoke to his crew. "Everyone make ready — Battle stations!!" Then he turned to Dr. Zuntor. "I know this Captain Sumoon! He's the biggest scum in this Sector. He takes advantage of ships by terrorizing them until they pay. Or else he actually destroys them - and their planet! Well, I think this time, he's picked on the wrong ship!"

Once again Sumoon tried to communicate with the Phantom II. "Calling the Phantom II — Come In."

This time, Captain Star answered him: "Hi, you space scum — This is Captain Star of the Phantom II. Tell me — who told you that you have the authority to collect a tariff on any ship in this sector? As I understand, this sector is still under the jurisdiction of the I.P.D. Command."

Answering him, Captain Sumoon said, "I should have known it was you! It just goes to show, that if I just have patience — all good things come to those who wait."

Then Captain Star sarcastically replied "Well — I'm so glad you waited." Since he knew that Captain Sumoon was a sneaky trickster, Captain Star was ready for the likes of him! In one move he switched on his ship's Reflector Image Eliminator and disappeared!

Not understanding what had happened, Captain Sumoon couldn't believe it! All he knew, was that the Phantom II had been in his laser cannon's sights, so he ordered his gunners to open fire where he thought Captain Star's ship was. He didn't know that Captain Star had swung the Phantom II around behind him and had its laser cannons lined up on his ship.

Turning off his Reflector Image Eliminator, Captain Star communicated with Captain Sumoon, saying, "First you see me — now you don't! But here I come again!"

Watching Captain Star on his Hologram Scanner Screen, Captain Sumoon was totally surprised that the Phantom II had flown around behind him and he hadn't even seen it happen! The next thing he saw was a big flash, and he heard the sound of laser rays hitting against his ship. The sound of his ship's fire alarms ringing and members of his crew running and looking for safety made him furious! Trying to reel his ship around so he could fire back at the Phantom II was a maneuver too difficult for his old model War-Starship. Zing! Zoom! Boom! went the laser cannons of the Phantom II, hitting his ship over and over again.

Realizing that their ship was no match for Captain Star's Phantom II I.P.D. War-Starship, one of Sumoon's officers screamed: "Let's get the hell out of here before it's too late!" But it was already too late! As soon as the words left his mouth, their ship blew up, and became an enormous fireball! So, just like the ship appeared — it disappeared!

"Wow!" said Dr. Zuntor, "you took care of him as fast as a flash of neutrons!"

"That's right," declared Star, "Believe me, with scum like that it doesn't pay to play around with them! I just hope he didn't alert anyone else that we're out here. If so, every crud out there will be after the serum, and our chances of fulfilling our mission will be small — if any!"

"You're right, Captain! But we still might have some tricks up our sleeves," said Dr. Zuntor. "And what might they be?" asked Captain Star.

"Well," Zuntor replied, "As of yet, we've not seen the orders from the Admiral, concerning the new weapons we have on board the Phantom!!"

"You're absolutely right, good buddy! And I think we had better check them out on our Hologram Scanner Screen, and see what his Memory Retainer Slide has to say," suggested the Captain.

Moments later the 3-D Hologram image of Admiral Fitchly appeared. "Captain Star, you and Dr. Zuntor both know that you're carrying a most dangerous cargo. It's highly possible that you will encounter some of the most ruthless space outlaws in our solar system. They'll be trying to get their hands on it. And there will be times when you will be greatly outnumbered. That's why I've installed some of the most sophisticated, state-of-the-art weapons on your Phantom II."

"First, you have a Mini-Swirling-Cluster Laser Cannon — the same type as the late Commander Booner had on his Monster-Mothership. The only difference is, that yours is much smaller and shoots much faster than his did. Next, we installed something we call an Image Duplicator. It creates a duplicate image of the Phantom II. Therefore, to your enemy, it looks as though he were facing more than one ship! If you set its computer correctly, you will be able to give the appearance that there are two – or, if necessary, even three – of the Phantom II. They will look so identical that your enemy won't be able to figure out which one is the image or which one is the real ship. Dr. Zuntor is already familiar with the computer settings, since it was mostly his invention. The last new extension to your ship is the Missile Boomerang Force Field. Its usage is important! If you are greatly outnumbered, and missiles are being shot at your ship by a group of War-Starships, and an enemy missile impacts on your force field, its swiveling rotation will return it back to the ship from which it came."

"These new additions, along with what the Phantom II already has, should give you a little more edge to fight with. Since you're out there on your own, remember, Captain Star, that Dr. Zuntor is an expert concerning these new weapons. So allow him to make your crew familiar with their usage. I sincerely hope the both of you have a safe and speedy journey. Over and Out!" His image slowly disappeared.

"Well Zuntor, it looks as if we might have a fighting chance after all," remarked Captain Star.

Dr. Zuntor proudly announced, "We might not have a fleet backing us Captain, but the Phantom II has got to be the best equipped War-Starship in the cosmos." They continued on their journey to the black hole, Bassera.

Captain Icpek stopped by the laboratory on board their Mothership. He addressed Dr. Poolong, "Doctor Poolong, have you heard that the Phantom II is headed this way, and that it's carrying 'our Serum' on board?"

"Wow! What a payload! If it's true, we're really in luck! With the mighty fleet we have, there is no way he can pass through our sector and live to talk about it! There is only one thing that disturbs me — if we know that they are headed this way, then everyone else knows too," said Dr. Poolong.

Captain Icpek exclaimed, "If that's the case, we had better move fast and intercept them before someone else does! I've got an old score to settle with that know-it-all, Captain Star. I made a vow to get even with him for what he did to my brother, and for what he did to me!"

"There it is, Commander Fexnob! Just as I thought it would be! The information we received from our surveillance equipment on the Eagerton Asteroid conveyed that it was in this vicinity," reported his First Lieutenant.

"If it is the Phantom II, then the Serum is on board!" Captain Fexnob was so excited, he could hardly contain himself. "I've heard so much about that Serum and how much power it has. The genetic properties of the ZYM230 Serum has proven to be incredible! It can perform miracles with any life form. And, it is indestructible! I've just got to have it!" declared the Commander.

"I've heard that the Phantom II is a dangerous ship, Sir. Do you have a plan as to how we'll be able to take her?" asked his First Lieutenant. "Yes, there is only one way! And that's with power! We'll use every ship we have to make sure she doesn't stand a chance!" With greed in his eyes, he passed down his orders: "Make all ships 'Battle Ready!' We don't have a second to waste!" In no time, his fleet was ready for war and in pursuit of Captain Star, the Phantom II, and the ZYM230 Serum!

Meanwhile, on board the Phantom II, Captain Star's Communications Officer exclaimed, "Captain! Look at our Proximetry Locator Screen — there's a group of ships headed right for us, Sir!" Watching their Locator Screen, both Captain Star and Dr. Zuntor knew they were in for some big-time trouble!

Captain Star made an announcement over the ship's In-Beam. "All crew members — man your battle stations!" Then he said to Dr. Zuntor, "It's a good thing we reviewed the instructions for our new weapons. If we hadn't, we would be in bad shape. Good Cosmic God! Look at all those enemy ships out there!"

"Well," said Dr. Zuntor, "We'll soon see if the Phantom II will stand up to our expectations!"

"There is no way that the Phantom II's Captain would be such a fool as to think he could win against a fleet like ours, Sir," said the First Lieutenant on Commander Fexnob's Mothership. Feeling confident that he could make a deal with the Phantom II's Captain, Commander Fexnob transmitted his image out to the Phantom II's Hologram Scanner Screen. He then announced: "This is Commander Fexnob of the Great-Mothership Airromus. You are now under the mercy of my powers! I'm going to give you only one chance to save your lives! Hand over the Serum at once! Then you will be able to go back to Duderyon in peace. If not, I promise you, you will pay the price with your life! I'm going to give you just ten seconds to make up your mind!"

"And counting ... nine ... eight ... seven .. six ... five ..."

Hundreds of small ships had exited from the huge Mothership, under the command of the infamous Fexnob! All of them were in strict formation, hovering around their Mothership, waiting for their command to attack. Seeing this, Captain Star said to Dr. Zuntor, "It looks like we don't have any other choice — we're gonna' have to fight! 'Cause there is no way I'm going to give up this Serum!"

"Do you have any plans, Captain?" asked Dr. Zuntor.

Captain Star replied, "Well, I think if we attack them, instead of waiting for them to attack us, and then of course, with the use of some of our new weapons (along with our standard ones), we might have more than a chance."

Knowing that his ten seconds were up, Captain Star accelerated the Phantom II into hyperdrive. Then he headed it into the direction of his enemy's entire fleet. Not believing the Phantom II's Captain could have that much nerve, Commander Fexnob – for a second, or two – was frozen! That was all the time Captain Star needed. He told Dr. Zuntor to make ready their Mini-Swirling-Cluster-Laser cannon, and to have all the gunners ready with their regular laser cannons. He then ordered Dr. Zuntor to activate their Reflective Image Eliminator!

"Where did they go?" was the thought of each pilot in Commander Fexnob's fleet. Then, over his communication In-Beam, the Commander said, to all of his War-Starship pilots, "Don't let this foolish trick stop you — Attack!!"

Seeing the attacking ships headed directly for them, and knowing that they were invisible, Captain Star ordered his Operations Officer, Mr. Pep, to maneuver the ship up and over the orbit of Commander

Fexnob's fleet. Now the Phantom II would be able to drive into their formation, attacking from above, using all the weapons he had readied for the battle.

Looking around, and watching his fleet firing their lasers at open space, Commander Fexnob knew that sooner or later, his fleet's lasers and cannons would hit something, even though it was invisible! "Sir, there's nothing out there!" called back one of his squadron Captains!

"I know you can't see them just now," roared the Commander, "But don't stop firing!"

Then, just like the Phantom II disappeared, it reappeared! Zooming down from the upper orbit. The Phantom II surprised the entire fleet! Lasers and rockets were killing ships that never had a chance. Zooming in and out of their formations, the Phantom II was flying like a dream!

After some time had passed, and they had taken a good beating, Commander Fexnob's ships began to regroup and fire back at the Phantom II. "O.K., now it's time for that New Canon! said Captain Star to Dr. Zuntor. Within seconds, the Mini-Swirling-Cluster-Laser Cannon went into action. The laser clusters were swirling in the midst of all their enemies' ships, taking them out, dozens at a time!

"What kind of ship is this Phantom II?" Commander Fexnob cried out as he continued to fight! But his fleet was no match for Captain Star's Phantom II!

Dr. Zuntor exclaimed, "Well Captain, it looks as if our Phantom II has taken the sting out of Commander Fexnob's fleet!"

"Yes, it looks that way. And, now that we have a chance, I think we should get out of here," said Star. He then made an announcement over the ship's In-Beam for everyone to cease firing! Soon, all weapons were silent and secure. He then called down to Mr. Pep and ordered him to guide their ship back on course, and to pick up its speed to 4.6 light-speed. Instantly, the Phantom II flew off into deep space, leaving the mangled, shot-up remembrance of a fleet, many light-years behind!

Millions of kilometers away from their battle with Commander Fexnob's fleet, the Phantom II was cruising at warp speed. Sometime later, their ship was approaching the planet Melobo; "Captain, it looks as if we're on course and back on schedule, Sir," said Mr. Pep over the In-Beam.

"Thank you, Mr. Pep," said Captain Star, as he stood, looking out of his window.

Looking at the three sets of rings around the planet Melobo, his mind was back on Duderyon — with his new wife, Lt. Tulley. He was looking out of the same window then, as he was now, while he remembered how they first kissed, so passionately...

Knowing just about what was on his mind, Dr. Zuntor said, "I miss Usar, too."

Turning away from the window, Captain Star asked Dr. Zuntor, "How did you know I was thinking about my Tulley?"

"Looking out at all those stars and those three beautiful rings around Melobo, I can't think of very many other things that would be on our minds," replied the Doctor. "Anyway, I've heard that the Planet Melobo is populated by 90% women!"

Then, Captain Star said, "Yeah! That's what I heard too! Wow! Before I got married to Tulley, I would have had to orbit around it and beam down until they ran me off the planet!!" Both of them began to laugh like a couple of schoolboys.

"Captain Vena — That's the Phantom II, and it's just now entering our sector. Should we prepare to attack?" asked one of the female officers on the all-female crew attached to the Melobo War-Starship!

"No, I don't think that will be necessary, Lt. Swefa. From what I understand, there's not a War-Starship in the entire solar system that can take on the Phantom II and survive," stated Captain Vena. "But it has that 'Serum' on board!" exclaimed Swefa.

"I know it's there, and with it, we will have all the power in the solar system! So, don't think I've given up on having it in these hands!" declared Captain Vena, as she threw up both hands and rolled her sexy eyes.

Even though one of her eyes was blue, and the other one was red. In fact, all of the women on the Planet Melobo had one eye of one color and the other eye of a different color. All of them had perfect figures, and were well over six-feet tall — looking like the ancient, perhaps mythical, Amazon women. They were also like black widow spiders. They would mate with males from their Planet (or even other planets) and then kill them ... after they had taken their pleasure! And as far as Star-Pilots were concerned, the Meloboin women were ranked among the very best Star-fighters in the universe.

"Captain Star, there is a Captain Vena on the Hologram Scanner Screen, insisting on seeing you!" reported Mr. Pep, over the In-Beam.

Looking at Dr. Zuntor, Star said, "This looks like real trouble!"

"What do you mean by 'trouble?'" demanded Dr. Zuntor.

"I've heard about that Captain Vena! She's a space-jockey's dream come true! And I've also heard that she's so beautiful, no one can resist her!" said Star!

"I know," said Zuntor, "but I also understand that the women of the Melobo kill their men soon after they mate!"

"Well," Star replied, "I won't have to worry about that now that I'm married!"

Dr. Zuntor was quick to remind his friend that "You wouldn't be the first husband to stray — so that's no guarantee."

"True, but they weren't married to my beautiful Tulley!" asserted the newly married Captain Star. The two good friends enjoy a hearty laugh together. Then, after regaining their composure, Star switched on the Hologram Scanner Screen.

"Hello, Captain Star! I'm Captain Vena. I heard you were in our sector and I thought it would be nice if we could show you and your crew some hospitality — to sort of help you along the way to your journey's destination," Captain Vena said, with her hot, sexy, voice.

"I'm impressed that you know my name, Captain Vena." remarked Captain Star.

"Captain Star, by now, everyone in the solar system has heard of the Phantom II and it's courageous Captain Raymond Star," said the Meloboin Captain, as she very slowly rolled her sexy, bi-colored eyes. Then she purred, "I've also heard that you never let a fellow Captain down, if they are in need! And," Captain Vena continued, "by looking at me, Captain Star, it's plain to see that I'm very much in need of your assistance!" she implored as she took a deep breath, showing off her immaculate body.

"And, how do you propose we do that?" asked Captain Star, realizing too late that he had fallen for her trickery.

Captain Vena asks, "Your ship or mine?"

"My ship — by all means", committed the reluctant Captain Star.

A short time later, the Melobo War-Starship orbited next to the Phantom II. Then a party of ten of the most beautiful Meloboin women – along with Captain Vena – were beamed aboard the Phantom II. Leaving the transport room and entering the luxurious entertainment area of the Phantom II, Captain Vena and her entourage were greeted by Captain Star, Dr. Zuntor, Mr. Pep, and a few well-chosen members of their crew.

Soon the two Captains and their crews sat down to cocktails and dinner. The lights were as romantic as any club in the solar system. Everyone was relaxing to the sweet music, as the Meloboin women were seductively trying to get information concerning the whereabouts of the Serum! Captain Vena thought if she could find out where it was stored, she would be able to maneuver her way to its location, and remove it without anyone knowing she had taken it.

Not knowing that Star had already informed his crew about what to expect from them, the very sexy Meloboin women were using all the tricks in the book of seduction, to find out what they wanted to know. But, Star's crewmen were having the time of their lives, playing the Meloboin game of seduction, along with these gorgeous women. In the meantime, Dr. Zuntor had slipped away from the party, and returned without anyone noticing. He then gave Captain Star the sign that everything had been made ready.

Knowing that their trap had been set, Captain Star said to the sexy Captain Vena, (pretending as though he had consumed too many cocktails): "I've enjoyed your company, Vena. You make me feel that I need to know you much better."

"Oh, Captain Star! I've dreamed of times like this with someone as important as you," said Captain Vena.

"I'm not important, Vena. I'm only a small-time I.P.D. Space Jockey, that's all," offered Captain Star, acting more intoxicated than ever.

"That's what you think, Captain. Everyone knows that you are the only Starship Captain in the Solar System that could be trusted with that Serum," cooed Captain Vena. But she was thinking that the time to get her hands on it was just about right!

"I don't know if all that is true, but sometimes I wish I had never seen it!" said Captain Star, knowing she had fallen into his trap. So Captain Star asked her, "Would you like to see what all the fuss is about, Vena?"

She quickly took the bait, and played her turn in the game, "I don't understand, Captain Star, we both know your orders are that no one can get close to that Serum except you and Dr. Zuntor."

"Why are you playing with me? You know, of course, I would be the envy of all the Captains in this solar system — being able to say that I had a chance to see it, yet lived to talk about it! Oh Wow! Come on, Captain Star, please don't say something like that and then you can't, or won't, do it — Please!" In the back of her mind, she was thinking: "Now I'll have a chance to steal the cylinders and sneak the Serum back to my ship."

"What do you mean, 'I can't do it?'" exclaimed Star (still playing his game).

"Well, if you do mean what you just said — then come on! Let's do it now!" cajoled Captain Vena.

They slowly stumbled to his cabin. The both of them entered. Then, Captain Vena's red and blue eyes searched around the room, as he stumbled over to his bar and mixed the both of them another drink. "Captain Star, I see your cabin is as attractive as your handsome face," she said, as she helped him take another sip of his cocktail. Then she said, "You know, it's getting on in time, and soon, my crew and I will have to go! So, if it's alright with you, could you show it to me now? And, if you are not playing games about letting me see it, I'll give you me — in a way that no man on any planet has ever had me before!"

She then threw him back onto his bed, and laid her hot, sexy, body on top of his and they began to kiss. All the time, Captain Star was acting more intoxicated than ever, saying, "If I had known that Meloboin women were as sweet and sexy as you Vena, I never would have taken so long to fly to this sector. But, since I've been in your presence, I know one thing for sure — I will be back!" He then gently rolled her from the top of him, got up, and stumbled over to a secret panel. He removed a small cylinder and handed it to her. Then he clumsily sat back down on the bed.

Captain Vena's heart began to beat faster than ever in her life. Her hands began to sweat. Her body was so excited, she was having an orgasm! (One behind another, as a matter-of-fact!) Then her mind began to run completely wild! She could only think of what powers she would have if only she could get off the Phantom II with the cylinder! That is, if she could get off the Phantom II, and still be alive! "How does it feel to have all the power in the solar system in your hands, Vena?" Asked Captain Star (who was still acting).

Unable to speak plainly, Captain Vena said, "It ... it feels too good ... and I owe it all to you, Captain Star. Let's have another drink, and then we'll celebrate ... just you and me!" Still holding onto the cylinder, Captain Vena rushed to the bar and began mixing them a drink, but this time, she deviously put a sleeping potion into his glass. She then returned to the bed where Captain Star was reclining. Handing him his drink, she acted as though she needed to have another one also.

She knew that she had to make him drink, but her mind was so caught up with the cylinder, and all the power it represented, that she didn't see him when he switched glasses. Thinking she had things under control, Vena picked up the one with the sleeping potion. She held up the lethal glass and said, "Here's to you, Captain Star." The both of them took a huge sip of their drink. Captain Star then pretended to fall into a deep sleep. Though his eyes were tightly closed, he could hear Vena trying to tip out of his room with the cylinder. But before she got to the door, Star heard her drop to the floor. She was out cold!!

Springing to his feet, he rushed over, picked her up in his arms, and carried her to the transport room. In the meantime, Dr. Zuntor had gathered up her crew; they were already in the transport room, waiting for Star. They were ready to be transported back to their ship. Star laid Vena down on a soft, velvet couch, with her inebriated crew standing around her, he placed the cylinder between her huge cleavage — then crossed her hands on top of it. The Captain kissed her gently. Then turning to Mr. Pep, he said, "Beam them back to their ship! We've already lost too much time!" He and Dr. Zuntor walked away.

Zooming through a super-cluster of stars, they were still headed for the black hole, Bassera. The Phantom II began to pick up a transmission from the Melobo sector. Mr. Pep called Star on his In-Beam, saying, "Captain, you have your most favorite Melobo Captain, on your Hologram Scanner Screen — and she is hot, Sir!"

It seemed that when she had awakened from her own drugs, she was back on her own ship. She knew he had played her for a fool. Not only did she feel bad about being tricked back to her ship, but when she opened the cylinder, it was full of sweet perfume, extracted from some old star-dust samples that Dr. Zuntor had been analyzing.

"Well Doctor, I guess I'll have to talk to her, so switch her on. Moments later, on his Hologram Scanner Screen, Captain Vena's 3-D image appeared. And was she ever steaming, as she shouted, "How could you do something like that to me! How could you!? I've never been used like this before. How could you, Captain Star?"

Zuntor and Star laughed so hard, tears were running from their eyes! After Star regained his composure, he turned the game around. "Hold it, Captain Vena! How could you say such a thing about me? Didn't I allow you and your crew to come aboard the Phantom II? I thought you had a wonderful time — especially after you partied so hard, that you finally fell into a deep sleep. All I did, was make sure you got safely back to your ship. Yes, not only safe, but you had within your possession a lovely gift!"

Even though she was upset, she also had to laugh at the thought of how she had fallen into her own little trap. Then, in her usual soft and sexy voice, she purred, "I must admit, it is the best-smelling perfume I've ever had. So please, tell Dr. Zuntor, I thank him also!" Deep in her heart, she had a small crush on Captain Star. Therefore, as she rolled her red and blue eyes, she felt compelled to say, "When you're on your way back, come this way, so that you can – as they used to say in ancient times – "Fly up and see me sometime!'" She then disappeared from his Hologram Scanner Screen.

"Mr. Pep! What is that on the Proximetry Locator Screen?" Star shouted into his communication In-Beam!

"I see it too, Captain! It looks like an Asteroid, Sir," suggested Mr. Pep.

"Then something is wrong!" interjected Star, "because looking at my charts, it's not supposed to be in this sector!"

"Then it must be a fragment from a destroyed planet, Sir" offered Mr. Pep. "Well, we best find out what it is, and where it came from," stated Dr. Zuntor, "because if something's out here that can cause something like that to happen, we'd better be aware of it!"

"You're right! I'll look into it, Sir!" answered Mr. Pep.

Captain Star inquired of Dr. Zuntor: "What does he think happened? Maybe we should take a small landing party down there and have a look around. We might be able to find out something! At any rate, we need to find out what's going on, and report it to I.P.D. Headquarters!" surmised Captain Star.

"Sure, you're right!" agreed the Doctor.

After giving Mr. Pep orders to orbit the Phantom II around the Asteroid, Captain Star, Dr. Zuntor, and five of their crew took a small shuttle and headed down to the rogue Asteroid. Touching down, they see hot steam coming from its surface. Riding around in a land rover, the scouting party looked around for some kind of clue that would tell them something about what had happened. They did not know that during this time, they were being watched. Hiding behind some boulders, monster-looking men were looking at them, and they were prepared to attack!

"Do you see anything, Captain?" asked Dr. Zuntor, as they rolled through an area that looked like the inside of a volcano.

"It's kind of eerie around here, Zuntor," said Captain Star. "I think it's best that we keep our laser guns ready, men."

"Do you expect trouble, Captain?" asked one of his men.

"I don't know, but stay on your guard!"

The land rover slowly passed under a bunch of large boulders. One of his men felt some small pebbles hitting him on his head. He looked up.

There he saw something that looked like men — but not like any men he had ever seen before. "Look! Look! Look up there! he shouted as he pointed his finger up toward the top of a huge pile of rocks over their heads!

"Where?" asked Star.

"Up there!" replied the crewman! But no one was there! Just like they appeared, they disappeared! "They were there just seconds ago!" insisted the crewman.

Then another crewman said, "He's just seeing things." The rest of the crew began to laugh.

However, a serious Captain Star interrupted the laughter, "All right, men! Don't take this as a joke — He might have seen something! No telling what's out here! So keep your eyes open!" He turned to Dr. Zuntor, "What do you think it was?"

Zuntor replied, "I think it was what he said! Because I've seen something, myself! I just didn't say anything because I didn't want to spook the men into imagining things!"

After a reasonable amount of time, Captain Star said, "I think we'll set up camp here." While the crew was setting up their camp, Star and Zuntor began to walk around the perimeter of their campsite.

"Look! Captain!" shouted Zuntor, when he saw a footprint in front of them. The two of them walked over to it. Captain Star put his foot inside of it. It was so much larger than his, even though he had his boots on. It still looked as though his foot was the size of a baby's foot inside their newly found footprints! Not only that, but the footprint had only three toes, and they looked like cups.

"Doctor, have you ever seen anything like this before?" asked Captain Star.

"No! not on Duderyon, or any other planet for that matter! For the depth and length of it, this thing must weigh at least five hundred pounds!"

"Oh my God!" Star suddenly got very quiet. "Just think, it might be that this entire planet is full of them!"

"Let's hope not!" said Dr. Zuntor.

"Well, whatever they are, we'll just have to wait and see, because I'm going to get some rest! Let's go back," said Captain Star. With that, they made their way back to their camp.

Soon, the camp had bedded down. It was so quiet, a person could hear their own heart beating. Suddenly, one of the men who was walking guard duty heard an unusual sound. Quickly looking in the direction of the sound, he thought he saw something moving. Holding his breath with fear, he slowly walked in the direction of the sound, with his laser gun in his hand, ready for whatever might be out there. Jumping from the top of a huge boulder, two of the "almost man-looking" creatures took him to the ground and ripped him apart! Then, they just quietly ran away. Unfortunately, the guard was unable to get off a single shot, which might have warned the camp!

The next morning, the crewman who was next in line to relieve him found him lying in a pool of blood, dead! He ran back to camp to inform Captain Star and Dr. Zuntor about what he had found! Grabbing up their laser guns, the both of them made their way back to the scene where the dead crew member was lying!

"Have you ever seen anything like this before, Dr. Zuntor?" asked Captain Star.

Looking at what was left of the dead crewman's body, Dr. Zuntor replied, "It looks as if it's been ripped apart! Something, or somebody, or whatever it was, must have been as strong as three of our men!" Then, he noticed footprints in the hot, soft, mud. He walked over to show the footprints to Star, and said, "They're the same kind of tracks we saw last evening, when we were out scouting, before we turned in! Not only that, but it appears as though there were two of them!"

"If that's the case, we had better follow these tracks to find out where they lead, before they take us out, one-by-one," suggested Captain Star. So some of the crew stayed behind, while the others went along with the Captain and the Doctor. None of them had any idea of what to expect as they followed the tracks through the rugged terrain of the Asteroid. Over hills and over streams of hot lava, they continued to follow the two sets of tracks.

Suddenly, Dr. Zuntor stopped! He motioned for everyone to get down. He whispered, "Look! Look down there!" Creeping to the edge of a dangerous cliff, they could see some kind of village. And, there they were! A small group of huge, almost man-looking, monsters! It appeared as if there were male, female, and children in the group. The adults seemed to stand well over eight feet tall, and weighed about five hundred pounds! The children must have been over two hundred pounds, and were five- to six-feet tall! Their heads looked like catfish, and they had long, thick, heavy tails. Even though they walked upright, they were covered with thick, alligator-like scales, more like water creatures than land creatures. They had large and extremely muscular forearms with dagger-like fingernails protruding from enormous hands. When they communicated, they made a deep, wavy sound.

Never having seen any creatures like this before, a confused Captain Star asked the Doctor if he knew what or who they were. Dr. Zuntor looked at him and replied, "I can't be sure, but I think they are called 'Hynipbos'." Repeating him, Captain Star questioned him: "Hynipbos? What in the Cosmos are they? And where in the Cosmos do they come from? And, how in the Cosmos do you know what they are?"

"Star, you know I've studied different life-forms on many planets for a long time — especially unusual ones!" Zuntor added, "And this is one of the most unusual, because Hynipbos are found only on the planet Nipkolor! — And it is billions of light-years away from this sector! That's why I can't believe that they are here, on this deserted Asteroid!"

Then Captain Star said, "Whatever you call them, and whether you believe it or not, there they are! And they have killed one of my crew!"

"Look Captain!" One of Star's crew, looking just past the camp of these strange beings, saw the wreckage of a War-Starship. He pointed his finger in that direction.

"It's a ship, and it's still smoldering," said Star to Dr. Zuntor. "We've got to get over there and find out if anyone on it is still alive, and try to learn where it came from!"

Dr. Zuntor cautioned, "We must be careful. Remember, we still have to keep in mind the importance of our mission."

"I know," said Star, "but if anything happens to us, Mr. Pep can still continue on. And, I'm also sure that the I.P.D. Command needs to know what is going on out here."

The determined Captain persisted, "So, we'll just have to take that chance, Zuntor!"

Giving in, Zuntor replied, "Well, if you feel that way, I've got to back you! So, let me see if I can draw their attention away from that ship long enough for you to check it out!"

Dr. Zuntor crept around to the opposite side of the alien camp as Captain Star was making his way toward the crashed ship. Zuntor and his men were soon in place. Looking over the top of the camp, he spotted some hanging rocks. Showing them to his men, they took their laser guns and fired, hitting the rocks. The force of the laser rays made them begin to roll down the hill, causing a rock avalanche!

The sound of the small avalanche coming down on their camp diverted the Hynipbos' attention away from the burning ship long enough for the Captain to make his way around them. Seeing a huge hole where he could enter the crashed ship, Star ran and dived into the still-smoking ship.

Once inside, he carefully looked around, hoping for some sign of life. All he could see were dead bodies that didn't survive the impact of the crash. Looking through the flight instruments, he found two small memory slides. Saying to himself, "These memory slides should have a hologram image and a message that might tell us what happened. He started to make his way back. When he was almost at the hole where he had entered the ship, one of the younger Hynipbos (about three-hundred-fifty pounds) slapped him down with the back of one of its forearms!

Rolling over onto the floor, almost out, Captain Star saw it coming at him! The Hynipbos turned around and lifted its long speckled tail, and tried to slam it down on Captain Star! Seeing what was about to happen, Star rolled over and out of the way of the blow, just in time, missing him by just a split second! Star pulled his laser gun, only to have it knocked out of his hand onto the floor by the charging Hynipbos' long arms! And before he knew it, there he was, with nothing to protect himself!

Captain Star tried to run, only to fall over a dead body of one of the ship's crew! Rushing over for the kill, the Hynipbos tried to grab him!! Rolling out of its reach, Captain Star picked up his laser gun and fired! Zunnn — Zunnn! went the laser gun, hitting the Hynipbos in the face, which exploded its head like a watermelon! Down it went to the floor, with yellow blood running out of it.

Slowly making his way out of the smoking ship, Star saw his chance to get back to the top of the hill, above the Hynipbos' camp. Seeing him coming, the Doctor rushed over to meet him. Helping him back to their camp, he asked what had happened. Captain Star replied, "I found these memory slides. And that's not all — I got acquainted with one of those... whatever you called it! It almost did me in! Together, they rapidly made their way back toward their own camp.

Unknowing to them, the Hynipbos were following their trail by their scent! They quickly broke camp and were heading back to their shuttle. But, before they could make it, they heard an ungodly noise coming from the top of the surrounding hills! When they looked, they saw hundreds of screaming Hynipbos running in their direction!

Captain Star screamed his orders: "Get back to the shuttle! Everyone! Run! Run!" He and Dr. Zuntor began to fire their laser guns at the monsters! The Hynipbos were throwing huge rocks. Even though they were falling as they were being hit by the laser fire, and even though some were being killed, there were just too many of them!

Realizing their men had made it to the inside of their shuttle, Captain Star and Dr. Zuntor began to run for their own lives! The Hynipbos were gaining on them! The only thing left for them to do was to continue running as fast as they could! As he ran, Captain Star shouted, "It looks as if we need a miracle to get us out of this one, Zuntor!" No sooner said, than done! A bright streak of blue and white light hit a group of Hynipbos! The force was so strong, it knocked them completely off the Asteroid!

The same flash was exploding all around them, and was killing the Hynipbos with pin-point accuracy. Little did Star and Zuntor know –

as they were still running for, and then climbing into, their shuttle – that their own Mr. Pep had seen everything on the 3-D Hologram scanner screen and had fired from the Phantom II. With this help from the Phantom II, Captain Star's small shuttle was back in its ship and headed for the Mothership!

"That was close, Dr. Zuntor! I can't wait to see what's on these Hologram Memory Slides. They might have some information about what happened on their ship, and how it arrived on that Asteroid." said Star. "One thing I'm trying to understand, is how did that Asteroid get into this system's orbit? Another thing is how did those Hynipbos' get there!?"

"Maybe those Hologram Memory Slides will give us a clue," said Dr. Zuntor. "Whatever is on them, Captain, we will at least have something to give to the I.P.D. Commission, so they will know that something is going on out here!"

"Dr. Poolong, I've gotten a message from Captain Barlow, of the Starship Sepito, saying they have just spotted the Phantom II. And, they are going to intercept it as soon as it arrives on the other side of the Kisalunt Quasar," said Captain Icpek over the communication In-Beam of their Mothership.

"Why is he in that Sector, Captain?" asked Dr. Poolong, "Shouldn't the Sepito be orbiting around the planet Nipkolor, waiting to hear from us?"

"They were!" answered Captain Icpek.

"Then why aren't they, now?" asked Dr. Poolong.

"As I understand," replied Captain Icpek, "he and some of his shipmates went to war with their Commander! Captain Barlow says that his Fleet Commander, Pratt, was too weak, so he took over."

Dr. Poolong stated, "I've been saying that all along. Captain Barlow and that scum of a fleet is much too ambitious for their own good. Now, he's talking about intercepting the Phantom II alone, with that small fleet! Believe me, all he's thinking about is getting his hands on that Serum, so that he alone will have the power to control the solar system!"

Captain Icpek asked, "If that's the case, then why did he let us know where he was planning to launch his attack on the Phantom II — if he's all for himself?"

"Can't you see?" replied Dr. Poolong, "for him to be willing to let us know where he is now, something bad must have happened on the Planet Nipkolor!"

At that very moment, Captain Icpek remembered that not too long ago, his ship's seismonitor and directional indicator had shown some unusual disturbances in the Nipkolor Sector. "I think you're right! Something did happen on Nipkolor! Give me a little time, to check the computers on my seismonitor Directional Indicator Unit. I know it has recorded a disturbance in that sector. It might take a little time, but it will tell me exactly what happened. As soon as I find out, I'll let you know."

At last, Captain Star and his crew docked their shuttle back on the Phantom II and rushed into the area where Mr. Pep was waiting for them. Star and Mr. Pep greeted each other like two long-lost brothers. Then, Star said, "Well, Mr. Pep, once again, you saved our lives! If you hadn't kept an eye on us, we would be dead for sure!"

Mr. Pep, looking like a true I.P.D. Officer, with his chest stuck out, said, "Captain, it's my duty to always keep things under control."

"Very good, Mr. Pep," said Star, "Now, there's something I need for you to do." He handed the Hologram Memory Slides over to him and issued his orders. "Take these H.M. Slides and compute them in our H.M. Scanner. When it pulls up its image, put it through the language translator, then let me know when it's ready."

"Will do, Captain!" replied Mr. Pep. The Captain and Dr. Zuntor made their way to the upper deck.

Sometime later, a call came over the In-Beam saying, "Captain Star, it's Mr. Pep, all things are ready as you ordered, Sir."

Answering him, Captain Star said, "Very good, Mr. Pep. We'll be there right away." Then he and the Doctor rushed down the ship's corridors, on their way to the main Hologram Section of the Phantom II.

As they opened the door and walked into the room, it was as if they were in the heart of everything that was happening. On the H.M. Slides, everything was life-size! After they had taken their seats, they were completely surrounded by the events that had been recorded on the two slides.

"Look, Zuntor! It's a Nipkolor Commander!" exclaimed Captain Star.

"How do you know, Captain?" asked Dr. Zuntor.

"I know the uniform and the crest on the ships," replied Star. Then he inquired of Mr. Pep, "Why isn't there any sound? I can't hear what's going on!"

"It's the slides, Sir. They must have gotten magnetized and lost some of their frequencies. But, I'll keep trying. Maybe all of the sound isn't lost."

"Well, do what you can, Mr. Pep," said Captain Star. "We need to know everything possible."

Still unable to hear, Captain Star and Dr. Zuntor were looking around at all of the stars, moons, and asteroids in the Planet Nipkolor's Sector. The view was as if he were the pilot on the Nipkolor's ship.

The reason they had picked the main hologram section for viewing was because he could control the angles of view. If he wanted to see from the outside of the ship to the interior, all he had to do was hit a switch on the arm of his chair. The same was true if he were on the inside, looking out. With the Phantom II's hologram computers, it could be as if he were actually there! Especially with its 3-dimensional viewing. Also, with the Master Control Switch, he could split an image into two parts. It could project a replay simultaneously, even as it continued to move forward!"

"It appears as if this ship were surrounded by a fleet of other Nipkolor War-Starships," said Star.

"I know, but I wonder why they're fighting each other," remarked a bewildered Doctor Zuntor. They continued to watch, as the battle between Captain Barlow and Commander Pratt continued. Actually, they were quarreling over who was going to have command of the fleet.

Then, just as when the sound went out, it came back on. At that moment, Mr. Pep's voice came over the In-Beam, saying, "Captain, the sound should work now. I've fixed it, Sir. You can run it back again, to the beginning of the Memory Slide, anytime you like."

"Very good, Mr. Pep! You never let me down," said Captain Star. They rolled it back to where the Memory Slides began.

The voice of Commander Pratt was saying (before the battle began), "Captain Barlow, don't be a power-hungry fool! I'm ordering you not to try and take the Phantom II alone! I've already explained to you that Dr. Poolong and Captain Icpek's fleet will join us in the Bassera Sector."

Determined to disobey orders, Captain Barlow said to his Commander, "I don't need anyone to help me take that Serum from the Phantom II. Me and my fleet are all I need!" As soon as the Commander heard him say, "my fleet", he knew then and there, that it was a case of stopping Captain Barlow by force, or be killed himself! Either way, he knew it had come to a showdown between the two of them. That's when the Commander gave orders to open fire on Captain Barlow, never dreaming that his own fleet would turn on him.

Of course, Pratt had no way of knowing that Barlow had already made a deal with the other ships in the fleet, to side with him. Barlow had convinced them that when they had taken the Serum from the Phantom II, they would all share the power that the Serum would bring. Soon, Commander Pratt's ship was taking hit after hit from Captain Barlow's ship, as well as from all the other ships in his fleet! Even though the Commander's ship, with his powerful Laser Cannons, had taken out some of Barlow's fleet, there were still too many for him alone!

Spinning out of orbit, Commander Pratt's ship soon crashed into the surface of the Planet Nipkolor. The enormous Mothership had carried an ample supply of nuclear fuel. And when it hit the planet, by coincidence, it exploded in the middle of a huge radioactive area. Therefore, upon impact, the combination of both nuclear elements caused a compound, thermonuclear explosion.

Since the planet Nipkolor was such a small planet, the tremendous force knocked it off its axis, and it catapulted out of orbit. Because it was now in an altogether new orbit, the unbalancing of that sector put a huge asteroid and the newly weakened planet Nipkolor onto the same orbital trajectory. In time, they collided. This caused both of them to be smashed into billions of small asteroids. Soon they found new orbits all over that sector. That's why the planet Nipkolor is no more.

Running that sequence over and over again, Dr. Zuntor scientifically explained to Captain Star what had happened. Star then asked Dr. Zuntor, "Where did the Hynipbos come from?"

"Let me try to explain what I believe happened," said the Doctor. "They were always on the Planet Nipkolor, and there was a huge population of them. But with the destruction of the planet, the thermonuclear explosion killed most of them! Only a few were able to survive. The speed of the planet, as it was knocked out of orbit and flung into space, caused the hot, nuclear energy to overheat the atmosphere. This generated a mutation in the few surviving Hynipbos! Before these things occurred, their intelligence was almost equal to ours. Even though they had turned into huge, wild beasts, they still had our characteristics. That's why we saw them living together and fighting as a unit!"

At this point, the Captain asked him, "Why did they try to kill us?"

Dr. Zuntor answered, "They were defending their territory, that's all."

The two of them looked at the images of the recorded slides over and over again. Not long after that, Star called over the In-Beam, just to say, "Thank you, Mr. Pep - Once again — Thank you! You did an excellent job!" Captain Star and Dr. Zuntor walked slowly back toward the upper decks, as they continued their discussion about all they had seen in the main hologram section of their Phantom II Starship.

Sitting back in the lounge area of their ship, Star was still trying to put the association between Dr. Poolong, Captain Icpek, and Captain Barlow together. He turned to Dr. Zuntor and said, "I wonder why they play games with each other. It's apparent that Dr. Poolong knows he can't trust Captain Barlow, because he knows that he has already double-crossed his own Commander. Also, as we know, Captain Barlow has no place to go, because his own planet has been destroyed! Not only that, but Captain Icpek knows he can't do a thing without the help of Dr. Poolong. So, this means, if he wants to stay alive, he has to protect Poolong from Captain Barlow! And, we both know Captain Barlow will be trying to get his hands on the Serum, so he can move in on the both of them, and take over!"

Dr. Zuntor said, "If that's the case, Dr. Poolong and Captain Icpek also know the same thing!"

"Well, that means they will also be on their way to the black hole! And they will be hoping to take the Serum from us before Barlow gets a chance to try!"

Captain Star said, "Knowing Captain Icpek as we do, he would much rather let Captain Barlow try to take the Serum from us first; and in the event that he can't, and we kill Barlow off, the Phantom II would probably be in such bad shape after the fight, that it wouldn't take very much for Icpek and his fleet to take it away from us! Then of course, he would destroy the Phantom II. And after that, all the ships in the solar system would be afraid of Icpek's reputation."

Dr. Zuntor interrupted, "I can see him now, thinking of a plan to take it all from Dr. Poolong, and keeping it all for himself! If he could get that lucky!"

With a cold stare, Captain Star looked at Dr. Zuntor eye-to-eye and stated, "Believe me — he'll NEVER get that lucky!! If anyone gets lucky, at all, it will be us! Because Poolong and Icpek will be trying to figure out what happened. But since we've seen these slides, we know what's happening. Now, what is also working in our favor, is they think we're not even aware of what's going on!" Thinking to himself for a moment, he gave Dr. Zuntor a smile of confidence and then said, "Let's give all three of them a big Phantom II surprise!" With that, the two men stood up and shook each other's hand.

After this conversation, Captain Star spoke to his entire crew, over the In-Beam: "This is Captain Star. We are about to be in the middle of one of the most awesome battles we have ever known — and we will be completely on our own! Now, listen up! All it is going to take, is for everyone to do their J-O-B to the best of their ability! So, make ready your posts so you will be prepared to go into battle at my command!"

He then turned his attention to Mr. Pep, saying, "Mr. Pep, put the Phantom II into hyperdrive — 4 point 7 warp speed. Let's get to that black hole — A.S.A.P.!" The Phantom II, with Dr. Zuntor's Serum aboard, zoomed faster than the speed of light — headed for war and Bassera, the black hole!

Captain Icpek announced to Dr. Poolong over their ship's In-Beam, "Dr. Poolong, I've checked on that disturbance in the Nipkolor sector. From all indications, it was Nipkolor itself that was disturbed."

I should have known!" exclaimed Dr. Poolong. "It's all beginning to make sense now," continued Captain Icpek. "Captain Barlow is trying to take over! He must have had something to do with the destruction of Nipkolor! Since the Planet Nipkolor has been destroyed, and if he is not successful in taking that Serum from the Phantom II, he will need some place to go! To him, we are just a safety valve if things go wrong for him!"

As he gave it a second thought, Icpek was becoming fearless. Slamming his hands down on the arm of his chair, he roared, "What does he think we are!? He must think we are fools! He actually believes we are not able to see through this game he's playing!"

Dr. Poolong said, "I only hope that Captain Star hasn't figured out what's going on yet. If so, he'll be prepared! And, without the element of surprise, it won't be so easy to take the Serum away from them. The only way we can be sure of getting our hands on that Serum, is to beat the Phantom II to the black hole, and join Captain Barlow's fleet!"

"With our huge fleet joined to Barlow's fleet," Captain Icpek added, "there is no way Captain Star can resist our demands. He will be forced to give up the Serum!"

Poolong said, "I believe you are right, Captain, but don't forget, that as soon as we get our hands on that Serum, we must do away with Barlow and his fleet. Remember, he is not like his Commander; Barlow absolutely cannot be trusted!"

"O.K. then," declared the determined Captain Icpek, "let's get everything ready! We can't waste any more time!" Soon everything was battle-ready, and the enormous Mothership of Dr. Poolong and Captain Icpek, with their huge fleet, was speeding toward their date with destiny!

Pacing the floor of his ship, Captain Barlow was impatiently waiting to intercept the Phantom II, before it got to Bassera. Barlow was thinking out loud: "Soon, I'll be so powerful — I'll be the 'Supreme Ruler' of this solar system! No one will be able to stand up against me! Not even those fools, Poolong and Icpek. How could those two idiots think I would ever give that Serum to them? Once I've taken it from that Captain Star, it will belong to me alone! And they will all know that I am the only worthy one!" Then, like all the others before him, the thought of himself having the Serum in his personal possession, caused him to cross over that thin line of sanity into madness! Barlow began laughing out loud; he sounded just like the insane creature he had become!

While these three players were making their way to the black hole Sector, another power-hopeful was on his ship intercepting the transmission, of the conversations, between Dr. Poolong and Captain Icpek. Indeed, he was learning all about their plans to take the Serum from the Phantom II.

He was an outlaw escapist from the I.P.D.'s prison asteroid, by the name of Negwa. He had once been a member of the Duderyon Intelligence Operations. During the deadly rampage of the two Killer

Drymahords, he and a group of his yes-men took advantage of the panic within the Duderyon population. This panic (of course) was caused by so much destructive disturbance taking place on their planet. Breaking into the Interplanetary Treasury, he stole over six billion gugee (dollars) and tried to get away. However, after the annihilation of the Killer Drymahords, along with the planet Getnor, things finally returned to normal. It was then that the theft was discovered, and he, with his crew, were put on the "wanted" list for the crime.

On his way to a far, distant planet, he was trapped by the I.P.D.. He fought with them, and before he was subdued, he had killed thousands of crew members on the three ships he had destroyed while trying to get away. After a long, and hard-fought trial, he and his crew were sentenced to life in exile. But on their way to be confined on the Prison Asteroid, the Super I.P.D. 77-B Mothership's crew and Captain were overpowered and killed. That ship, from then until now, belonged to Negwa, who now called himself "Captain" Negwa. Ever since he highjacked the I.P.D. Ship, he ravaged the solar system! He went throughout that galaxy killing and destroying asteroids and small planets! Simultaneously, this space pirate recruited ships from these desolated hot spots, until he had become a gigantic force to be reckoned with!

Negwa was speaking on the In/Out-Beam with Xergot, his Co-Captain. Xergot was in command of the other Mothership, which was flying along-side Negwa's ship. "I've just heard a conversation over my I.C.I., (Interplanetary Communications Interceptor,) that put the entire solar system into our hands! I'm ordering you to change course for the Sector of the black hole!"

Xergot, on the other Mothership inquired, "Do you mean the black hole Sector that was named Bassera? If so, we're taking a big chance!"

Captain Negwa demanded, "What do you mean by 'a big chance'?"

Xergot insisted, "Captain, so many ships have been lost in Bassera, that anything can happen! What is so important that you want us to take such chances?"

Upset at having his authority questioned, Captain Negwa asserted in no uncertain terms, "Listen you fool, all of these ships in this fleet belong to me! And if I give an order, I expect it to be obeyed without question! Do you understand!?" However, after thinking about it for a few seconds, Captain Negwa, knowing he needed all the help he could get, decided to tell his Co-Captain all the details he had heard — especially about the Serum.

After listening to the entire story, the reluctant officer said, "What are we waiting on? With that kind of power, it's worth taking the chance of being sucked into that bitch of a black hole!" The outlaw fleet immediately routed all their ships toward their rendezvous with destiny, full light-speed ahead!!

The In-Beam on board the Phantom II was also busy. Mr. Pep was consulting with Captain Star, "Captain, I've been picking up transmissions from all over the Bassera Sector. It seems as though every small-time captain or fleet commander out there has an eye out for us! It looks like we had better put a little fear of the Phantom II into their hearts! Then, Sir, everyone will think a second time before they try to attack us."

"Mr. Pep, you sound a little upset. What have you heard?" asked Captain Star.

Answering him, Mr. Pep said, "I recorded it for you, Sir. I'll patch it through to your area, so you and Dr. Zuntor can hear it. It will only take me a moment, Sir." Within seconds, the two of them were listening to several conversations concerning plans to intercept the Phantom II, in hopes of taking the Serum.

Dr. Zuntor remarked, "You were right, Captain, for making everything ready — because I do believe the hunt is on!"

Within seconds after uttering those words, Mr. Pep called the Captain saying, "Captain Star, check out your Proximetry Locator Screen. There's a group of ships headed this way! I think, as usual, they're up to no good, Sir!"

Looking at his P.L.S., Captain Star said, "You're right, Mr. Pep. It seems to be time to let the games begin!" He ordered everyone to man their battle stations.

It was a group of power-hopefuls, trying their luck — believing they could take the Serum for their own gains. There were about five outlaw ships on the attack! The lead ship was the most aggressive. Its Captain flew their ship directly across the front of the Phantom II's path. "Fire!" ordered Captain Star.

He ordered his laser cannon's gunner to fire on the lead ship. This ship took a full hit in its energy section. Then another three hits that exploded it into space dust! Rolling over from side-to-side, the Phantom II out-maneuvered the other ships in such a way, that it was able to kill off another one of the attacking ships.

Swinging its laser cannons in a 160-degree angle, the Phantom II rolled and looped as if it were a smaller ship. It then killed off two more of the attacking ships! With only one more ship to go, Star knew it was a waste of time to kill it off, so he ordered Mr. Pep to switch on their Reflective Image Eliminator Unit. This made the Phantom II disappear!

Never having seen anything like this before, the marauding captain of the last attacking ship was so confused he turned his ship around, threw it into hyperdrive, and zoomed out of the area of battle as fast as possible! He declared to his crew, "I heard that the Phantom II could fight, but I had no idea it was that much of a killer! Not only that, but if I hadn't seen it for myself, I would never have believed it could fly so fast! It just disappeared into space! Wow! We were lucky to get away with our lives!" He then sped away to tell all the other ships in the sector to stay away from the Phantom II!

Watching the remaining attack ship fly off in the other direction, Captain Star began to laugh, knowing he had used him to spread the word about the fantastic Phantom II! After making sure that it was safe, he told Mr. Pep to switch off the R.I.E. Unit, and return the ship to normal.

Then he announced to his crew, "This is the Captain speaking, I want to let you know what a good job you did in that little conflict. But don't let yourself think there won't be more of those kinds of attacks on us, because there certainly will be! In fact, I thoroughly expect them to be even more vicious! So stay sharp!"

As they continued toward the black hole, Bassera, once again, someone else thought they could take on the Phantom II. It was the War-Starship Nozach! Its Captain was one of the most ruthless space-killers in this solar system! At one time, Captain Sidman had taken control over three, populated asteroids. The I.P.D. had a reward of one-million Gugees on his head, dead-or-alive! But no one was able to collect. His ship was one of the most sophisticated in this system. And Captain Sidman knew if he gained possession of the Serum, there would be no doubt about it — nothing could stop him! So, he was literally, on a "do-or-die" mission!

"Captain Sidman! — It's the Phantom II," announced his First Mate!

"Finally!" Sidman exclaimed, "At last I have my chance! Prepare to attack! Use every laser and cannon we have! I want that ship lit up like it's full of sun rays!" Not long after he had given the order, Sidman's ship was on the attack. "Fire!" — He kept shouting to his gunners, over and over again. The Phantom II was returning the fire, but both ships' force fields were repelling the rays and missiles from their ships, as they continued to do battle.

Captain Sidman's First Mate, trying to encourage his Captain and himself, made the following grandiose statement: "The Phantom II can't stand up to us!! Yours is the only ship that will be able to take it! We have nothing to worry about!"

The two ships fought all over the sector. It looked as if neither ship would give in, until Captain Star switched on his Image Duplicator! Then, within seconds, instead of one Phantom II, there were three of them! Now Captain Sidman really was confused! He didn't know which one to fire upon. Not only that, but it was like a reflection in a mirror. When one Phantom II made a move or shot a weapon, all three of them did the same thing, at the same time. When the Phantom II attacked Sidman with lasers and cannons, it looked as though an entire fleet was firing at them at the same time! There were so many beams of laser light simultaneously coming toward his ship, that Sidman was unable to switch his force field fast enough to keep up! So, from time-to-time, the Phantom II was getting in some good hits on the War-Starship Nozach.

Captain Sidman was losing control of the Nozach, because it was becoming helpless after taking so many hits from the Phantom II. Fire and smoke had begun to move through the enormous War-Starship! His crew knew that it wouldn't be long before their ship would be lost. Even though the Nozach was in danger of exploding at any time, Captain Sidman was still fighting! "Fire my double-laser cannons!" he ordered his gunners! Soon, five double-laser cannons appeared, and within seconds, laser-rays were lighting up the force field around the Phantom II.

"Dr. Zuntor, I don't know if our force field can hold off so many laser hits much longer," said Captain Star. Looking at the Hologram Scanner Screen, Dr. Zuntor could see, that the double-laser cannons of Captain Sidman were firing extremely fast!

Even though to the enemy it appeared as though there were three Phantom II's, all three of them were being hit each time the original was hit. He also knew it wouldn't be long before Captain Sidman would figure out that two of the Phantom II's were only reflections of the original! He knew he had to think of something else, fast!

Then it came to him! Saying to himself, "That ship's lasers are firing faster than I've ever before seen laser-cannons fire! There's only one way to defend ourselves from so much firepower, and that is to use our Missile-Boomerang Force Field! Even though they are not firing many missiles, I do believe it should also boomerang their laser-fire back to them — Back to the Nozach from where it originated!"

After firing its double-laser cannons at all three of the Phantom II's, some of the rays eventually got past the force-field and hit the Phantom II! Hit so many times that flames began racing out of a small hole in one of the shuttles that was docked on the port side of the Phantom II. Seeing this, Captain Sidman realized it was some kind of reflected image of the Phantom II. He knew his double-laser cannons had hit only one of the three ships he saw; yet all three of them were flaming, in the same spot!?

"Captain Star, Sir! We've been hit!" shouted Mr. Pep!

"What's the damage, Mr. Pep?" asked Captain Star.

"It's in the shuttle docking area, Sir. I think it's only one of our shuttles that's been hit," replied Mr. Pep.

"Well," said Captain Star, "Do what you think is best, Pep. I'll leave it up to you." Moments later, seeing that it was only one of their shuttles burning, Mr. Pep detached it from the Phantom II, and sent it drifting slowly off into space.

To the crew of the Phantom II, it was only one flaming shuttle falling from the shuttle docks, but to Captain Sidman, it was one of three, simultaneously falling out of the docks of the Phantom II. At that very moment, a surprised Captain Sidman knew it was a reflection trick. He gleefully turned to his First Mate, and declared, "Ah Hah! I knew it was a trick! At first I couldn't figure it out — but now I know!"

He ordered his gunners to test fire at sections of the area in which the three Phantom II's were located. In seconds only, he knew which one of them was the real Phantom II! Using his computers to zero in on the target, Captain Sidman began to fire his double-laser cannons, full speed, at the real Phantom II. He not only fired laser cannons, but he also fired missiles! He shot everything he had at the Phantom II! He was hoping to disarm it enough, so that it would give up! If so, then they could board it, and take the Serum!

"Fire!" He was shouting to his gunners. "Give it all you've got! Fire!" The projectiles were leaving his ship in waves.

As he watched the huge War-Starship, Nozach, firing at them, Dr. Zuntor analyzed the situation and said to himself, "He's firing just enough for me to take him out with his own weapons!" Calling Mr. Pep, he asked, "Are all those things that I ordered you to assemble, for use against Captain Sidman's ship, ready?"

Mr. Pep answered, "Everything is ready, Sir!"

Calling Captain Star, on the In-Beam, Dr. Zuntor said, "Captain, swing our ship around about 45 degrees, and hold it there about six seconds. Then, as soon as I say 'GO!' let's get the hell out of this sector as fast as possible!"

"Got You!" concurred The Captain!

While still firing at the Nozach, Captain Star maneuvered the Phantom II, just as the Doctor had requested him to do. The Phantom II had swung to a 45-degree angle from its original position across from the Nozach. This maneuver put their ship behind Captain Sidman's Nozach.

Just as Captain Star was making the 45-degree sweep, Dr. Zuntor switched on their Missile-Boomerang Force field; all of Captain Sidman's missiles and some of his laser-rays were caught up in the boomerang effect of the Phantom II unit! Instantly, it reflected all of them back to the Nozach!

Knowing that the laser-rays and missiles had been reflected and were hitting Captain Sidman's ship; the Phantom II, as it was zooming out into deep space, began to spray him with its Weapons! The Nozach was simultaneously being hit by tons of missiles and laser rays! It began to glow with a bright halo flashing around it, until it exploded into a mass of space dust! If the Phantom II had not pulled out of the area at top warp-speed, it would also have been destroyed. The shock-waves caused disturbances for thousands of kilometers throughout the sector.

"Hey Doc! It's a good thing you told me to zoom away from that ship as soon as you did! If not, the Phantom II would only be a memory!" said a thankful Captain Star, as the Phantom II continued on its way to Bassera, the black hole.

"We should be picking up the Phantom II on our Proximetry Locator Screen, pretty soon now," ascertained Captain Pratt, of the second Mothership, which was flying alongside Captain Barlow's Mothership, the Sepito.

Captain Barlow replied, "I should think that by now, we would have already picked it up."

"Some other fleet may have intercepted it before it got here," surmised Captain Pratt.

"I don't think so. If it had been intercepted, all of the ships in our solar system would have heard the news. It's coming — just keep your eyes on your Proximetry Locator Screen," ordered Captain Barlow. They continued on their way to the Bassera Sector.

"We're almost there, Captain. Just a few light-years away," said Dr. Zuntor.

"I know, Zuntor, but I'm sure we're not out of danger yet," said Captain Star.

A hopeful Dr. Zuntor offered, "Maybe after all those other ships were unable to take the Serum from us, the word got out that the Phantom II is too much of a Warship for any ship to take on!"

"Yeah!" Star agreed. "I do believe most of the ships that are out here right now are afraid to take a chance with us. But, we still have to deal with Dr. Poolong, Captain Icpek, and that mad Captain Barlow and his cohort, Captain Pratt! No matter what might have happened with the other ships, those four are still going to be out there waiting for us!" After a short pause, Captain Star continued, "Now that I think about it, we should be running into one or another of them pretty damned soon!"

"What do you think they're gonna do first?" asked the doctor.

"I don't understand what you mean by 'going to do first?'" queried Star.

Dr. Zuntor said, "I'm talking about what kind of attack they might use. The reason I'm asking is because there is probably going to be so many of them; it's important for us to have some kind of battle plan in advance."

"Is that all?" quipped a thoughtful Star. "Well, you've got a good point there, Zuntor! I believe they're going to group-up and set-up a solid screen of firepower, hoping it might cripple us! Then, they will probably send out some small fighters, thinking they can keep us off balance, so that they will be able to surround us and hit us with heavy fire from their Motherships!

"So once again, Doc, I must agree with you. We have to come up with a plan, before we go into battle! Do you have any ideas?" An eager Doctor Zuntor declared, "First of all, we both know that no one can fly the Phantom II, or any other ship, better than you. So! You man the controls, and use your hand-lasers and cannons. In the meantime, I can employ a few tricks I picked up from you. Such as the 'Now you see us, and now you don't, and now you see us again!' But this time, there will be three of us!"

"Gotcha' Zuntor!" Star exclaimed! "They have never seen the Phantom II in action before, so they won't know what to expect. In other words, when they see us, they will attack! But before they make contact, we will switch on our Image Duplicator, and they will immediately be thrown off guard! Because then there will be three of us, and before they realize what is happening, we will attack them with all our ship's standard arsenal! When they believe that's all we have, I'm sure they'll try to rush us — sending out all the little ships they have! And, that's when we use our Mini-Swirling-Cluster Laser Cannons!" "You know — the ones the I.P.D. engineers just installed? We adopted them from those that

Commander Booner used on us, with his 'Monster-Mothership'. And, we know what those Laser-Cluster-Missiles can do to a small group of War-Starships, don't we?!"

"Right!" agreed Zuntor, as he continued, "After the Mothership's see what happens to their smaller ships, they will attack — with everything their 'big' ships have. That's when we can use our Missile-Boomerang Force Field, along with our Reflective Image Eliminator — switching it on and off. They won't be able to tell where we are!"

"Wow!" said Captain Star, "You and Mr. Pep will have a big job, trying to pull off all of that!"

"I know, but it can be done," affirmed Zuntor. "That is, if it's all right with you, Captain?"

"If it's all right with me?! What in the galaxy are you talking about, Zuntor? That's the best plan I've ever heard. To tell the truth, I was really uncertain about which way to go. I remember now, that Admiral Fitchly advised me to let you help if I got into real trouble — because you know these weapons better than anyone! So you and Mr. Pep had better make everything ready before we run into the real battle!" ordered Captain Star.

A few light-years closer to their destination, all weapons were ready. Each individual member of the Phantom II crew had been briefed for their own personal job. Everyone now knew exactly what they needed to do.

"How do you intend to stop most of the fighter Starships from being sucked into that black hole, Dr. Poolong?" asked Captain Icpek.

"I've been thinking about that," said Poolong, "ever since I found out that the Phantom II had that Serum, and was headed this way." He then pulled a small, black disk from a case and showed it to Captain Icpek. He put the disk into a small computer, and after pushing some buttons using a group of numbers, the screen showed a computer image of a ship that was being sucked into a black hole! It just disappeared! Then it showed the same image of the same ship being sucked down into the same black hole But this time, the ship flew out of the black hole at top speed!

Seeing this, an excited Captain Icpek exclaimed, "There is only one way that ship was able to free itself from out of that black hole! It has to be the same kind of Gravity Equivalent Reversal Power (GERP) Unit as our Mothership has. But, how were you able to come up with a unit small enough to be installed on all of our War-Starships?"

After Captain Icpek asked this question, Dr. Poolong gave him a look that announced, "Don "t ask such foolish questions!"

Captain Icpek got the message. He looked at Dr. Poolong like a kid who had gotten caught with his hand in the cookie jar. He meekly said, "Forgive me, Dr. Poolong, I must never forget that you are the most brilliant scientist in the solar system."

Dr. Poolong continued, "I've already put one of those units on all of the ships within our Mothership!"

Captain Icpek paused, and then asked, "What about all the other ships that are in our fleet? Those that are flying in formation around our Mother?"

Looking at Captain Icpek with a greedy smile, he said softly, "Who cares what happens to them! After we get the Serum, the fewer Captains we have to deal with, the better off we will be." They both began to laugh.

After they had their laugh, Captain Icpek spoke, "That means that we have the only ship with this GERP."

He once again began to laugh as he said, "Captain Barlow with his two Motherships, and his scum of a fleet, doesn't have it! So all we'll have to do is use Barlow and his fleet to soften up the Phantom II for us then we'll trick them into the area where Bassera has the greatest gravitational pull, and let 'the Bitch' do the work for us!"

His eyes (all three of them) lit up as he walked away laughing, and saying to himself, "Dr. Poolong, you are a genius, an absolute genius!"

Their Mothership (along with their huge fleet) continued on. Getting closer to the black hole — closer to the "Bassera Bitch" than any of the other ships, Sepito the Mothership, was cruising around the Planet Elondo. Elondo was only one planet away from Bassera. At this time, a transmission came to their ship from the Elondo Defense. Their Patrol Commander announced, "This is Commander Penazer, of the Elondo Defense Patrol - Come in Sepito."

"It looks as if that ship from Elondo is looking for trouble", said Captain Barlow to his Co-Captain, Pratt, on his other Mothership, which was flying alongside him. After a second call came through, Captain Barlow decided to answer. "This is Captain Barlow speaking. What do you want with me?!"

Commander Penazer bellowed, "You have not had permission to enter our sector! Why are you trespassing?"

Captain Barlow replied, "We are just passing through. Do you have any problem with that?"

That's when Commander Penazer, in a voice that was much more calm, said, "I have orders from the I.P.D. Command not to let any unidentified ship fly through our sector without asking them to fly around us. But seeing how powerful your fleet is, I can tell you are not on a mission of peace. Therefore, I am ordering you and your fleet to turn around, and go back from where you came!"

Knowing he was not going to turn around, because nothing was going to stop him from getting his hands on that Serum, Captain Barlow answered, "What kind of fool are you, Commander? Can't you see there are too many of us? You cannot stop us!"

Commander Penazer knew, by what Captain Barlow had said when he was ordered to turn around, that he was a man without understanding. So Commander Penazer gave a signal, and from behind a small asteroid, ten Elondo Defense War-Starships appeared, and took positions next to his ship for support! Thinking that his back—up ships should have made a difference, he demanded once again for Captain Barlow to turn around!

But instead of turning around, Captain Barlow gave orders to open fire on the small fleet of the planet Elondo! The very first round of laser fire hit one of the ships three times, causing it to explode! Seeing this, Captain Barlow became even more confident that his fleet could handle them. So he gave orders to his Co-Captain Pratt, and some of the ships that were in his fleet: "I don't have time for this small battle — I've got to intercept the Phantom II before Dr. Poolong and Captain Icpek do. Therefore, I'm leaving this little fray in your hands! Later, when it's over, you can join me."

Answering him, Co-Captain Pratt said, "Go Sir! This won't take long!"

Captain Barlow and most of his fleet continued on their way to the black hole, while his other ships remained in the Elondo sector to finish the battle with Commander Penazer and his small fleet.

Feeling as though he were guaranteed to win the battle with the I.P.D.s, Elondo Defense Patrol's small fleet, Captain Barlow's Co-Captain was thinking, "Now that I have survived Captain Barlow, all I have to do is take care of these fools, then really take my time in re—joining Captain Barlow at that black hole. I'll wait long enough for him, or Dr. Poolong and that Captain Icpek, to kill off the Phantom II, and take the Serum!" He began to laugh as he continued thinking, "I can see it now. After one of them gets their hands on it, they're going to kill one another off until there is only one of them left alive. That surviving one will have the Serum! Then, I can come along and take it away from the survivor!"

Seeing his dreams coming into focus, he and his ships began to fight more treacherously. "Fire!" was all he was saying to his ships over and over again! Even though Pratt was most ambitious and had confidence, the Elondo Defense Patrol War-Starships were too much for him! Captain Pratt even ordered his small ships (from inside his Mothership's hangar) into battle. He used every laser he had, but the I.P.D.-trained Elondo Defense pilots were flying rings around them. Indeed, they were killing off every ship he had!

Then it came down to just him and his ship! Realizing he was all alone, and that it was finished, his panic took control! He saw all of his dreams flying away from – just as fast as they had flown into – his head in the first place!

Captain Barlow's Co-Captain was like the others who had dreamed of having Dr. Zuntor's Serum in their hands. Like the others that came before him, dreaming that with the power of the Serum, they could rule the solar system. Like the others, his dream was no more. His ship exploded into a huge, nuclear, mushroom cloud!

Finally, Captain Barlow and his ruthless fleet were entering the sector of the black hole, Bassera! Since they were the first ones to arrive, they were able to hover in an area that was to their advantage. They were now in a position to attack anyone who entered their arena before they could even prepare themselves for battle.

Looking at his Proximetry Locator Unit, Barlow could see a group of ships coming in his direction, speeding fast!! The group of ships was too small to be Captain Icpek's fleet, and they were coming from the wrong direction for it to be his own Co-Captain. He adjusted his Proximetry Locator Screen so he could have a 3-D view of the oncoming ships. The ships had an unfamiliar symbol on them. As he was looking at, them, he said to himself, "I wonder who this could be?" But, as they came closer, it turned out to be the Phantom II.

Dr. Zuntor had switched on their Image Duplicator Unit, and it appeared as if there were three Phantom IIs — all spitting hot laser rays! Never had anyone, in Barlow's contingency, ever seen three ships flying in battle formation, rolling, dipping, looping, and firing lasers and cannons simultaneously — killing the enemy fleet at will. Then, just like they came, they disappeared!

"Where did they go?" asked Captain Barlow over his Beam to anyone who was listening. Before his crew could get reorganized, the Phantom II reappeared and did the same thing again. Zoom! Boom! Zoom! went its cannons, taking out five more ships of Captain Barlow's fleet! Then something went wrong with the Image Duplicator Unit, and the Phantom II was only one ship again!

Still not knowing what kind of trick had been used on him, Captain Barlow thought the other two ships had turned and flown away. Calling his fleet, Captain Barlow shouted, "They're running away! There is only one of them left! Fire on it! Fire on it!!" Soon, the entire fleet was firing on the Phantom II.

"What happened, Dr. Zuntor?" Star yelled as he continued rolling his ship and firing his cannons.

"I don't know, Captain, answered Dr. Zuntor. "I'll have to check with Mr. Pep. But in the meantime, I'm switching over to the Reflective Image Eliminator. While Captain Star was firing lasers and streaking in between enemy ships, the Phantom II disappeared!

More confused than ever, Captain Barlow was about to go crazy. "Fire!!" he was shouting to his fleet, but even though they were following his orders, there was no target to fire at. The invisible Phantom II had orbited to the other side of the battle zone!

Then Dr. Zuntor switched off the Reflective Image Eliminator, and the Phantom II reappeared! But this time, it was using one of its Mini-Swirling-Cluster Laser Cannons, along with all of its regular lasers and missiles.

Captain Barlow's fleet never knew what hit them! The missiles, full of laser clusters, would fly between a group of ships and explode. Then the laser clusters would spread throughout a group of ships, killing off three to five of them at a time!

Beginning to realize that his fleet was no match for the Phantom II, Barlow started releasing all of his smaller ships from his Mothership's hangar. Popping out by the hundreds, the small War-Starships were attacking the Phantom
II like flies on honey.

"Our force field is holding up for now, Captain Star, but we've taken so many hits from those damnable little ships, I don't know how much longer she'll be able to take it", exclaimed Mr. Pep, over the In—Beam.

"Just keep trying to fix our Reflective Image Eliminator Unit, and I'll take care of those little ships!" shouted Captain Star!

Just arriving at the battle arena in the Bassera sector, Dr. Poolong and Captain Icpek, accompanied by their huge fleet, could see the battle over their hologram scanner. Captain Icpek, with heat in his eyes, announced, "It's the Phantom II, and it looks like it's in trouble!" Captain Icpek continued speaking, except that now, he was speaking only to himself. "Well, Captain Star! I told you I would see you again! And that I would have a fleet so strong, the solar sky would be black with so many of my ships. Well, here I am!"

Dr. Poolong spoke to him, over the Beam, "I told you Captain Barlow would be trying to take the Serum before we arrived here at the black hole Sector. Now is our chance to get both of them at the same time! I can't wait! I'm sending out my fleet to help Captain Barlow with the attack!"

Pep urgently announced, "Captain Star! Here comes what looks like a thousand more War-Starships! They must be coming out of that huge Mothership that just arrived!"

"I can see them coming!" answered Star. "How are you progressing with that R.I.E. Unit?" asked Star.

"It shouldn't take much longer, Sir. replied Mr. Pep.

Having more ships to battle than ever before, Captain Star could think of only one thing that might save his ship. "We'll have to employ the Gravity Equivalent Reversal Power Unit; then we will fly the ship into the middle of the black hole!" As he was heading his ship into Bassera, he called Mr. Pep saying, "Have you gotten that Reflective Image Eliminator fixed yet?"

Mr. Pep answered, "I've found the trouble. It won't be much longer now, Sir."

Star then asked Dr. Zuntor to be ready to switch on the Unit as soon as he gave him the signal. The battle was so intense that the laser fire was like a million stars exploding at the same time. Even though the Phantom II was killing off ships from the two fleets, it was still taking hits. Smoke was coming out of one of its rear engines. It had taken a rocket hit from Captain Barlow's ship, the Sepito!

"Look, Captain! We hit it!" shouted one of the officers who was talking to Captain Barlow, on board the Mothership Sepito.

"I know", Barlow answered. "Now he knows that he, too, can be knocked out of the universe!" But at this point, Captain Barlow saw the other fleets of Dr. Poolong and Captain Icpek arriving. Slamming his hands down on the arms of the controller's seat, he cried, "Those fools would have to come just in time to get in my way. I almost had this battle under my control. Now there are so many ships out there, firing at the Phantom II, they are getting into each other's line of fire!"

What Captain Barlow was saying was the truth! Captain Star was flying the Phantom II so skillfully and acrobatically, that ships were flying into one another and exploding. They were firing missiles that were missing their targets and exploding their own ships. The Phantom II was still killing them off with every weapon it had.

Switching over to all of its mini-Swirling-cluster laser cannons, its enemy-ships were being killed and knocked out of action in waves. The laser cluster missiles were exploding in the middle of groups of ships. Laser flashes were spraying all over the battle arena.

Realizing that his fleet, along with Captain Barlow's fleet, were still unable able to bring the Phantom II into submission, Dr. Poolong knew the battle was not going well for them. That's when he called over to Captain Star, saying, "Calling the Phantom II - This is Dr. Poolong - Come in Phantom II..."

Captain Star knew there was no good reason to respond because he already knew what Poolong was going to say. Instead, Captain Star called

Dr. Zuntor. "Hold onto your switches — here we go!" The Phantom II was thrown into hyperdrive and dove faster and deeper into the black hole! Hundreds of both fleets followed them! Soon the gravitational pull began to suck all the ships deeper and deeper inside Bassera! The speed caused by the gravitational pull also caused many of the ships to lose control. Some tried to turn around, but found it impossible!

Seeing the Phantom II still headed deeper into the black hole gave the pilots the confidence to follow! And some of the ship's pilots, not knowing how strong the pull was, were still flying their ships toward the periphery of the hole, thinking they would be able to engage in battle. More and more of the enemy ships continued to follow the pursuing ships into Bassera. The gravitational pull of the black hole was wide at the edge, and became narrower and stronger as they got deeper inside! It was as if they were going down into a funnel.

The Phantom II was traveling ten times the speed of light. The huge ship was vibrating so intensely its pipes were popping and shooting out steam. The smaller ships couldn't take as much pressure as the Phantom II. They were exploding like popcorn!

Calling to Mr. Pep, Captain Star said, "Mr. Pep, what about the Reflective Image Eliminator Unit? I need it now! It's now or never!"

Their ship was vibrating so intensely, Mr. Pep's voice was vibrating also, as he replied, "You got it Sir! It's working again! Just tell me when!"

Answering him, Captain Star said, "I knew you could do it!" He then called Dr. Zuntor and said, "When I count to three, switch on the Gravity Equivalent Reversal Power Unit." Then, he said over the ship's In—Beam, "This is your Captain. When we come up from out of this black hole, I want everyone to fire their weapons at anything and everything that is flying out there! ... All right you spaceijockeys, here we go!"

He began to count "One ... two ... three. NOW!" On this command, both Dr. Zuntor and Mr. Pep switched on their units. At that instant, the Phantom II disappeared — and at the same time, reversed its direction, with more than its own thrust. The power of the gravitational pull of the black hole had also been reversed! The thrust that was equivalent of the pull had turned into a push! The now projecting powers, along with the Phantom II's own power, shot the magnificent Phantom II up and out of the black hole like a champagne cork! And it was still invisible!

Observing all that had happened on their hologram scanner screen, both Mothership Captains could not believe their eyes! They had just witnessed both of their fleets sucked into Bassera. Not only that, they were also thinking they had seen their dreams go down into it because they thought the Phantom II and its fleet had been lost with the Serum on board.

Captain Barlow was all-the-way upset. He thought he was about to turn the tide on the Phantom II before Captain Icpek and Dr. Pooloon's fleet came along and got in his way. Now he had nothing! As far as he was concerned, all he had left was his huge empty Mothership and ten or maybe twenty ships. His plan was no longer valid because the Phantom II had been destroyed. All these things would never have happened if it were not for Captain Icpek and Dr. Poolong.

At the same time, Dr. Poolong was also upset. All of his dreams were lost, along with the loss of the Phantom II, in that bitch of a black hole! He was out of control! He raged out loud, "That fool Barlow! If he hadn't been so power-greedy, I would have had that Serum! Now, it's gone forever!"

Of all of the players, Captain Icpek thought he had lost the most. Not only had he lost most of his fleet, he didn't even get the chance to kill Captain Star himself. After all, it was Captain Star who had killed his brother, another reason he needed revenge. All he could do within the stupor his stunned brain had placed him in was to say to himself, "That Captain Barlow — I'm going to kill him!" He continued repeating this over and over again!

Icpek thought (as did Dr. Poolong) that Captain Barlow was too power crazy, and that he had taken too many power moves, too soon. Not only that, but he had double—crossed everybody at the same time!

Icpek was thinking about how he must destroy Captain Barlow and his fleet. Even though they had lost most of their fleet, they still had some ships in their Mothership's hangar. So, equipped with Dr. Poo-long's Gravitational Reversal Unit, there didn't seem to be any reason for him to be afraid of being sucked into the Bitch.

Still invisible, the Phantom II had at last maneuvered itself from out of the capture and imprisonment by Bassera. They were free!   And, even though the remaining enemy ships couldn't see the Phantom II, Star's crew could see them, and see what was going on between them.

"It worked! It worked!" shouted the excited Captain Star, while he was still trying to gain control of his ship. The Phantom II was flying so fast that it went into a higher orbit than the other ships. After he had entered the new orbit, it didn't take long for him to regain control of his ship. And there they were, looking down on all of their enemy's ships, while their adversaries had no idea, because the Phantom II was still invisible!

"Dr. Zuntor, I can't stop thinking about how many ships got lost down in that black hole. They just disappeared into nowhere! At first, they were behind us, by the hundreds. And now, they are simply gone! Each and every one of them! I can't believe it ..." said Star!

"I understand what you are saying, Captain", replied Dr. Zuntor. "The same thing was on my mind. And, if it weren't for Little Orcal, the Phantom II would be gone also, just like the others..." said Zuntor.

Suddenly, their conversation was interrupted when Mr. Pep called over the Beam to Captain Star, "Look, Captain! Look at your hologram scanner screen! You won't believe your eyes!" Within seconds, both Captain Star and Dr. Zuntor were watching the screen. They both had hoped it would happen, and now, it really was happening. Captain Icpek had launched an attack on Captain Barlow! And, what was so ironic was that neither of them had any idea that the Phantom II was just one orbit above them, watching the entire battle!

Swirling out of the path of a huge missile, the Mothership Sepito returned fire with a barrage of missiles at the Motherships of Icpek and Poolong! Then, the smaller ships that were left of Captain Barlow's fleet went on the attack!

Seeing them coming, Captain Icpek ordered his reserve ships inside his Mothership's hangar to intercept them! Before long, the sector had once again become a war zone, except that this time, the two motherships were battling each other!

It was a case of give and take. Each Captain's smaller War-Starships were looping and rolling as they continued firing lasers and cannons at one another. The two Motherships were firing at each other with huge lasers. They were both taking so many hits that their force fields were glowing red hot from so much strain.

Remembering how the Phantom II had lured most of their fleet into that hungry black hole, Captain Icpek ordered his smaller ships (those equipped with the Mini— Gravitational Reversal Unit) to lure Captain Barlow's smaller ships into the black hole: "This is Captain Icpek speaking. As you already know, each of your ships has the new Gravitation Reversal Unit on board. So, go into your hit—and—run tactic. Fire on your enemy's ships, then make at least one of them follow you into that black hole! Once your ships have been caught up in the gravitational pull, you can use the advantage you will have that they don't have, which is they don't have that unit! Remember now, don't switch it on until both ships have begun to plunge into the black hole! Then, you can escape; they cannot! Repeat this operation over and over again. Do you understand me?"

Soon, the hit—and—run, ship—killing party was on! Captain Icpek's ships were leading Barlow's ships into the Bitch Bassera's mouth, thus killing their enemy's ships nonstop!

Unaware that his ships were falling into Icpek's trap, Captain Barlow was thinking that both of them were losing ships to the black hole! That is, until he realized that some of Icpek's smaller ships were coming back out, while none of his own were coming out. Once he realized that he had fallen into a trap, he called over the Beam, telling his pilots not to follow Captain Icpek's ships into that blasted hole!

"It looks as if they're killing each other off for us", declared Star to Dr. Zuntor. They were still watching the battle on their huge 3-D hologram scanner screen. They knew they had a chance to slip back into the black hole; and they were thinking, finally, they could at last fire off the rocket that contained the cylinder with the ZYM—23Ø.6 Serum. Star, who was still manually flying the invisible Phantom II, headed her back in the direction of that terrifying black hole.

"Good thing we're still invisible, Doctor. It would be impossible to fly through that war zone and get away without another battle, and almost certain death!"

After rocketing back into the orbit where the battle raged, the Phantom II had ended up in the middle of the arena, without either side knowing they were there. Seeing both sides fighting all around them, the Phantom II (still invisible) slowly cruised between them. It became amusing to Star and Zuntor, seeing both of their enemies fighting one another over them, while the Serum would be lost, down there somewhere inside the black hole. Yet, here the Phantom II was, with neither of the Motherships' Captains having any idea that it was there! Star had to swing and swirl the Phantom II out of the way of oncoming ships, as it continued creeping through the battle area!

Suddenly, as luck would have it, the Reflective Image Eliminator went back on the fritz, shorting out all the way! An image of the Phantom II was flashing into sight, then back out of sight, over and over again, when it suddenly became completely visible! Both Motherships' Captains were lost for any kind of rational thinking! They were both floundering for a logical train of thought!

"Oh Boy! We are in deep—trash trouble now!" exclaimed Captain Star to Dr. Zuntor, when he realized that the Phantom II was no longer invisible. They were now trapped in the middle of the battle! Captain

Star threw his engines into hyperdrive! The Phantom II took off, and they were firing everything they had, at every ship in sight!

Most of the ships were so surprised at the sudden appearance of the Phantom II that they were unable to respond in time to prevent it from firing on them first. Taking advantage of this element of surprise, the Phantom II was killing ships as fast as it could get off a shott. Rolling from side—to—side, the Phantom II was firing all the lasers, cannons, and missiles it had, even their Mini—Cluster Missiles.

Captain Barlow's quick mind was recovering and he was saying to himself, overjoyed with that thought, "I don't know what has happened, but it looks as if I've got another chance to capture that, Serum! I've got to take the Phantom II before Captain Icpek and Dr. Poolong do!" He also knew he had to come up with one helluva good plan!

Seeing his wish come true – that the Phantom II was once again in his sight – Captain Icpek stopped thinking about trying to destroy the Sepito. He was only thinking about killing Captain Star. The Serum didn't even seem to matter to him anymore. All he wanted at that moment, was his decades-long need and compulsion to take Captain Star's life!

Dr. Poolong could once again feel the power of becoming the ruler of the solar system. Knowing that the Phantom II had somehow returned from out of the black hole – with the Serum on board – he thought he still had a great chance to capture it!

Heading toward the black hole as fast as the battle would allow, the Phantom II was fighting off the smaller ships and having its own way, until both the huge Motherships converged on it at the same time, lasers blazing! Captain Star knew he would be caught up in a deadly trap if he didn't immediately change directions. Diving below the Sepito, the Phantom II, trying to elude its laser fire, got in three clean hits in the Sepito's hangar area.

The Sepito was rocking from side-to-side because of the enormous hole in its belly! Barlow knew he had to prepare an escape just in case his ship was destroyed! Seeing flames coming from the Sepito, Captain Icpek said to Dr. Poolong, "By the appearance of his ship, it looks as if we might not have to deal with Captain Barlow much longer!" Poolong concurred, "We don't need him anyway! Let's just help put him out of his misery!" So, their Mothership began to fire tons of missiles at the Sepito, hitting it time-after-time! Even though they were being hit, the Sepito gunners continued firing at both the Phantom II, and Captain Icpek's ship!

Captain Barlow's crew had panicked as they tried to escape before the Sepito exploded. As he made his way to a shuttle, Captain Barlow stumbled and fell over a dead crew member. Fire and smoke were every-where! One of his crew, seeing him helpless on the floor, rushed over to help him up and carried him to the area where the shuttles were docked. In the meantime, parts of the Sepito were falling out into space, after taking so many hits from both Motherships. With the help of his crew members, he climbed on board one of the shuttles. Barlow stopped in the shuttle doorway, and turned around for one last look at his ship. The last thing he could see was the destruction that had taken place. With tears in his eyes, he slowly walked in and strapped himself into his seat, and ordered his pilot to blast off and away from his flaming Mothership!

Watching the Sepito burn (while still being bombarded by the Phantom II) Captain Icpek said, "I never did have much use or need for him anyway!" He ordered his gunners to continue firing on her! At last the Mothership, Sepito, exploded into a mass of nuclear flames. While Captain Barlow's shuttle was streaking deeper into outer space, he watched. He watched until he saw his beloved Mothership explode! He started to think about how close he had gotten to having the Serum in his hands. He began to cry. He sobbed like a baby! Then, knowing he had no place to go, and knowing his entire fleet was gone, he took out his laser gun, put it to his head, and pulled the trigger.

Realizing he didn't have to deal with the Sepito any longer, Captain Star, with lasers still firing, began to turn his ship back around, and head into the direction of Bassera.

"I've got him this time!" declared Captain Icpek. All of his ships were firing at the Phantom II, except that now there were only about fifty smaller ships left to pursue; Captain Star was still out—flying them! "Well, I'm not going to keep running from these ships!" Star said to Zuntor. "It's time for us to stop and fight!"

Even though he was flying as fast as he could to get away, he now quickly stopped the Phantom II, making a U-turn, and the Phantom II now hovered in orbit, like a gunfighter in the Old West.

Captain Star fired every weapon possible at the smaller ships. Boom! Zoom! Zamm! The sound of its cannons, lasers, and missiles was awesome! Star and his men were killing them off like fish in a barrel.

Seeing his smaller ships being killed, Captain Icpek screamed, and with both hands, raked his face in anger! He ordered his gunners to fire at the Phantom II with everything they had!

"Zuntor, switch on our Missile Boomerang Force." He knew his force field was overstrained with so many hits; he also knew that somehow he had to trick them. In his mind, he said, "I'll let them think they have a chance to hit us then, I'll run away slowly, until they catch us! That's when the Missile Boomerang Force Field will sting them with their own missiles! In the meantime, we'll continue blasting them with our mini-Swirling-cluster, laser cannons! I've got to get rid of these mosquitos, so I can get down to business with that Mothership!"

Soon, all things were ready. The Phantom II slowed down, allowing the smaller ships to surround it. It then began to spit out Laser-Cluster-Missiles into groups of enemy ships. Suddenly the entire battle arena exploded with streaks of laser rays in all directions! The smaller ships began to fire their missiles and lasers at the Phantom II, but that only made the bad situation worse. Their missiles were caught up in the boomerangs and were flung back at them, exploding and destroying them with their own missiles

"How do they do it?" Dr. Poolong was asking himself, as he was watching his 3-D hologram scanner screen, seeing his ships being killed with their own missiles. "I've got to do something about this, or soon I won't have a single ship left!" He was right, because in time, the attacking ships were down to only five. All the others had been shot and exploded with their own missiles, while the Phantom II continued to destroy them with its powerful laser rays.
Realizing that most of their fellow ships had been destroyed, the remainder of Icpek's fleet turned and ran away off into deep space!

Now it was only the two of them, as it was once before, when Captain Star had run him off, Poolong's ship smoking from a laser ray fire. Indeed, it was a long time ago.

"This simply cannot be!" Dr. Poolong was thinking. "How could one ship kill off such a mighty fleet as we had? What kind of ship is this Phantom II? No!" he screamed out loud, "This can't be." Holding his head with his hands, he was repeating this over and over again. He knew that without a fleet, there was no way he could ever put his hands on that Serum. The very thought of him losing his fleet to the Phantom II caused him to repeat his mantra... "No! This can't be." Indeed, there was no doubt — Dr. Poolong had begun to lose his mind.

There was an audio transmission coming in over their hologram scanner, saying: "Captain Icpek! This is the one who is going to blow you out of the solar system!" Like in a bad dream, Captain Icpek switched the scanner on, and there he was! Now he could see the one he hates the most. It was, of course, Captain Star!

Answering him, Icpek said, "I see we meet again, Captain! I must congratulate you on your victory over all those ships. I have to admit that your Phantom II is one of a kind! But, it's not the ship," continued Icpek, "it's the pilot! And I am a better fighter pilot than you. So, if you think you have a chance, meet me out in open space in one of your shuttles. Then, we will see who shall live or who shall die!"

"I think you just might have something with that idea, Icpek", replied Captain Star. "There is no need for anyone else, on your ship being killed. This time, I'm going to kill you!"

"What do you mean, Star? Kill me? Star? Fool! There is no way you will ever be that lucky!" challenged Icpek.

"Well", retorted Star, as he accepted the challenge, "if you agree, give me a moment to make things ready, and not only will I meet you out there, but I'll beat you out there!" He switched off his hologram scanner.

"You're not serious about fighting with him out there, are you, Captain?" asked Dr. Zuntor.

"I'm just playing a game with them", said Star. "The Phantom II has taken too many hits. I don't think we can take much more. Captain Icpek can fly that big Mothership well enough, but with the Phantom II being all shot up, we might have a better chance if I can get him out of it and into a one-on-one fight. Now, if he comes out, you and Mr. Pep attack their ship and kill it! And, I mean, KILL IT!" By the look in Star's eyes, Dr. Zuntor knew he was more than serious.

"Dr. Poolong, keep up with my shuttle on our Proximetry Locator Screen. As soon as you get a fix on us, fire your lasers at his shuttle. We have to kill him no matter what it takes. Once we get him out of the way, the taking of the Phantom II will be no problem. Remember, the Serum is still on board his ship. So, with me firing at him and keeping him busy fighting me, you will have a clear field to fire on him, from an unexpected direction! He can't get away. After we get him and his shuttle, all we have to do then is take on the Phantom II. Without him on board to maneuver her, it will be an easy task. The Serum will soon be ours!"

Down in the shuttle area, Captain Star asked Dr. Zuntor what his engineers were doing to his shuttle. "I'm adding something special to your shuttle — something special that might give you a little advantage." Then he asked Captain Star to sit in his pilot seat. He had installed a Mini-Reflective Image Eliminator, and a Mini-Double-Laser Cannon that swirled. After he showed him how to operate his shuttle's new weapons, he said, "With these, you won't have any trouble fighting him off. But... I've installed just one more feature. It's a compound hyper-drive switch!" Pointing to the switch, Dr. Zuntor said, "When you hit this switch, your shuttle will double its rocket power and jump to over six-point-77 warp speed in five seconds!"

"That's even faster than the Phantom II!" exclaimed Star. Captain Star then looked Dr. Zuntor in the eye and very seriously voiced his feelings. "Look, Zuntor... No matter what happens to me out there, don't give up that Serum! And, if something does happen, tell Tulley that even up to my last moment, I was still thanking her for loving me and tell her she will always be in my heart." He then strapped himself down, and began to pump up for the face—off.

Taking off like two comets from out of their respective Motherships, with Captain Star in one shuttle, and Captain Icpek in the other, they were on their way to the big showdown. Both pilots were firing lasers at one another and rolling out of the way of the other's laser rays, as their ships passed each other. Looping in a figure eight, Captain Star's shuttle shot a missile at his enemy, only to miss him by nearly six feet.

Zinnnng! went a laser cannon from Captain Icpek's shuttle. It scraped the port side of Captain Star's shuttle!
If not for his fast reflexes and reactions, his little ship would have been hit broadside! Around and around, the two shuttles went dodging one another as they fired at one another.

Then Icpek fired his Double—Automatic Cannon. The fire from this cannon comes so fast that an entire area lights up with the rays from the lasers. Rolling and looping, with Icpek on his tail, Captain Star was thinking, "Come on, keep it up! You're doing just what I want you to do!" He knew he needed Icpek to fire at his ship even more, so that he would be able to use his Boomerang—Missile Force Field. But it was also dangerous, because with so much firepower aimed at his shuttle, it was quite possible that his ship could take a big hit and explode. Icpek was flying his shuttle so close behind Star's ship that Star knew, sooner or later, he was going to be hit unless he did something. Thinking fast, he began flying his shuttle in a figure eight, making double loops over and over — until at last, the shuttle that was once being chased was now doing the chasing!

Once Star had looped himself in behind Captain Icpek, he began to fire at the stern of Icpek's shuttle. Zoom! Bang! Boom! went his laser cannons! It was nothing but an old-fashioned dog fight! Now and then, one of the ships would take a hit or two, but nothing that would cause critical damage to either shuttle.

Noticing that Dr. Poolong's Mothership was paying more attention to the battle between the two shuttles than to the Phantom II, Dr. Zuntor called Mr. Pep and said, "Mr. Pep, ready all weapons and take command of the gunners. I'm going to fly the Phantom II myself!"

Answering, Mr. Pep complied, "O.K.! Will do, Sir! But did I hear you say you were going to fly the Phantom II yourself, Sir?"

"That's correct, flying her myself! And why not? I'm the one who designed her! So, believe me, I'm flying her! Now, let's move! Time is running out!" Zuntor rushed down to the cockpit of the Phantom II and strapped himself into the pilot's seat. He switched all pilot weapons to manual and took off after Poolong's Mothership! Dr. Poolong, seeing the Phantom II coming, stood there in disbelief.

"Fire, Mr. Pep! Fire all cannons!" commanded Dr. Zuntor over the ship's In—Beam. As they passed by the huge Mothership, the Phantom II's laser canons and missiles must have hit it at least twenty times. Even though Poolong's Motherahip was being hit, its force field was still holding up. Then Dr. Poolong fired on the Phantom II but missed it because Dr. Zuntor had rolled his ship out of the line of fire.

The two huge ships were firing on each other and taking hits from each other. Then, Dr. Zuntor remembered an old trick Captain Star had told him about, on how to get an enemy ship to overshoot your ship and put you in a position to kill it from behind.

Dr. Poolong's Mothership had taken so many hits that he knew there was no way that he was ever going to get his hands on that Serum! The only thing that was on his mind now was staying alive! He ordered his gunners to fire at the Phantom II with everything they had.

Certain that Dr. Poolong was getting desperate, Dr. Zuntor knew that now was the best time to make his move.

After making a pass in front of Poolong's Mothership, Dr. Zuntor slowed down so that his enemy could take a shot at him. Poolong took the bait! He thought he had a chance to hit the Phantom II! So, Dr. Poolong ordered his gunners to fire!

Knowing he was going to be fired upon, Dr. Zuntor had rolled his ship out of the line of fire. He then threw the Phantom II into hyperdrive and took off, heading into deep space. Thinking that at last he had the Phantom II on the run, Poolong ordered his pilot to take off after her. Chasing after the Phantom II at over 5.7 warp speed, Poolong felt that at last he might have a chance to destroy her!

In another area of that same sector, Captain Star was still battling with his old nemesis, Captain Icpek. They were throwing verbal barbs at each other over their In/Out Beams. As he fired on his shuttle, Icpek declared, "It looks to me, Star, like you've lost some of your trick-flying abilities" while Star, flying upside down, performed a quick roll—over, and dodged one of Icpek's missiles.

"Icpek, I thought you knew how to fire that weapon better than that. Now, let me show you how it's really done!" That's when he threw his ship into hyperdrive and took off! A few seconds later, he switched into low-drag. This caused his shuttle to quickly brake its speed. At that instant, he rolled and made a very quick turn to the right! Trying to keep up with him, Icpek found himself facing Captain Star's laser cannons.

And there Icpek was, ducking and dodging laser rays. He put all his skill to work, but even so, his shuttle was hit in the engine power section! Smoke began to pour out of his shuttle from the huge hit it took! Icpek punched a button that activated his shuttle's fire extinguisher. Even though his shuttle was aflame, Captain Icpek never stopped firing at Captain Star's shuttle!

Trying to make him nervous, Star scoffed at him over his In/Out Beam, "I've got you now, Icpek! Your shuttle can't fly as swift as mine! Do you remember the last time I had you in this predicament? You got away then, but not this time!" Captain Star, realizing Icpek's ship was shot up pretty badly; he knew he only had to out-fly him until he could get a good, clear shot!

As he swung his shuttle around, Icpek found himself in the path of another of Captain Star's missiles! His shuttle began to spit out even more flames! Overly anxious, Captain Star tried to kill him off too soon, and thus, made his first mistake! He flew too close to the enemy's ship, and a big slab of Captain Icpek's injured shuttle fell off and hit his shuttle in the vacuum area of his engine, temporarily stalling it!

When his rocket engines shorted out, this caused his shuttle to take a dive – almost into another orbit – before he was able to get it back under control. By the time he was able to fly back where Icpek's shuttle was, his ship's energy meter was in the danger zone. Thinking he didn"t have much time left, Captain Star's mind was racing to think of another trick that might work.

"Come on, come on! Just a little faster!" Dr. Zuntor was saying, hoping that Dr. Poolong's Mothership would pick up enough speed for him to overshoot the Phantom II. Seconds later, the two huge ships were at top speed. Dr. Poolong's Mothership was on the tail of the Phantom II. Each time the Phantom would make a move, Poolong's Mothership would make the same move. This went on until Dr. Zuntor knew the timing was just right. He threw the Phantom II into drag mode, then made a 160-degree dive and instantly leveled her off!

This maneuver was so abrupt that Poolong's huge Mothership didn't have a chance to brake enough to make that same move. There wasn't anything left to do but fly over the top of the Phantom II, putting the Phantom into a lower orbit than the pursuing Mothership. This also put the Phantom II behind Dr. Poolong's Mothership. Within a few seconds, Dr. Zuntor had made the necessary adjustments and was firing lasers, missiles, and cannons at the stern of Dr. Poolong's huge Mothership.

One hit after another caused Poolong's ship to wobble and lose speed. Five more hits from the Phantom II's huge lasers caused large chunks of the ship to fall off into space. Dr. Zuntor began to gain altitude, and before long, the Phantom II was diving down on top of its enemy's ship, aiming every weapon it was able to fire.

Crossing the orbit in which Dr. Poolong's Mothership was, the Phantom II raked the starboard side with cannons. Small explosions were occurring each time it took a hit from these small missiles. Dr. Poolong's pilot was losing control of the huge Mothership. His crew was running around, trying to find a safe place on the ship — one that was not on fire. The thought of all of his power slipping away threw Dr. Poolong into a daze; he could only stand there in total disbelief!

Coming in for the final kill, Dr. Zuntor flew the Phantom II around the huge Mothership in loops. He continued to fire as he made a full circle around her. He then took off into deep space. Watching his huge 3-D Hologram—Scanner screen as he streaked deeper into space, Dr. Zuntor could see the great Mothership, along with Dr. Poolong and his crew, blow into a trillion small nuclear fragments!

"You did it! Dr. Zuntor, You did it!" cried a voice that came from over the Beam. It was Mr. Pep with the entire crew, congratulating him on the victory over Dr. Poolong and Captain Icpek's huge Mothership. Suddenly, it came to him that Captain Star was still out there, battling with Captain Icpek! He quickly turned the Phantom II around so he could go and help his friend.

Of course he didn't know if he needed help or not, but nevertheless, he was on his way! Watching his Proximetry Locator Indicator, he was hoping to pick up the image of the two shuttles if they were still battling. Or, pick up the image of one shuttle if the battle were over. When the Proximetry Locator Indicator picked up the image, he would know in which sector they were and would be able to set course for that location. The Phantom II would be able to retrieve its shuttle and take Captain Star on board. Then, barring any further interruptions, they could fire the rocket that would shoot his ZYM Serum into the hungriest black hole in the universe! Indeed, she deserved her common name — "Bassera, The Bitch!"

After locating the shuttles – still battling – Dr. Zuntor and the Phantom II rushed toward them! Upon arrival at the battle arena, he could see Captain Star's shuttle hitting Icpek's shuttle with his laser cannons, over and over again! But from where the Phantom II was located, it appeared as though Captain Star could have killed off the shuttle anytime he wanted! The longer he watched, the more Dr. Zuntor realized what Star was most likely thinking.

As the two shuttles continued the dogfight, Dr. Zuntor had Mr. Pep monitor the conversation that was going on between the two warring Captains, as they continued to fire at one another. Over the In/ Out Beam of the Phantom II, the entire crew could hear both Captain Star and Captain Icpek, as they tried to psych each other out.

Knowing Icpek was still able to fight and because he wanted him to suffer a little for all the low-down traitorous things he had done, Captain Star taunted his long-time enemy: "I'm gonna take my time before I put an end to you, Icpek." As soon as he had said these words, he hit

Icpek's shuttle in the starboard side with two more small rockets. This exploded one of his engines! This near lethal hit was seen on the Phantom II's 3-D Hologram screen. Every member of its crew gave out a loud cheer.

Continuing to try every trick he could think of, in hopes he could turn the momentum of the battle in his favor, Captain Icpek retorted, "I've taken the best you got! And you still can't kill me off, Star. Doesn't that tell you something?"

Warning him, Captain Star answered, "Yes, it tells me that I've played with you too long! And, it tells me that I had best get this over with NOW!" That's when he looped backwards in a reversal maneuver that put his shuttle in behind Icpek's shuttle. As he fired with all that he had, he shouted, "Got You!" This final onslaught was more than enough to do the job. At long last, Captain Icpek's shuttle exploded! Seconds before the explosion, the sound of his voice screaming was heard over the Phantom II's In—Beam.

Star's ship was also ablaze! Dr. Zuntor informed him that the Phantom II was in the area and that they had seen the whole thing. Answering him, Captain Star said, "It's a good thing you're close by, because if you weren't, I would have to walk back to Duderyon!"

"I can see what you're talking about, Captain", observed Dr. Zuntor. "From the condition of your ship, you won't be able to make it back to the Phantom II!"

Not knowing of anything he could do, Star spoke quietly to the Doctor, "Well Zuntor, it looks as if this is also the end for me. Remember what I told you to tell Tulley. I really never thought it would end like this."

Aboard the Phantom II, after a few seconds of silence, the only sound coming in over the In—Beam was the racking cough and labored breathing of Captain Star. Then more silence. After what seemed to be an impossible length of time, Dr. Zuntor cried out, "Wait! I have an idea!"

Captain Star spoke in a voice that was just barely above a whisper, "Well, you had better make it quick, Doctor. The heat and the smoke is getting serious in here!"

Zuntor exclaimed, "All you have to do is just walk home!"

Still coughing and choking, Captain Star, in a voice barely above a whisper, demanded, "What are you talking about, Zuntor? Are you losing it, or what?"

"No, I'm serious!" insisted the Doctor. "Just walk home. Now, listen to me carefully: all you have to do is make it to the rear exit of your shuttle."

Star interjected, "I don't think I can make it."

Dr. Zuntor bellowed, "You can make it. Star, you can do this! Just get up and start moving!" Zuntor paused for a second, and continued, "Look in the compartment next to the door. There you will find a hydro—rocket suit. Put it on and pull the emergency lock on the shuttle's door. Then turn on the suit rackets and simply walk out the door. I"ll track you on our Proximetry Locator Screen, and send another shuttle to pick you up!"

Feeling much better, now that he knew he had a chance, Star said, "Zuntor, no wonder they call you The Amazing Dr. Zuntor!" Having said that, he put his shuttle on automatic pilot and quickly did just what the Doctor had instructed him to do. Not long after putting on the rocket suit, Captain Star blew open the shuttle's door and flew out, into space like a missile! They could see him on the Hologram Scanner Screen flying through space in the rocket suit, just before his shuttle exploded! The loud silence on board the Phantom II also exploded, as the entire crew screamed with joy!

A voice came over the Beam to the Phantom II, saying, "This is your Captain speaking... can you hear me?"

"Yee! We can hear you!" shouted an elated Dr. Zuntor.

Star then remarked, "I've never used one of these rocket suits before. If I would have known how great it feels to fly in one of these things, I would have done it a long time ago!" After some maneuvering, the dispatched shuttle was in the area where Captain Star was flying and picked him up. Not long after that, the shuttle docked into the Phantom II's hangar.

Receiving a hero's welcome from his crew, a very grateful Captain Star convened a meeting between Dr. Zuntor, Mr. Pep, and himself. Once they were all together, the three of them began to laugh and talk like schoolgirls. They were talking so much and so loudly about the battles that the entire crew could hear everything they were saying.
"Did you see this happen? ... Did you see that happen?" Each one of them had their own story to tell. And each one of them put more into it than what had really happened. Even though each of them was bragging, they all knew it was the Phantom II that deserved most of the credit!

So, as they raised their glasses of Noxoper in a gesture of a toast, all three of them saluted the Phantom II! They then drank the rest of the Noxoper and threw their glasses to the floor as they hooked hands. As is usual, too soon, the time had come for all good things to come to an end. Since there was still the deployment of Dr, Zuntor's ZYM Serum into the black hole, their little celebration was cut short. After all, their mission had not yet been completed.

"Captain, I have an idea, Sir", said Mr. Pep. "If I may speak concerning the Serum?" he inquired.

"Go right ahead, Mr. Pep", said Captain Star.

"Well, the Phantom II has kinda gotten beat up! She's been through so many battles, it might be wise if we didn't take the risk of getting her caught up in Bassera's gravitational pull!"

Dr. Zuntor agreed, "It's possible she just might be pulled apart!"

"Yeah, you're right!" said Captain Star, "But, what can we do? We have to do something, and soon!"

"As I was saying, I've got an idea", said Mr. Pep once again. "Why don't we take one of our shuttles and fly it into the black hole, by remote control. Then have the shuttle fire a missile as it is being sucked into the abyss. We could monitor the shuttle's flight as it is being pulled into Bassera's intense gravity."

Zuntor interjected, "You might have something there, Mr. Pep. We need to know more about what goes on inside black holes, anyway. What do you think, Captain?"

After he had given it some thought, Star replied, "It sounds like a good idea, but we will be taking a big chance. What if something goes wrong and we lose the shuttle, and the Serum ends up someplace other than inside Bassera? What would we do then?" They all just looked at one another.

At last, Captain Star made up his mind. He turned to the others and said, "All of us have only one life to give for our planetary system. We are all committed with our lives to the Imperial Planetary Defense — to protect all of the inhabitants within the borders of this solar system. The population is so large, and there are so many of us, we are actually without number, which makes this an awesome task! Trying to play it safe now, after all we've been through, is not the way. Therefore, whatever it takes to fulfill our mission is what we have to do. To tell the truth, it really was a good idea, but I'll have to say NO! We simply wouldn't have complete control, and that is an absolute necessity!"

He turned and looked out of the window at the constellations streaking by as he sped deeper into space, headed toward the black hole. He took a deep breath and continued, "We all may feel that the Phantom II might be a little beat up, but so are we! And, if we are not giving up, then why should the Phantom? She has never failed us yet, so let's continue to put our faith in her! After all, she is one helluva superior craft!"

After he said all that, both the Doctor and Mr. Pep understood how he felt. Mr. Pep announced, "No need of me relaxing up here with you Captain, I've got work to do!"

Zuntor asserted, "You took the words right out of my mouth. I've also got work to do!"

With that, the mood became more energetic. Before long, all three of them were doing everything they could to tighten and fix up the Phantom II for its flight down into the unknown and dangerous abyss of the black hole, the "Bitch", Bassera!

The engineers were fixing pipes and gadgets. Mr. Pep and Dr. Zuntor were working on all the special features, such as the G.E.R.P. Unit, the Image Duplicator Unit, the Swirling-Cluster Laser Cannons, and many more of the ship's special units. Captain Star was working (along with his weapons engineers) on the rockets he was planning to use to discharge the Serum into the depths of the black hole. Everyone on the Phantom II was working, with all their spirit and energy, to put their ship back into as near-perfect working order as possible!

Looking out of the ship's windows, Star could see his engineers outside of the ship, wearing rocket suits and tethered with long cords. They were patching up the damage that their beloved ship had sustained during the many hits it had taken while engaged in the recent battles.

Before long, all things were ready, and the Phantom II was once again on its way to Bassera. Knowing that all the work had been done, Captain Star spoke to his crew over the In-Beam, saying, "This is your Captain. I want you all to know that you did an excellent job repairing the Phantom II. As you know, we have had a most difficult journey. But with the cooperation of each individual, and against all odds, were able to survive! Now we are going back into that same black hole we went into before, when we were being pursued by hundreds of enemy War-Starships! At that time, our Gravity Equivalent Reversal Power Unit was in perfect working order. Since that time, our G.E.R.P. Unit has had a tremendous amount of strain put on it. But with the help of Dr. Zuntor and Mr. Pep, this unit has been put back into working order. There is no way we can test it out here, until we actually re—enter that bitch of a black hole!"

"Now, if all things work properly, all will be well... But if not, we will never know it. I know you remember what happened to those ships that followed us inside the last time. Well, the same thing can happen to us! That is a chance that 'I' have to take! But for you members of the crew, you do not have to take this extra chance. This extra duty will put your life into double jeopardy, so to speak, since you have already been there once. That is unless you choose to go again. If you decide not to go with us in the Phantom II, it will be all right, because you have already fulfilled your commitment well beyond the call of duty. And, if you decide not to take this second trip with us, we will have shuttles prepared for you. Those of us who do make the trip and survive will pick you up on our way back to Duderyon. So now I'll give you a few minutes to make up your minds. In— Beam, Over and Out!!"

Committed and loyal, every single Duderyon I.P.D. crew member said, "Captain, wherever you and Dr. Zuntor go in this Phantom II, we will go also!"

As they slowly approached the black hole, Captain Star and Dr. Zuntor were making last-minute adjustments to the rocket that had the ZYM Serum encapsulated within it. "Captain," said Mr. Pep, "I think that if anything can, this rocket has enough power to fly all the way through that black hole."

Dr. Zuntor informed Captain Star that as a special feature, he had added a remote camera to the nose of the rocket. Captain Star asked, "Why have you added a camera to the rocket if no one aboard is supposed to know where it ends up?"

Dr. Zuntor said, "No one knows what its cargo is. But the important thing is, no one knows what's deep inside Bassera since no one who went deep down inside has survived to be able to report it. Who knows, with this special camera sending back those images, we might be able to record what is on the other side of it. We might even discover another solar system. Who knows?"

Star replied, "Once again, I have to say that I can see why they call you The Amazing Dr. Zuntor!" They shook each other's hands and headed the ship straight into Bassera, the bitch!

The ship began to pick up speed. The gravitational pull from the black hole was extremely intense. The Phantom II began to vibrate as if it were in a blender. Pipes were popping; steam and sparks were springing up everywhere. The frightened crew was holding on to anything within reach!

Dr. Zuntor was strapped into the co-pilot's seat, waiting to switch on their GREP Unit as soon as he received the order from Captain Star. Mr. Pep, strapped down, was watching all the gauges, dials, and switches that were in his Central Control area. Captain Star was piloting the Phantom II with his finger on the button that would fire the rocket that would carry the ZYM Serum so deep into the black hole that no ship in the solar system would ever be able to retrieve it.

Looking out of the pilot window, Star could see everything disappearing, such as asteroids, comets, stars, and even light! The gravitational pull from the black hole caused the Phantom II to pick up more and more speed! As he was watching this extraordinary event, he was thinking about all the things that had happened up until this very moment: How he and Captain Octerfree had helped defeat Commander Booner's fleet; how the two Killer Drymahords almost destroyed the solar system; how he escaped from that asteroid after fighting with the Hynipbos; how he had fallen in love with Lt. Tulley.

All these things, and hundreds more, had been centered around Dr. Zuntor's ZYM23Ø.6 Serum. And, now at last, it was on its way to being eliminated once and for all. Suddenly, it occurred to him that he, and he alone, had this awesome power at his fingertips! Then his mind flashed back, and he started thinking about how the most powerful tyrants in the solar system had died, and how entire War Star-Fleets had been killed and destroyed while trying to put their hands on it.

Now it was up to him... Should he take it back to Duderyon? Maybe he should keep it? Because there wasn't anyone or anything that could stop him — it was all up to him! What would he do?

Snapping him out of his thoughts, came a voice saying, "Captain, how much deeper do you think we need to go into this blasted hole before you fire that rocket?" It was Dr. Zuntor, looking over at him. Captain Star could see the doctor's body vibrating so intensely that he was almost a blur.

He looked at his instrument panels, all in the danger zone. So he closed his eyes and pushed the little red button! The kick from the rocket, blasting free from the Phantom II, shook them so violently that it reminded him of when their ship had taken that huge direct hit from the mothership of one of their past enemies!

Knowing that the rocket had been shot completely and successfully into the black hole, he hit the switch to their Gravity Equivalent Reversal Power Unit, and then began to pray. Within seconds, the Phantom II began to slow down enough for the Captain to turn it around. And once again it began to pick up speed. Before long, it had gained up to 11.6 light speed, and was still climbing. Seconds later, like a cork, it shot up and out of the black hole and on into deep space!

Realizing that all things had worked according to their plans, the crew, along with Captain Star and Dr. Zuntor, began to cheer and scream with relief and joy! Soon, the Phantom II was on its way back to their home planet Duderyon.

The flight was smooth and peaceful. Calling Captain Star and Dr. Zuntor over the ship's In—Beam, was Mr. Pep, saying, "I have prepared the 3-D Hologram Scanning room as you requested, and I'll be in there waiting, Sir." Rushing to the Hologram Scanning Room and opening the door, both of them saw Mr. Pep sitting in his seat surrounded by trazillions of stars, small planets, and every kind of object in the heavens. The sight was so awesome, that as both of them took their seats, they were absolutely speechless!

That special camera, installed by Dr. Zuntor on the nose of the rocket that carried his ZYM2Ø3.6 Serum into infinity, was showing the first, and hopefully the last, view of the inside of...
"THE BLACK HOLE"

THE BIRTH OF HIP HOP
" RAPPER'S DELIGHT "
The
GENE ANDERSON
Story

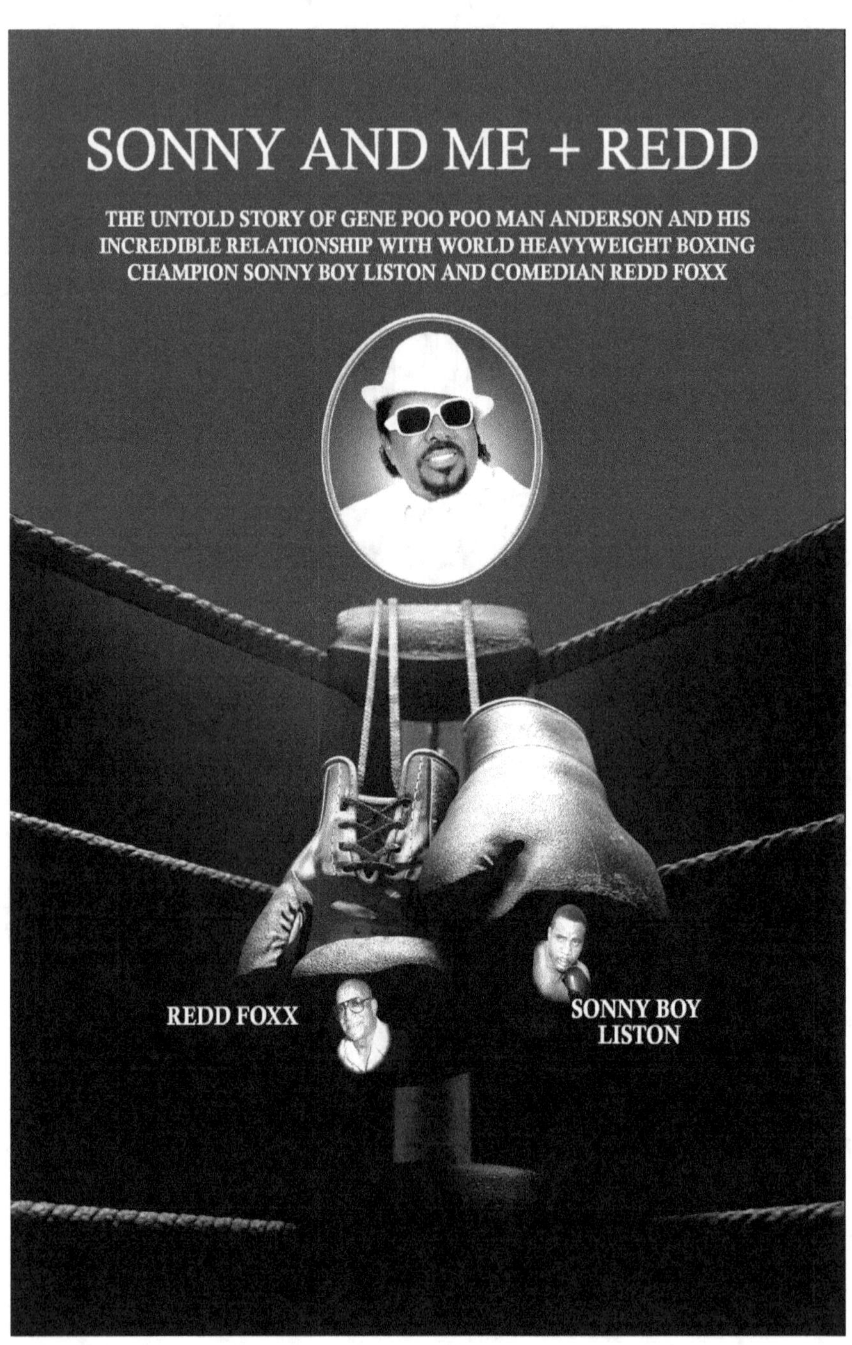

SONNY AND ME + REDD
THE UNTOLD STORY OF GENE POO POO MAN ANDERSON AND HIS INCREDIBLE RELATIONSHIP WITH WORLD HEAVYWEIGHT BOXING CHAMPION SONNY BOY LISTON AND COMEDIAN REDD FOXX
REDD FOXX
SONNY BOY LISTON
TheGeneAndersonStory.Com